Manuscript *for* Murder

Also by B. F. Monachino

Confessions of an Accidental Sleuth

Manuscript
for Murder

B. F. MONACHINO

ARCHWAY
PUBLISHING

Archway Publishing books may be ordered through booksellers or by contacting:

Archway Publishing
1663 Liberty Drive
Bloomington, IN 47403
www.archwaypublishing.com
844-669-3957

ISBN: 978-1-4808-9796-0 (sc)
ISBN: 978-1-4808-9797-7 (hc)
ISBN: 978-1-4808-9795-3 (e)

Library of Congress Control Number: 2020920443

Print information available on the last page.

Archway Publishing rev. date: 02/16/2021

To Mike
for his steadfast encouragement,
and
for Mom.
Wish you could be here to read this.

Prologue

SHE CLOSED THE BOOK, CARE-fully separating the back of the dust jacket from the cover to reveal the author's image. A pair of heavily lidded eyes reminiscent of those of a king cobra about to strike its prey stared back at her. A cold fear gripped her. From the dim recesses of her memory, a blurry image surfaced for an instant and just as quickly vanished. She rubbed her eyes. As hard as she tried, she could not retrieve it. Wearied by the effort, she slumped in her chair and closed her eyes. She had seen that face somewhere before, but where? The answer eluded her.

Restless, she rose, wrapped herself in a sweater, and stepped out into the night. She made her way to the edge of her property—a precipice suspended halfway between the panoply of constellations above and the black void of the Dordogne Valley below. Where once she had found solace in the beauty of the night, now there was only apprehension at the darkness enveloping her. Without a backward glance, she hurried back to the house.

After throwing off her sweater, she stoked the fire and

added more wood. When the fire was blazing, she went over to a rough-hewn wooden cabinet. She hesitated for a moment before pushing lightly on one of the panels. It sprang out, revealing a brown accordion-style envelope with edges bleached tan by age. The black string wrapped around the fastener resisted her efforts to untangle it but finally yielded. She thumbed through the contents and removed an envelope. She hesitated again and then opened the envelope and pulled out a thick sheaf of faded yellow carbon sheets. For a moment, she stared at the pages, and then she turned one page after the other.

The sound of gunshots startled her. She sat upright, her heart racing. Her eyes darted around to find the source.

She realized it was just the rat-a-tat-tat of sleet smashing against the slate roof. Coaxing her sclerotic limbs into a standing position, she glanced around the room. Everything looked the same as it had last night, yet nothing would ever—could ever—be the same again.

Wracked by indecision, she paced the floor.

For more than forty years, she had despaired of unearthing the truth of his disappearance. But now, with her own death imminent, she sensed the answers she sought, once seemingly beyond her grasp, were tantalizingly close. The prospect of her death troubled her not in the least. She had had a good, long life, and she was ready to go. Pursuing those answers would fulfill a promise she had made to herself on that first night and allow her to die in peace. But that same pursuit would mean breaking a promise she had made a long time ago to another.

The living would bear the pain of her decision.

1

NEW YORK

On December 11, 2009, I was occupying my usual position at Everything Used and Rare, the bookstore I owned in Manhattan with my two partners: my wife, Maggie Parker, and our friend George Zoski. I was contemplating, without much enthusiasm, the task those same partners had assigned me—cataloging a collection of books belonging to a now-deceased not-much-loved, rapacious hedge-fund manager, which had been entrusted to our care by the executor of the estate, his equally rapacious widow.

I had been admonished to complete the task by the time they returned from meeting with a potential buyer for a scarce and precious 1640 first English edition of Machiavelli's *The Prince*. Their admonitions had been stern—and probably rightly so since I was known to be a terrible procrastinator when it came to that task, which was my least favorite part of the business. I had hoped our trustworthy sidekick, Miss Harriet Brewster, would be available to relieve me of the burden of the task, but she wouldn't be back in the store until the end of the week.

Our Miss Harriet was a PhD candidate at Columbia. Her

passion, wholly lost on Maggie and me, was medieval English literature—Chaucer, to be precise—but the job market for PhDs in medieval literature and, in particular, the nuances of Chaucerian prose (or was it considered poetry?) was pretty limited in our current economy, so to supplement her grants and scholarships, she'd joined Used and Rare as our resident Person Friday, cataloging manuscripts and books as well as other literary memorabilia, researching market values, going to auctions, looking after the cash register, and such. We loved Harriet because she shared our passion for books. Unfortunately for me, that week, she was preparing to defend her thesis on some obscure aspect of Chaucerian literature, and her love for our humble bookstore was no match for the passion she felt for her dissertation. Needless to say, it was a welcome distraction when a cold blast of air announced the arrival of a customer.

I glanced up to see an elderly man sporting an incongruous homburg, his cheeks ruddy from being exposed to the winter elements, pause inside the door. He looked from side to side and then behind him, whereupon he fastened his gaze on the umbrella stand that occupied a small niche next to the door. After deliberating for a few seconds, he deposited his walking stick in the stand. He transferred his briefcase to his left hand, removed his rimless spectacles, and held them at arm's length while he waited for the fog to recede from the lenses. Satisfied that they were sufficiently clear to permit navigation of the aisles, he replaced them on the end of his nose and proceeded toward me. He stopped in front of me, unbuttoned his thick wool overcoat, removed his homburg, and peeled off his gloves, which he then placed in the well of the homburg before turning his attention to me.

"Mr. Kramer?"

My eyebrows flew up. I wasn't sure what surprised me

more—hearing a complete stranger call me by my name or the disconnect between the deep basso voice and the less-than-imposing physical stature of the person before me. Regardless, he had my attention.

Seeing my surprised look, he pointed at my name badge, which revealed in no uncertain terms that I was Harry Kramer, the proprietor.

"And you are?" I said.

The man peered around as if to make sure no one was listening. I followed his gaze.

"Arthur Babcock." He held out his hand, and I shook it. He then handed me his business card, which identified the holder as Arthur Babcock of Babcock and Wilson, attorneys at law.

"What can I do for you, Mr. Babcock?"

He walked over to a reading desk, put his briefcase on top of it, opened it, plucked a somewhat-tattered envelope from its interior, and got right to the point. "I've been retained by a client who wishes to have a manuscript examined with a view to establishing the authorship of same. I did some research and came across the name of your bookstore."

That confirms we've had at least one hit on our website, I thought wryly.

"We do offer that service," I said, "but in the interests of full disclosure, you should know we contract it out to a third party."

He dismissed my full disclosure with a wave of his hand. "How you conduct your business is strictly up to you. If you are interested, I'll leave the manuscript with you so you can consult with your partners."

"Well?"

"Good," said Mr. Babcock. He opened the envelope and withdrew a bundle of yellow paper—the kind used to make carbon copies of documents in the days before spell-check and the backspace key made such paper obsolete. He placed the sheets of paper on the table. The type was faded. There was no title and no author's name.

"What can you tell me about the manuscript?" I asked.

He gave me an enigmatic smile. "My client would prefer you look over the manuscript first, and then she will meet with you to tell you herself about its origins."

"Can you tell us anything about who the purported author might be?"

"My client is the best person to talk to about that," he said.

"Who is your client?" I asked.

His fingers drummed the top of the yellow sheets. I sensed he was getting impatient with all of my questions.

He exhaled slowly. "I'm not at liberty to disclose that information right now. Once you have perused the manuscript, if you decide to undertake the task of establishing the identity of the author, my client will meet with you to give you and your partners all the information you need to get the job done." He put the manuscript back in the envelope and handed it to me. "I trust you have a place of safekeeping. This is the only copy extant."

Before I could answer, he stood up and said, "Please call or email me when you have had a chance to read it. My contact details are on the card." He buttoned his coat, placed the homburg on his head, and marched to the door, pausing only long enough to retrieve his walking stick. A blast of cold air announced his departure, as it had his arrival, leaving me holding the bag, so to speak.

2

I was still puzzling over the mysterious visit of Mr. Arthur Babcock and his even more mysterious client, when the door opened again, and in blew Maggie and George, the Mutt and Jeff of Used and Rare. Maggie, tall and elegant, was swathed in politically incorrect fur, and George, square of stature, was wearing his latest thrift store acquisition: a gray flannel overcoat that strained at the buttons and almost touched the floor. Judging by the jubilant looks on their faces, I assumed the pursuit of the buyer for the Machiavelli had been successful, which meant the bookstore could hold its own without an infusion of funds from our personal bank accounts.

Maggie breezed up, gave my nose an affectionate tweak, and gave me a peck on the cheek. I was about to turn that peck into a full-fledged exercise in mouth-to-mouth resuscitation, when I heard a gentle cough from behind.

I turned around to find George with a broad grin forming on his lips. "You don't want to make an old man envious, do you?"

I grinned back, but my smile was wiped off my face in the next instant.

"How's the cataloging going, darling?" Maggie asked.

I turned to face her with chagrin, or maybe guilt, written large over my middle-aged face.

"Harry—"

Before she could scold me, I interjected. "It's not my fault."

"Well, if it isn't your fault, whose is it? Are there more than three partners in this store? Really, Harry, you are incorrigible."

I pointed at the manuscript.

She gave it a cursory look. "And?"

"I had an unexpected customer. He has a client who wants us to try to identify the author of this manuscript."

George picked up some books in need of shelving and looked at me. "Who is the client?"

"He didn't tell me. He said his client wanted us to look at the manuscript, and if we are interested, we should let him know, and he will then have the client contact us directly to talk about the provenance of the manuscript."

With a hint of impatience, Maggie asked, "So who is the customer?"

I picked up the business card. "A lawyer by the name of Arthur Babcock."

The thud of books hitting the floor interrupted me. I turned around to discover that the books George had been about to shelve had found a new home on the floor.

"Dear, dear, I am getting clumsy," he said. "I should know better than to try to shelve more than one book at a time."

I reached down and picked up the books. "Oh, don't worry about these. Just some new release by a guy named Black. It just came in, so I thought I'd make a small display in the new-additions section."

George took the books from me and headed to the non-fiction section.

Maggie tapped her fingers on the counter. "Babcock—that name sounds familiar. George, isn't he one of Daddy's cronies?"

Without turning around, George said, "Hmm, your father has a lot of cronies. I suppose it's possible."

If anyone would have known, it would have been George. He and Maggie's father had been friends since George opened his first antiquarian bookstore in Manhattan in the 1950s.

Maggie picked up the manuscript. "*Stealth Victory: A History of the French Resistance in Occupied France, 1940–1944.* That's quite a mouthful," she said.

"Where did you find the title? I looked when Mr. Babcock brought it in and couldn't see one."

"Oh, it looks just like the opening line of the book."

"Well, what do you think?"

"Probably no harm in looking it over—we can decide a bit later if we want to commit to a major attribution project."

George interjected. "Well, you two are on your own on this one. I'm leaving for Jerusalem next week."

I had forgotten. We had a trade-off: George made his annual pilgrimage to Jerusalem, and as soon as he returned, we made our yearly pilgrimage to Saint Barth, where we spent our honeymoon.

When Maggie asked me to marry her a few years ago, I accepted with unseemly, bordering-on-indecent haste—which, for me, was probably a mark on the right side of my ledger since I dithered for years before she took matters in hand—and off we went to city hall forty-eight hours later. That was in October. The following February, in the midst of a fierce nor'easter that had already dumped two feet of snow on the city, she plopped down beside me and announced that we were going to have a honeymoon. Familiar with that certain firmness of tone, I knew it was pointless to debate the merits of the idea, so my only question was "Anywhere in particular?"

Her reply came in the form of two plane tickets and a reservation for a week's stay at a beachside hotel in Saint Barth. We never looked back.

Our friends raised eyebrows when we mentioned that we were spending time in Saint Barth. We knew what they were thinking: *You're just booksellers—how can you afford a month in Saint Barth?* We just looked at each other, secretly smiled, and said nothing. Little did they know.

Maggie was my guru in all matters financial. The woman had the Midas touch when it came to making money and making it grow. She had looked after my financial affairs for years, and as a result, I was a modestly well-off person.

Just before we married, we solved a mystery involving a particular baseball scorecard I discovered in George's original store, which was later destroyed by arson. To make a long story short, we solved the crime; returned the scorecard to its rightful owner, who happened to be Maggie's father; and uncovered financial skullduggery on the part of Maggie's ex-husband, and I got the girl.

Maggie knew that books were my first love, so we teamed up with George, rebuilt the store, and stocked it with a lot of books that George had inherited from his father. We opened up business as Everything Used and Rare, which was a bit of a misnomer because we also sold current titles to help pay the bills while we awaited big payoffs, such as the sale of the Machiavelli. Maggie handled all matters financial and, incidentally, added George as a client. I was the gofer, running around checking out estate sales, garage sales, and the like and foraging for new stock for our old bookstore, and George was the real bookman. He was making a herculean effort to turn me into the real deal, but I knew I'd never be as good as he was. He had more book sense and knowledge in his little finger than I could have hoped to pick up in a lifetime.

We were something of a family. We rebuilt the store as a four-story brownstone: two stories for the business, one story for George, and one story for Maggie and me, which was a huge sacrifice for Maggie, as she had to give up her beloved loft in Tribeca. One thing we all agreed on was that the commute was great.

"I have a feeling this project will be resolved long before you return," I told George. "Besides, what can it hurt to read the manuscript?"

He looked doubtful. "Never underestimate how time-consuming attribution issues can be."

As it turned out, no truer words ever had been spoken.

3

After much discussion, Maggie and I agreed we would not tackle the manuscript unless we knew who the client was and, more importantly, could determine the client's ability to pay. Attribution issues were never simple and always expensive. Besides, we wanted to get a better idea of what exactly would be involved.

The next morning, after dropping George off at the airport, I called Mr. Babcock and told him of our decision. He didn't sound pleased about it but said he would speak to his client about our position and get back to us.

Late in the afternoon, as my thoughts were turning to the icy martini I would be imbibing in a short while, the bells over the entranceway tinkled, signaling the arrival of a late-in-the-day customer. I sighed and mentally put the cold martini back in the freezer. Our attitude toward our customers was somewhat laissez-faire. We let them browse without interruption in the belief that if help was needed, they would inevitably ask for it. Besides, after trial and error, we had found that it only annoyed them when someone raced up to them and asked, "May we be of help? Is there anything in particular you are looking for?" and other inane questions. However, such a policy resulted in flexible closing hours.

Over the top of my glasses, I observed an older woman swathed in cherry red from head to toe carefully close the door without a sound. I liked her already. Nothing made us crazier than people who walked in and slammed the door as if it were made of steel instead of glass.

She brushed the scarf from her head, revealing an angular face laced with lines—she was perhaps eightyish, maybe older. Wisps of snow-white hair escaped from the constraints of a loosely wound French roll. With graceful movements reminiscent of a ballerina, she made her way down the center aisle, unhurried, pausing now and again to lift a book, open it briefly, and return it neatly to its place.

She approached the counter. "Are you Mr. Kramer?" Her voice was low and husky, with just a hint of an accent.

I found myself staring into eyes that were an unusual shade of hazel dotted with tiny flecks of gold. Despite the fact that her face was crisscrossed with creases, the color of her skin was such a soft, creamy alabaster that I was almost overcome by an irresistible urge to reach out and stroke it. No matter her age, she was a great beauty. She showed no signs of impatience as she waited for my answer, as if she were used to having this effect on men. Maggie, on the other hand, was less patient.

"He is," she said, answering for me.

"I am," I muttered, unnecessarily since my beloved wife had already identified me. "Is there something I can help you with?"

"I hope so." She turned to Maggie and smiled.

"Oh, I'm sorry," I said. "This is my wife, Maggie. We own the store together."

The woman peeled off a glove, revealing a perfectly

manicured hand in the same almost translucent shade of alabaster, marred only by a mottled brown birthmark just above her wrist. She extended her hand toward me. Her grip, though not strong, was firm. She turned to Maggie and took her hand. "My name is Sally Bedford. I believe you have already met my attorney, Arthur Babcock."

The mystery client stood before us.

She continued. "I understand from Mr. Babcock that you are not willing to accept commissions to perform attributions unless you first meet the client." There was no reproach in her words, just a simple reconfirmation of the facts as she knew them. "That makes eminent sense to me. I apologize for not phoning in advance of my visit, but as you can tell, I am of advancing age, and I want to begin this process as soon as possible."

Maggie recovered first. "Harry, please get a chair for Mrs. Bedford."

I did as I was told, and presently, Mrs. Bedford was sitting. She sat at the edge of the chair with her spine erect and her hands crossed and relaxed in her lap. Her eyes sized us up in a neutral way. She waited.

"Mrs. Bedford," I said, "we did not mean to offend you by—"

"No offense was taken, Mr. Kramer. I think it is a very reasonable thing to request."

Somehow, I knew we were going to say yes to Mrs. Bedford, no matter what we learned in the next few minutes.

"Would you please bring me the manuscript?" she asked.

Maggie stood up and returned a few minutes later with the thick manila envelope that held the manuscript and handed it to her. Mrs. Bedford placed it on the counter, rose, and strode over to the new-arrivals display. She paused briefly. A momentary look of distaste flitted over her face. She plucked a book from the display. She brought it back to the counter and placed it next to the manila envelope. We leaned over to see what her selection was. *Secret Victory: French Resistance in Occupied France, 1940–1944* by Arnold Black peered back at us. It was the book we had received a few days earlier from a small publishing house we had not heard of. Puzzled, Maggie and I looked at each other and then at Mrs. Bedford.

Before we could say anything, Mrs. Bedford opened the manila envelope and removed the manuscript. With a long, elegant index finger, she tapped the book, and then she ran her fingers gently over the manuscript.

Turning the book over, she pointed at the author's picture and said, "I want you to prove that this man could not possibly have written this book."

The ticking of the grandfather clock was almost deafening.

"What makes you think he didn't write it?" I asked.

"Because my husband wrote it."

4

"Perhaps we would be more comfortable discussing this in the office," Maggie said.

Mrs. Bedford clasped the manuscript to her. Maggie picked up the Black book, and I brought up the rear. I motioned to Mrs. Bedford to take the great big old club chair.

"Let me take your coat," I said. Removing her coat, even with my help, seemed to sap whatever remaining energy she possessed. She sank into the chair.

"May I offer you some tea?" Maggie asked.

She nodded without saying a word. We waited in companionable silence until Maggie returned with steaming-hot cups of tea.

Maggie placed a cup of tea in front of Mrs. Bedford and offered sugar and milk, both of which she declined. She stared at the curls of steam rising lazily from the cup and rubbed her hands over the porcelain surface. Her smile was dreamy and distant. "You serve tea just as your mother does, in a proper china cup."

Maggie laughed and placed her hand gently over Mrs. Bedford's. "I'm not sure where I picked this habit up. My mother died when I was very young, and truth be told, I have no memory of her."

Mrs. Bedford gave Maggie a sympathetic smile and gave her hand a light squeeze. The room was hushed but for the whir of the overhead fan.

I picked up the book, took a quick peek at the author biography, and then turned it over to look at his picture. Glancing up, I said, "Do you know this Arnold Black?"

"I have never seen him and hadn't heard of him until I came across this book." She hesitated for a moment. "At least I don't think I have ever seen him."

Maggie's eyebrows arched. "Forgive me, Mrs.—"

Mrs. Bedford interrupted in a brisk voice. "Please, let's not rest on formality. Do call me Sally."

"Sally," Maggie said, "if you have never met this man, how could he possibly have written the same book as the one you say your husband wrote?"

She motioned for me to hand her the manuscript. "Mr. Kramer—"

I held up my hand and grinned. "Remember, no formality here. Call me Harry."

She gave me a weak smile. "Harry, please read the opening line from that book."

I did as requested. After I finished, she picked up the yellowed manuscript and turned to the opening page. She read the first line. The two lines were word-for-word identical.

She put the manuscript down.

"May I see it?" I asked, pointing at the manuscript, and she pushed it toward me. I looked at the title of the Black book and then at the title of the manuscript. I had to admit the title of Black's book bore a passing resemblance to the title of the manuscript. I passed the manuscript to Maggie. She looked at the front and then went to the back page.

"Don't waste your time, my dear," Sally said. "Nick, my husband's name, appears nowhere as the author of the manuscript."

"But shouldn't your husband confront him?" I said.

She looked up at me, her eyes watery. When she spoke, her voice was tight. "Oh, that is not possible. He is quite dead."

I turned beet red.

Maggie leaned over and took her thin hand. "I am so sorry, Mrs.—er, Sally. We seem to have foot-in-mouth disease today."

Sally burst out laughing, and the tension dissipated. "Not to worry. I suffer from the same disease myself from time to time. I shouldn't have been so blunt. My husband disappeared from our home in France in the early fifties. No trace was ever found of him. He has been declared legally dead. The original of this manuscript disappeared with Nick when he disappeared. But it is most assuredly his work, as I was his reader and first editor."

"Why don't you just go to the police with your information?" I asked.

"And say what?" Her voice was bleak. "That Arnold Black, someone I have no recollection of meeting, is a thief and a plagiarist who copied a fifty-year-old manuscript with no name attached to it? No, I must be able to definitively prove that this manuscript was authored by my husband and not this Arnold Black person."

She paused and bowed her head. When she looked up, her eyes glittered. She stabbed at Black's photograph. "I want you to prove that this man is a thief and that my husband is, without question, the author of this manuscript. More than that, I want to know how Arnold Black came into possession of the original of this manuscript. I am convinced this man knows something about my husband's disappearance, and I want you to find out what that something is."

5

Streetlights flickered on outside our front windows, reminding me that evening was drawing in. I reached over and switched on a lamp.

Maggie looked at her watch and muttered, "It's late, Harry. Let's lock up."

Where had the afternoon gone? I locked up, turned on the display lights, and said, "Let's move upstairs." I gathered Sally's coat. Maggie picked up the book and manuscript, and we headed upstairs. I turned on the fireplace, and we gathered around the coffee table.

"May I get you a drink, Sally?" Maggie asked.

"A gin martini would be lovely, my dear."

"A woman after my own heart," I said.

"I think we all need one," Maggie added.

I turned to Sally. "Olives or twist?"

"Olives."

"Olives all around it is."

Maggie went to the side cabinet and made three perfect martinis. When she returned, we all raised our glasses, paid homage to a great elixir, and took a sip. For the moment, we were all content to stare at the flames darting in and out of the logs.

Finally, Sally spoke. "I am sure you must wonder if some deranged person has walked through your door, but I assure you, even at my advanced age, I am, as lawyers would say, perfectly compos mentis."

I hesitated, feeling I had to choose my words carefully. "To allege literary larceny is one thing, but to suggest theft and complicity in someone's disappearance is tantamount to making an accusation of criminal activity. What makes you think this Black person was involved in the disappearance of your husband?"

"There is only one way someone could have possession of the original manuscript, and that is if they took it from our home in France. The only way it could have been taken is by force."

She paused to take a sip of her martini. "Let me explain. After the war, Nick and I bought an old farmhouse in the Dordogne area of France. We had grown to love the area as a result of our activities in France during the war, and Nick found it very conducive to his research and drafting of this manuscript.

"The day Nick disappeared, I was in Cahors, our nearest city, doing errands. When I left it was a beautiful morning, and then the weather turned miserable—torrential rains, mudslides, and the like. On the way home, I was held up at a roadblock. The road to our farmhouse had flooded and was impassable, so I had to take a longer alternate route. It was late evening when I finally pulled into the yard. That was when I had my first premonition that something was wrong. The house was dark, and no smoke rose from the chimney—we always had a big wood fire going at that time of the year.

"It was dark, but as I got closer, I noticed the front door

was slightly ajar. That in and of itself was not unusual. We never locked our doors, and they weren't particularly well made. The wind often blew them ajar. I thought perhaps Nick had decided to go to the local village to pick up some newspapers and had gotten caught up in the same weather-related delays, so I picked up some firewood to get the fire going and went on in. I was perplexed by what I found."

"What did you find?" I asked.

"Nothing. That was what was so disconcerting. Everything was neat as a pin, including Nick's desk. When I'd left in the morning, it had been in total disarray. He'd had all kinds of research papers spread out. I was always chiding him about his messy writing habits, and he had promised me he would tidy up on the weekend. Before I'd left, he'd told me that he had come across something interesting but needed to do a little more digging and that he'd tell me all about it in the evening when I returned.

"I went back to the great room. The fire was almost entirely extinguished, so I started to stoke it up again, and that was when I saw it."

"Saw what?" Maggie asked.

"This," she said. She pulled out a clear plastic bag containing some partially singed scraps of paper curled at the edge. She laid the bag carefully on the table.

"What do you think they are?" I asked.

"I'm not sure, but when I look closely, some appear to be bits of newsprint, and some appear to be notes, possibly some of Nick's research notes. If they are research notes or part of his research, why would he destroy them? He never destroyed anything. He was, as you say, the proverbial pack rat."

She paused for a sip of her drink. We waited.

"I think whoever stole the original manuscript destroyed these notes."

Maggie looked perplexed. "But why?"

"I believe Nick stumbled across something that someone didn't want him to know about—whatever interesting information he was going to tell me about. I think these scraps of paper are somehow related to what he discovered."

"Any idea what that something might have been?" I asked.

"Since he was writing about the French Resistance and since we were active with the resistance in World War Two, I assume it had something to do with that."

Seeing the dumbfounded looks on our faces, she smiled. "Yes, I was an American in the French Resistance. It was quite happenstance, really. When the war broke out, I was in Paris. I suppose I should have left. Goodness knows my parents begged me to come home, but I was eighteen and labored under the dual handicaps of youth: I was full of idealism and certain I was invincible. I hated fascism and what it was doing to Europe, so I thought I should do more than just talk; I should work actively to defeat Hitler."

"What were you doing in Paris?" Maggie asked.

"I was enrolled in a finishing school in Switzerland. I was to spend the summer with friends of my parents, perfecting my already pretty good French, and then go on in September to Geneva for a year. The war broke out that September. Without telling my parents, I got a job at a news agency by lying about my age. I started out as a general dogsbody but eventually served as a translator for some American reporters based there.

"When the Germans invaded France in May 1940, I fled to London. At that time, anyone who came off a boat was interviewed. I had heard rumors about a secret organization that was recruiting civilians like me to work behind enemy lines. Of course, no one admitted to such a thing, but a few days later, I was invited to a dinner party and was placed next to a woman who said she would like to talk more about my experiences in France. To make a long story short, that woman recruited me. The group was called the Special Operations Executive. They recognized my value as an American who could travel freely on the continent and send back much-needed intelligence. America was not yet at war with Germany, so I must admit I didn't see that much danger. At that time, the French Resistance was still in its nascent stages, but we had received information that we could make connections in Vichy, France. So I was sent to Vichy, where I registered with the American embassy and with the Vichy government as a reporter. I did make several contacts with the resistance and sent back several reports. Once America joined the war, I was repatriated to London. That is where I met Nick."

I tried hard to tamp down the familiar and, in that case, unwelcome tingling sensation that ran up and down my spine when I knew my curiosity was about to get the better of me. "You were a spy?"

She leaned back in her chair and closed her eyes. "More of that later."

Maggie looked at her watch. "Sally, it's almost eight o'clock. Please join us for dinner. You must be famished."

"That's very kind of you, and I will accept. I believe I detect the presence of a very fine lamb navarin."

While I had prevailed on the location of our new home and bookstore, Maggie had prevailed on the design for the space; thus, we had a large, open loftlike space with the kitchen open to the living and dining areas. We could cook, talk, and entertain and never feel as if we were missing anything.

"This reminds me very much of my farmhouse in France," Sally said in a wistful tone.

"When will you go back?" I asked.

Her voice hardened. "When I know the truth."

6

Maggie leaned forward. "But where will you stay while—"

"While I wait for the truth to find me," Sally said. "I have a small pied-à-terre on Gracie Square, so I will be in close proximity when you need to update me or if you need to consult with me."

Maggie poured some wine into my glass, but Sally put her hand over her glass and said, "I am a nonagenarian, after all, and my doctor, who is a bit of a pill, wants me to limit myself to a glass of red wine a day. Of course, I don't heed that advice. He'd probably have heart failure if he knew I was having a martini every night as well."

She took a sip of what remained in her glass and carefully replaced it on the table. "I believe there is a direct connection between this blatant act of plagiarism and my husband's disappearance, and I intend, one way or the other, to find out what that is. You will take on the job, won't you?"

Maggie and I were neither literary nor private detectives, and I felt we should advise Sally that we were not really equipped to take on such a project. I cleared my throat. But as had happened more than once in our married life, Maggie, employing the royal *we*, answered, "Of course we will."

Ignoring my reproachful stare, she turned to Sally. "But before we do, do you have any idea why he would copy an entire manuscript? And what makes you think he is implicated in any way with your husband's disappearance?"

"As I said before, I do not recollect ever meeting this man, and when Nick was alive, he never mentioned such a person. However, I feel certain that Nick must have known him. There are only two copies of the manuscript." Sally lightly tapped the yellow carbon copy. "This one and the original." She placed the yellow carbon copy on the table between us. "Someone removed the original from our home, and somehow Black came to have possession of it. If you can find out how he came into possession of it, I am certain we will get to the bottom of what happened to Nick and why."

"But why would he choose to publish at this time?" Maggie asked.

She pursed her lips. "Why indeed. We can only speculate on his motives, but perhaps the better question is, why not? Permit me to speculate for a moment. However Black came into possession of the manuscript, he knew it wasn't his work. He would also know that whoever gave it to him could ruin him, unless the person he obtained it from was in no position to do so or was already dead and therefore couldn't challenge him."

"But what about you? You would surely represent a threat to him."

She took another sip of wine. "I considered that and discounted it. There is really nothing to connect me to the book. Nick and I were only married well after the war ended. And even if he had known Nick had a wife, he might easily have assumed I was dead. You have no idea how many Sally Bedfords there are in this world."

"You had a copy," I said.

"Yes, but it was never kept in the farmhouse. At that time, we thought it wise to keep a copy in a safe-deposit box at our local bank. Our farmhouse was very old, and who knew when the chimneys had last been cleaned? We thought it safer to keep a copy elsewhere. Speaking of which, please remember, this is my only copy. Would you mind making a digital copy for me?"

"Not at all. Is there anything else you can tell us that might act as a differentiating feature between this copy and his book?"

"I thought I noticed some pages that were different, and I noted them in Black's book, which is at my apartment, and you are welcome to it. The most glaring difference is what is not in it."

"What do you mean?"

"You will note that there are no photographs in Black's book. Nick always planned to have photographs and made little *p* notations at points where he was going to insert them. Black wouldn't have known what the little *p* stood for, and even if he did, he could not put any photos in, because the photographs that were to be included are still in my possession. The day Nick disappeared, I dropped off the negatives of the pictures at a photography studio to be printed. I forgot about them for several months after Nick's disappearance, until the owner of the shop called me and reminded me that he still had the pictures and negatives. Some of them are at my home in France, and a few are here in safekeeping in the event anything happens to me."

Wineglasses poised midway from table to lips settled on the table again.

A weak smile formed on her lips. "As I said earlier, I am a nonagenarian, and as a result of the hardships of the war and my resistance activities, I acquired a weak heart. What keeps me going is the thought that finally, I will find out what happened to Nick."

"Let us suppose for a moment that we can prove that your husband wrote this manuscript and that this Black person has appropriated it," I said. "Tying him to Nick's disappearance will still present a challenge."

"I don't disagree, but I feel in my bones he is the one who knows what happened that day." Sally's body sagged in her chair; exhaustion was evident in every movement.

Maggie stood up, came over, and knelt before her, placing her hands on Sally's knees. "It's very late, and you must be exhausted. Would you like us to call for a taxi and take you home? We can meet again tomorrow and decide what to do."

Sally waved us off. "It is painful to speak of him, but the pain is because I do not know what happened to him. I don't want to die without closing this door. I know it happened a long time ago, and all my previous attempts have failed to unearth anything new, but"—she tapped the book—"this book opens up new avenues, and now at least I have a name to work with. All I ask is that you give it your best try. And now you are quite right; I really must go home and rest."

Maggie and I rose. "We'll get a taxi for you," I said.

"It's only a few blocks, and the fresh air will do me good," Sally said.

Maggie would have none of it. "It's far too cold and too late, so we'll get a cab and go with you."

Sally patted Maggie on the cheek. "You are a lovely girl. You've done your parents proud."

"Well, I can't speak for my father, but he gives me every indication he believes I've turned out reasonably well."

Sally's hand tightened over Maggie's hand for just a

moment. "Perhaps I could lean on you for a moment while I put my coat on."

A short while later, the cab dropped us off at Sally's building, and we waited until she was safely inside. As a doorman held the door open for her, she turned to face us. "Why don't you come over for tea tomorrow, and I will finish my story? I'll let the doormen know and leave my door open for you."

We watched until the doorman escorted her to the elevator. Then Maggie turned to me. "Well?"

"Well what?"

"You know perfectly well what I mean, Harry Kramer. Are you going to help her or not?"

"*Moi*?"

"Yes, you."

"What about you?"

"I've already said I would help her."

"If my memory serves me correctly, you used the royal *we*, as in 'Of course *we* will,' which sort of told me I was committed too."

"Admit it, Harry: you had that tingling sensation running up and down your spine again."

It made me crotchety when she did that to me.

"I know because you sat straight up as if you had to scratch your back and wiggled against the back of the couch to get comfortable for a long story."

Am I that readable? I wondered.

"And yes, you are like an open book—well, at least to me."

By then, we were at the door to the store. I stuck the key in and opened the door.

She brushed by me and flicked her gloves at me. "You know that to be true."

I gave up. "We'll talk about it in the morning."

"I'll take that as a yes."

7

Morning had an unpleasant habit of casting doubt on one's supposed clarity of thought. What had seemed like the right thing to do the night before seemed like a minefield the morning after.

"We need to tread carefully, Harry. We can't just bandy about accusations of theft and plagiarism," Maggie said.

"I agree. We need definitive proof, or we will find ourselves at the wrong end of a lawsuit," I said.

"Suppose we do come to the conclusion that the book bears more than a passing resemblance to the manuscript ..." She trailed off.

"How do we decide who the real author is? Right now, it's one elderly woman's word against the published author's."

She nodded. "And if we can somehow prove the writing is that of a man long dead, then what?"

"It will open up a whole other can of worms."

"Like how did Black come to have possession of a copy of the manuscript?"

I felt a gigantic headache coming on. "It could be dicey, especially since Black is somewhat of a public figure."

Paraphrasing *Hamlet* ever so slightly, I thought, *To do or not to do? That is the question. Do we undertake an enquiry that will, in all probability, be fruitless to satisfy an elderly woman's quest for vindication and closure, one that might have the unintended result of landing us and our business in a legal quagmire, or do we turn down the commission and possibly allow someone to get away with literary larceny?* Either way, my gut told me this would be nothing but trouble. I hated making decisions, so I did what I always did: tried to hit the middle ground.

"I guess it can't do any harm to at least compare the two books to determine how significant the similarities are. If it is just a matter of poaching a few sentences here and there, that may be the end of it. There's no copyright on ideas, so Sally would be out of luck."

"If it looks like there is some substance to her complaint, we'll call Syd in for her opinion," Maggie said.

Ever since she helped us solve an ownership issue using fingerprint technology, our friend Syd Madison had been our go-to literary archaeologist when issues of attribution or authenticity arose in relation to manuscripts or other written material of unknown provenance placed in our hands for resale. Most of her work was done for the big auction houses, but being an old friend, she helped us out on an as-needed basis at much-reduced prices.

"Yeah," I agreed, "that's probably the way to go, but let's do some legwork ourselves. As soon as Harriet scans the manuscript, I'll make a copy, and we can figure out the best way to compare the two manuscripts."

At that moment, the door to the shop swung open.

"Speak of the devil," I said.

Our indispensable assistant, Harriet, bore a striking resemblance to a six-foot beanstalk topped off with a tightly wound chestnut chignon. Resting perilously close to the precipice of a nose shaped like a ski jump was a pair of spectacles much like those worn by the wizard Harry Potter. Behind the spectacles were enormous blue eyes that missed nothing, and behind the enormous blue eyes rested brain cells worthy of Einstein. She was sort of our own little wizard.

I retrieved the manuscript from the vault and explained what I needed.

"Whose is it?" she asked.

I was having a moment of indecision about whether to fill Harriet in on our meeting with Sally and what she wanted us to do, when Maggie spoke up. "Well, actually, Harriet, we have a client who has reason to believe parts of the book were plagiarized, and we have been asked to examine the manuscript to determine if that is the case."

"Cool," said Harriet. "Who is the alleged literary vandal?"

I picked up Black's book, turned it over, and pointed at Black's picture. "This man."

She sniffed. "Nothing would surprise me."

"You know him?"

"I don't know him personally, but I know of him, mostly from what I read in the *Times*. He was a director of a national intelligence service involved in covert operations that weren't exactly sanctioned by either the Constitution or Congress. A few years back, there were big congressional hearings about illegal activities, like sales of weapons to countries on the US arms embargo list. Someone had to be the scapegoat, and that turned out to be him. He didn't resurface until his book was published.

"I found out from a friend of mine who works at the International Institute for Conservative Values that he was hired there to consult on identifying nations with conservative values that the US should support. She says it really means identifying any right-wing regime that might be an ally to the US. According to her, everyone is mystified by his choice of the French Resistance as a subject for a book. You can see from the jacket bio that his background doesn't seem to lend itself to the topic. As far as anyone can tell, he had no involvement in World War II, and frankly, word is, he never expressed any interest. My friend said the book just appeared one day."

I glanced over the brief author biography and turned to Harriet. "It says here he's a linguist. Maybe he did some undergraduate work in history."

"Could be, but even my friend who works there says his background is on the sketchy side. He never talks about his past. I get the feeling from looking at his photograph that he's a snake in the grass. I mean, think about it. Here is a man whose politics are to the right of center, yet he writes this book, which is sympathetic to, and even approving of, a movement that, to a large degree, was made up of socialists, communists, and a ragtag band of other center-of-left groups. Unless he's had some sort of sudden conversion, why would he do that, unless he's trying to rehabilitate himself? No, snake in the grass is what I think."

"All the more reason for us all to exercise discretion and keep this as confidential as possible. The last thing we need is to become embroiled in any kind of litigation."

"No problem. Are you calling Syd in?"

"Eventually, but right now, we are going to do a bit of our own legwork first."

Part of me was convinced that a little bit of legwork would put the matter to rest, but another part of me wasn't so sure.

8

After Harriet headed downstairs to start scanning the manuscript, Maggie and I tossed around what we were going to do or, more to the point, what we thought we could do.

"I think we should start by doing a preliminary comparison of random pages to determine if there is a frequency of similarity that would raise red flags," I said.

"And if there is, Harry, then what? How do we prove that Sally's husband wrote the manuscript or disprove that Black was the author?"

"At that stage, we may have to call in Syd. In the meantime, when we meet with Sally this afternoon, let's get as much information as we can about the manuscript, like what model of typewriter was used, if there are research notes, names of persons we could contact—that kind of thing."

Maggie looked at her watch. "Gotta go, sweetheart—I have a meeting with the bankers this morning."

I grinned. "Better you than me."

She wiggled her index finger. "You promised me you would finish cataloging the Richards collection."

My grin quickly turned into a groan.

"And you might want to check this Arnold Black out—see whether we can confirm any of Harriet's information." With that, she grabbed her coat and headed out the door, leaving a trail of Joy behind her.

In keeping with my proclivity to procrastinate whenever the subject of cataloging was raised, the minute Maggie was out of earshot, I turned that chore over to Miss Harriet and decided to do some research on Arnold Black. I had seen the name somewhere but couldn't place where or when. I took a look at the book jacket, but the information was sparse. He was a linguist by background, had worked in government, and was now an éminence grise at the International Institute for Conservative Values. There was no other personal background information. It appeared he had written no other books.

I looked at the author photograph. A tight-lipped, unsmiling man stared back at me. His face was thin, and his hair was slicked back from a receding hairline. The eyes made me shiver. Harriet had a point—he did look like a snake in the grass.

I shook my head. *It's just a picture.*

I consulted a couple of bibliography reference books, but the information was even sparser—in fact, it was nonexistent. I reflected on that for a moment. I checked the publication date of the reference books I had consulted. They were the most recent editions but were two years old. I checked the publication date of Black's book. It was just a couple of months ago. *Curious*, I thought. This was his first book. With all his experience, why had he waited four decades to write a book in an area of no relevance whatsoever to his work? More interestingly, an Internet search turned up nothing. Even the International Institute for Conservative Values didn't show up.

The opening of the shop door put an end to my authorial

sleuthing. I made a mental note to consult all the usual digital sources of personal information and then looked up to greet what I hoped would be a paying customer. No such luck—Maggie was back. She started toward me with a smile, took one look at my face, and stopped and put her hands on her hips.

Before she had a chance to say a word, I leaped in. "The cataloging of the Richards collection is in the far more capable hands of our Miss Harriet." I then filled her in on the results—or, rather, lack thereof—of my research.

"Well, maybe Sally will be able to tell us something that opens other doors," she said. "Speaking of whom, we'd better get going, or we'll be late."

We swaddled ourselves in parkas so voluminous that only our noses showed, with the comic effect that in the slanting rays of the early winter sun, our silhouettes resembled elongated amoeba blobs. The red brick of Sally's building glowed in the waning daylight, and rusticated limestone pilasters took on a honeyed hue. It was a handsome building facing Carl Schurz Park. As we approached the front entrance, the doors were flung open, and a gaggle of adolescents tumbled out, all screams and giggles. We moved to the side to avoid the onslaught but not quite quickly enough to avoid a collision with a hooded boy in standard-issue borderline-rear-end-baring blue jeans shuffling out with his hands in his pockets. His hood fell away, and black eyes glared at me as he grabbed the hood and drew it down over his brow.

"Teenagers," said Maggie, rolling her eyes, as she glanced after the retreating mass.

We announced ourselves to a doorman, who in turn announced us to Sally.

The elevator bore us in silence to the fourteenth floor. We let ourselves in and stepped into a foyer of such elegance and graceful proportions that I wondered if we had stopped at the wrong floor. That definitely was not what I had envisioned a pied-à-terre to be. A stairwell, dotted floor to ceiling with works on paper that even my amateur eyes knew were Picassos, curved its way to the second floor. An antique Chinese writing desk made a splash of vermillion against the starkness of white walls and marble floors. A soft cough drew our attention to the hallway.

"After we chat, you may wander around and look at the art as long as you would like," Sally said.

We were so engrossed in looking at our setting that we hadn't heard our hostess approach.

"What an absolutely perfect space," said Maggie as she leaned over to kiss Sally on each cheek. "I love my home, but I think I want yours."

I nodded my agreement, took Sally's elegant hand, and kissed it in homage to her good taste.

"You are kind, but I have had the good fortune of being in the right place at the right time and with excellent advice on matters such as these. Let's make ourselves comfortable in the living room." She motioned for us to follow.

The hallway gave way to an exemplar of gracious living. The walls were a dusty cream color, except for the wall surrounding the fireplace, which was glazed in deep chocolate. A Frank Stella in vivid blue, yellow, and red hung above the fireplace. A blazing fire beckoned, and we did not resist. We sat, and Sally poured coffee for us. After we were settled, she said, "Now, what are these questions you have for me?"

"More information than questions," I said.

She nodded, indicating we should go on.

Maggie asked, "Do you know anything at all about this man Black?"

"As I mentioned in the bookstore, I have never set eyes on

him before and didn't know of him until I picked up his book. At least I don't think I have."

She paused and took a sip of her coffee before continuing. "In his role as liaison officer, Nick met and knew a lot of people during the war. Because of the Chinese walls we built for our own protection, I never really met any of his colleagues. That doesn't mean I never crossed paths with them; I just wouldn't have known who they were, and they would have thought I was just a local. I never spoke English, only French."

"And you don't think you ever saw this person?"

She shrugged apologetically. "I don't think so, and yet ..."

"And yet?" I said.

She sighed. "And yet I sense I have seen him. But where I may have seen him eludes me. I even went through Nick's old photographs, but they were so deteriorated it was hard to tell if he was in any of them."

"Did Nick ever talk about an Arnold Black?" I asked.

She shook her head. "No, but again, that doesn't mean he didn't know an Arnold Black. He might have known him by a code name, or he didn't mention him because he didn't think it mattered at the time." Sally's face was drained of color and drawn.

I leaned over and took her hand. It felt damp. "Are you feeling all right, Sally?" I asked with concern in my voice.

She patted my hand. "We must continue. During his research, Nick came across something. As I told you, he said he would tell me all about it when I returned from Cahors the day he disappeared. I'm not sure exactly what he found, but I suspect it had something to do with his suspicion that during the war, there was a traitor among us."

"Did he ever tell you what made him suspicious?" Maggie asked.

"From time to time, odd things would happen. Arms

drops would be intercepted just before we got to the drop point, or safe houses would be raided just before we were going to move out the occupants. And very near the end, Nick said that just as he and ..." She paused for a moment. "Just as his unit was about to make contact with the Allied troops in the region, they fell into a German ambush. Only two people knew the rendezvous point initially: Nick and myself. I never told anyone, because no one else had a need to know, but Nick was the liaison, so he had to take a couple of his unit members into his confidence. During the fight that ensued, one of his comrades was killed. Nick told me afterward that he had told only two others about the rendezvous, and one of the two had been the man who died in the fighting."

"And the other?" Maggie asked.

"Nick did not seem to question his loyalty and ruled him out as a possible culprit. Whatever Nick found out in his research led him to believe that the person he told who had been killed may have been the culprit."

"But what does this have to do with Arnold Black?" I asked

She leaned back in her chair and closed her eyes for a moment. "I believe the dead man is Arnold Black."

9

The only sound in the room was the hiss and spatter of the flames in the fireplace. Barely a smudge of daylight remained, just enough that through the windows, I could see the branches of the trees in the park being tossed in every direction.

Maggie sipped her coffee and then placed her cup on the coffee table before speaking. "So you think the man they believed died actually survived the attack?"

"I am beginning to think he was never injured in the attack." Before we could interrupt her, she held her hand up to silence us. "It was always a bit of a mystery. When Nick told me about the incident months later, he said the attack began with a single sniper shot that hit the man who died. The rest of the unit scattered immediately and took shelter behind a small hillock about a hundred yards away, where they were pinned down until darkness fell. When they returned in the morning, there was no body. Everyone assumed he must have lived but been captured. When no word was received, everyone assumed he was dead. It wasn't an unusual occurrence. The Germans often grabbed wounded fighters, tortured them for information, and then dumped their bodies."

"Why do you think it was any different in this case?" I asked.

Sally tapped her fingers on the arm of the chair. "Because he was the only one hit. Nick always thought it was odd that with a whole group clustered together, only one person took a direct hit. I remember him saying that after the first shot, there was a pause—not long but a pause nevertheless. That was what gave everyone else a chance to make it to the hillock. Nothing could be observed from there, because they were pinned down."

"What was the name of the man who was shot?"

"Nick referred to him as Jean Marcoux."

We waited.

Sally rose, grasping the chair's arm for balance. "I'm afraid I'm going to have to rest. I've had a bit of stomach flu and can't seem to shake it. Perhaps you could come back tomorrow, and I could show you some of the old photographs." Her voice trailed off. She swayed slightly.

Alarmed, I rose and put my arm around her waist just as she fainted. Maggie leaped off the couch, and I placed Sally gently down where Maggie had been sitting. Maggie took her pulse, and I went looking for the kitchen to get a glass of water and a towel. When I returned, Maggie had already called 911 and alerted the doormen.

I placed the damp towel on Sally's forehead. Her eyes fluttered open briefly, and she held my gaze. Gripping my hand, she said in a hoarse whisper, "Marcou—"

She drifted out of consciousness. I heard the door open and felt myself being pushed aside by the medics.

Time compressed. One of the doormen hovered; the anxious look on his face was tinged with fear. The medics took

Sally's vitals and, after establishing they were normal, gently lifted her onto a stretcher and took her to her bedroom. By that time, she was conscious and gave us a feeble smile. The medics hovered for a moment, but she waved them off with an impatient brush of her hand.

"I'm still a little exhausted from my flight over. It's really nothing to worry about." She signed a release, and the medics left.

Maggie and I sat on opposite sides of the bed. Maggie took her hand. "Are you sure we can't call a doctor for you?" she asked with concern in her voice.

"I'm perfectly fine," Sally said. Seeing the doubtful looks in our eyes, she added with a weak attempt at humor, "Remember, I am a nonagenarian. What do you expect—handstands?"

I chuckled at the incongruity of that vision. Even Maggie managed a giggle.

"Now, I am a little tired, so we will have to continue with this conversation tomorrow afternoon, if that is convenient for you."

We nodded.

"Good. In the kitchen, there is a key rack in the pantry. There are a couple of rings with keys on them. Take one, and let yourselves in. I'll let the desk downstairs know you are coming and that I have given you a key."

Maggie took her hand again. "It's very late. Can we order some dinner for you?"

"No, my dear, I'm quite fine. Le Petit Bistro delivered a lovely salad just before you came. However, if you wouldn't mind, I would appreciate it if you would open a bottle of Burgundy for me and bring me a glass. The rest can go in the fridge."

I left Maggie with Sally and went out to the kitchen. After foraging in the pantry, I found both the keys and the

Burgundy. I opened the bottle, found a glass, and made a nice, healthy pour. I snooped in the fridge just to make sure she did have food, and indeed, there were some neat little containers from Le Petit Bistro.

On my way back to the bedroom, I stopped in the hallway to admire a fine Jasper Johns from the early 1960s. On the console table below were several photographs. A black-and-white photograph of a couple caught my eye. I picked it up. Staring back at me were a beautiful, elegant young Sally and a handsome young man, presumably Nick, both in evening dress, entering some function. They were smiling. Whatever the occasion was, it seemed to be a joyous one. Other couples were in the background, all in evening dress. It was hard to determine where the photograph had been taken. There was some lettering visible on the back wall in the picture, but a man's head obscured it. The photo looked to be from the early 1950s, I thought, judging by the dress. I sighed. Sometimes I thought I had been born a generation too late. That sort of dress and elegance was almost never seen in New York anymore.

I put down the picture. Next to it was a faded sepia-toned photograph of three men: two kneeling, looking directly at the camera, and one standing with his head bowed, looking at the tops of the heads of the other two. Staring at the man kneeling on the right, I thought, *I know you.*

The sound of laughter coming from the bedroom brought me back to the present. After putting down the picture, I walked toward the bedroom. Standing in the shadow of the doorway, I saw Maggie and Sally leaning toward each other, their faces in profile. They both had high cheekbones and small, straight noses. Sally's profile was more angular because of her age, and Maggie's was softer because of her age. I had the disconcerting feeling that I was interrupting an intimate moment, so I hesitated. Just then, Maggie looked up and smiled.

"There you are, darling. I was just telling Sally that she shouldn't have mentioned food, especially French food, to you—that you might be doing a little sampling." She winked at me, and the sensation of my being an interloper vanished. I placed the glass of wine on the night table.

"It was tempting," I said. "But I reminded myself that we are heading to Saint Barth for a month, so I have to get down to a fighting weight."

Sally thanked me for the wine and took a sip. "When you come here tomorrow, remind me to take out some of my old photos from the early days of Saint Barth before it became the destination it is today. Did you find the keys?"

"I did, and now, with your leave, we will be on our way and let you rest."

"Please take your time, and if you want to look at the pictures, do so. Just lock the door on your way out."

10

A blustery wind kicked up whorls of freshly fallen snow and hurled them helter-skelter across sidewalks and down streets, forming rivulets of white powder. In just a few hours, those same pristine snowflakes would be reduced to a grimy slush, coloring the city a grim shade of gray. Deciding to brave the elements, we set out on foot to Sally's place in midafternoon, stopping along the way to pick up a wine and cheese basket we had ordered earlier.

We paused to admire once again the location of Sally's building overlooking the park. In a few short months a canopy of green would fan out beneath her windows. The wind picked up in ferocity, putting an end to any further musings on the joys Mother Nature might bestow, assuming spring actually arrived in a few short months. As we approached the front entrance, the door flung open, and the same sullen teenager who had run into us the day before brushed by us. Pulling his hood tightly to his face and exhibiting a rudeness that, sadly, many associated with New York, he let the door slam in our faces.

"Don't these kids ever go to school?" I griped.

We stopped at the concierge desk and introduced ourselves to the doorman, whose name tag identified him as Robbie. He checked a binder and said, "Oh yes, Mrs. Bedford phoned down to let us know you would be coming and going on a regular basis." He handed us a sheet of paper. "It's an authorization form," he said by way of explanation. "All visitors who have keys have to be signed in. Just drop it off on the way out."

"No problem," Maggie said. "Is there anything else we can take up for you?"

Robbie scanned another binder for a moment. "Nope, she's already had her delivery from Le Petit Bistro, and I don't see any other packages or letters listed."

We thanked him and headed to the elevator.

"I wonder if we should have brought the manuscript with us just in case she needs to refer to it," Maggie said.

I shook my head. "She seemed to be very concerned that it is in a secure place. We'll bring the digitized copy next time we meet with her."

We let ourselves in. The apartment was so quiet that the ticking of a small clock on the foyer table was almost deafening.

"Sally, we're here!" Maggie called out. She turned to me. "She's probably resting."

"Why don't you go upstairs and check to see if she needs anything from downstairs while I put the wine and cheese in the fridge?" I said.

Maggie headed upstairs, and I made for the kitchen. I sighed. It was neat as a pin, unlike ours, but on the other hand, ours was a working kitchen. I put the wine and cheese in the fridge and then tossed the carrying bag into the garbage.

A scream sent me scurrying upstairs. Maggie stood framed by the doorway, her arms rigid at her side. I squeezed in front of her. Her face was drained of all color. At her feet, the bedside lamp lay shattered in a thousand pieces.

"What happened?" I looked over to the bed. Sally lay there inert. Her lips were blue, and her eyes were closed. I grabbed her wrist. It was still warm. I felt for a pulse but couldn't detect any. I let go of her wrist, and her arm flopped over the edge of the bed.

I grabbed my cell phone, called 911, and put in an urgent request for help, but somehow, I knew there was nothing to be done. I turned my attention to Maggie and put my arms around her. Her whole body was trembling. I led her downstairs and sat her down on the couch.

She looked up at me and whispered, "Is she ..."

"I believe so."

For a long moment, we sat motionless, unwilling to believe what our senses told us. Shaking myself out of my stupor, I reached for my cell phone and said, "I've called 911; the paramedics should be here any moment. I'll alert the doorman."

Within minutes, a scene of déjà vu unfolded, only it wasn't quite déjà vu. This time, Sally would not be coming to.

11

I had only the faintest sense of the passage of time. The efforts to revive Sally were in vain, and the paramedics pronounced her dead at the scene, the victim of a heart attack. We were told there was no need for us to accompany her to the morgue, as we had identified her, and our contact details were on a form we had to sign. After the stretcher with her body was removed, we were left with the excruciating silence of the apartment.

"What do you think we should do, Harry?"

I took a deep breath. "I guess we should inspect the apartment just to make sure we know what state it was in when we arrived and when we left. After that, we had better phone Mr. Babcock. He'll know who the next of kin are, and we can return the keys and the manuscript."

We started upstairs in the bedroom. Maggie, in an unconscious reflex, tidied the bed, just as she did every morning at our own home. Everything was neat and tidy. In the closets, all the dresses were hung by length; all the pants and blouses were lined up, all by color. Shelves with cubbyholes of shoes ran the length of one side of the closet. Maggie took out her notebook and made a few notes.

I gave the landing a cursory glance and then stopped and took a closer look.

"What's the matter, Harry?

I stood in front of the Jasper Johns.

Maggie came up and gave my arm a gentle tug. "This is not the time to be casting envious eyes on artwork."

I turned to face her. "It's not the Johns, Maggie."

She crooked her neck and squinted at me. "Well, what is it then?"

I pointed at a space next to the picture of Sally and Nick.

"It's an empty spot—so what?" Maggie said.

"It wasn't empty yesterday—that's what." I told her that I had stopped to admire the Johns on the way back to the bedroom and noticed the large picture of Sally and Nick. Next to it had been a smaller sepia-toned photograph of three men.

Maggie shrugged. "Maybe she had a cleaning woman, and the woman moved it. You know what Astrid is like." Astrid was our cleaning woman. When she worked herself into a cleaning frenzy, nothing ever found its way back to its proper place.

"If there was a cleaning lady here, she wasn't very good." I pointed to a thin line where the surface of the console table was polished, surrounded by a film of dust. "There was something about that photo that caught my eye. I had the most disconcerting feeling that I knew one of the figures in the photograph."

"Well, Nick was probably one of them, so maybe after looking at the large photo, you just recognized him." She glanced at the large photo. "They certainly were a handsome couple, weren't they?"

I nodded, still pondering the blank space.

"Let's keep going, Harry. I'm beginning to feel like an intruder."

Downstairs, I did a last check of the kitchen, removing the wine and cheese basket. There was no telling when someone might be in there next or who it would be. The last thing one wanted to find was a fuzzy green monster facing him or her down. The takeout from Le Petit Bistro was gone. *At least she had a nice last dinner,* I thought. I pulled out the trash bin to retrieve the plastic bag we'd brought the gift basket in and was about to close it, when I checked again, and then I checked the fridge again. *How odd. Someone must have been here before us.* There was no evidence of the delivery from Le Petit Bistro. I couldn't imagine Sally, in her condition, making a point of taking out the garbage. Before I could consider it further, I heard Maggie calling to me.

"Harry, you had better not be eating anything in that cheese basket!"

My dietary restrictions were always foremost in her mind.

I followed the direction of the voice and found Maggie in the library, checking the desk. I glanced over the books.

It must have been a bit more than a glance, because Maggie admonished me. "Harry, this is no time to indulge in wishful thinking about the books."

"And just what are you up to, Ms. Nosy Parker?"

"Just checking for mail or documents left out, so I can tell Mr. Babcock. The last thing we need is to have accusations made that we were careless when we were in the place. But as you can see, like me, she maintains a very tidy office."

I let her little dig go by unanswered.

We finished the circuit and found ourselves in the foyer, satisfied that we were leaving the apartment as we had found it. After taking one last look, we got into the elevator and left.

Downstairs, Robbie was pacing furiously and wringing his hands. He raced up to us. "Mr. and Mrs. Kramer, I can't tell you how upsetting this is."

I thought he was going to burst into tears. Maggie must have had the same thought, because in a preemptive gesture, she whipped out a Kleenex from her bag.

Ignoring the proffered Kleenex, Robbie said, "I'm just not certain what I should do."

Maggie put a comforting hand on his shoulder. "There's nothing else you can do, really. I'm sure her next of kin will be calling the building."

"Oh no, I don't expect that to happen. Mrs. Bedford told me once that she was an only child and had no children." He paused for a moment, as if considering what he was about to say next. His lowered his voice and, in a confidential whisper, asked, "Do you think I should call her lawyer?"

"You know her lawyer?" I asked.

He seemed surprised by my question. "Oh yes, Mr. Babcock always phoned to let us know when Mrs. Bedford would be arriving, and he was a regular visitor whenever she was in town."

Maggie adopted her most soothing voice. "We'll do that. We have to make arrangements to return Mrs. Bedford's keys anyway."

He gave Maggie a grateful smile. "I'm sorry I'm not much help right now, but this is just so upsetting. I can't believe it happened so quickly."

"Death usually does," said Maggie without a trace of irony. She put her arm in mine, and we started for the door.

The doorman scampered ahead to hold the door open. "I mean, the delivery boy had just come down, and he didn't mention anything unusual."

I stopped and swiveled around. "What do you mean?"

"Well, the delivery boy dropped off the usual dinner from Le Petit Bistro maybe five minutes before you arrived, and he didn't mention anything about Mrs. Bedford not looking well."

Maggie and I looked at each other. "Was this her regular delivery person?" I asked.

He gave us a sheepish grin. "They all kind of look alike— you know, with their hoods pulled up and their jeans halfway down to their ankles. It could have been, I guess."

"Don't you ask for ID or phone up?" asked Maggie.

His face turned beet red, and he stammered, "Actually, I didn't see him come in. I just saw him leave. He had been in the day before with a delivery, so I just assumed Mrs. Bedford had put in another order. We always have two doormen on duty as a rule, but today the other scheduled doorman called in sick, so I'm the only doorman here right now, and I slipped out to the bathroom." A nervous tic appeared on the left side of his face. "You're not going to mention this to anyone, are you? I could lose my job."

"Of course not," said Maggie. "We'll have Mr. Babcock phone you with any further instructions, and we'll be sure to let him know how helpful you have been."

It was well after seven by the time we extricated ourselves from Robbie. Paying no attention to the bitter wind coming off the East River, we walked home in silence. The store was closed, so we let ourselves in the side entrance. It seemed like a lifetime since we had been there.

We shed our coats, made a drink, sat down in the darkness, held hands, and cried.

12

In the confusion of the previous evening, we had forgotten to phone Mr. Babcock, so it fell to me the next morning to deliver the bad news.

The silence on the other end of the line was so protracted that I finally asked, "Mr. Babcock, are you still there?"

I could hear his breath coming in shallow gasps. I grew nervous. Was I going to have a second heart attack on my hands? "Mr. Babcock, are you okay?"

"Yes, yes," he finally muttered. "I knew she had a weak heart, but she had been in the most robust health I had seen for several years. I am shocked, to say the least."

I tried to console him. "We didn't know her for long, but like you, we didn't sense any real difficulties until yesterday."

I filled him in on the events of the last two days. "We have the manuscript in our safe. We can send it by courier to your office if you would like."

Ignoring my offer, he said, "If it is not inconvenient, I would like to drop by the store this afternoon. Sally left me with specific instructions to follow in the event of her death, one of which was to deliver a letter to you and your wife."

"Well, yes, of course, we'll be here all day," I said.

After I hung up the phone, I told Maggie about the conversation.

"How did he sound?"

"I'm not sure. He said he was shocked and that she had been in, as he described it, the most robust health of late. Yet ..."

"Yet what?"

"He seemed to compose himself quickly, as if he actually had been expecting something like this. He immediately wanted to see us about this letter she wrote."

"Hmm, well, I guess we'll just have to wait and see." With that, she gave me a peck on the cheek and went to check on some orders.

I decided to catch up on all the neglected mail of the last two days, first snail mail and then email. Apart from the usual requests for information about out-of-print books and pleas from college students for internships, there was an odd assortment of banking, credit card, and personal emails. I tackled the book-related emails first and then the pleas for jobs, followed by banking and credit card missives.

I was about to shut it down, when I noticed that the spam bucket had a lot of unread emails. I sighed. *There is no end to the inventiveness of spammers and phishers to get into your system.* I clicked on the folder and was about to hit the Delete All tab, when I noticed a message from an address beginning with *sbedford.*

Once I recovered from the shock of seeing Sally's name, I opened the email. It was blank but had a forwarded message attached to it. I tensed. The original email had been sent to Arnold Black. *How did she manage to find that?* I wondered. The message was terse and to the point: "I have the missing pages."

I stared for a moment. What on earth was she talking about? Why hadn't she mentioned the email when we saw her? Then I checked the dates.

I called Maggie over. I pointed at the screen. "Look at this."

She read. Her eyes widened.

"Not only that, but look at the dates," I said. The original had been sent to Arnold Black a week earlier. "Sally forwarded it to us yesterday. And more to the point, look at the time."

She followed the direction of the top line. The time was listed as 12:30 p.m. Sally still had been alive just two hours before our visit.

I said, "If only ..."

Maggie gave the bald spot on my head an affectionate rub. "Don't beat yourself up, Harry. Our appointment time was what it was. What I'm curious about is what she meant, and how did she get Arnold Black's email?"

I looked again. "It looks like an email address at the International Institute for Conservative Values."

The door chimes tinkled. We looked up to see Mr. Babcock striding briskly toward us. His face, pinched and ruddy from contact with the frigid air outside, belied any emotion he might have been feeling about Sally's demise.

We left the front of the bookstore in Harriet's capable hands and retreated to the office. Mr. Babcock removed his coat and folded it neatly over the back of his chair. After removing his glasses, he extracted a handkerchief from his pocket and proceeded to clean off the vapor created by the warm air of the store making contact with the lenses. When satisfied that all evidence of moisture had been banished, he replaced them on his nose and said, "Before we talk about Sally—er, Mrs. Bedford—here is the letter she asked me to deliver."

I walked over to the desk, grabbed a paper knife, and slit the envelope open. Inside was a single sheet of paper. I sat down next to Maggie, and we read together. The letter was dated the same day as our first meeting.

Dear Harry and Margaret,

It was such a pleasure to meet you today. I am very grateful that you have agreed to investigate the authorship of my manuscript. I believe that resolving the authorship issue will ultimately lead to uncovering the circumstances of Nick's death. I don't care so much about the manuscript, but I would like to know once and for all what happened to my beloved husband. However, sadly, I am not sure I will live to hear the truth. For the last few days, I have been beset by the premonition that my death is imminent. If something should happen to me, I beg you to continue on with your investigation. I have left this letter with my dear friend and attorney, Mr. Arthur Babcock, whom you have already met, together with directions for, among other matters, this investigation and the reimbursement of your costs.

Arthur has keys to my homes in New York and France, as well as a key for my safe-deposit box. He can provide you with all the details. Most of my papers relating to the manuscript and any photographs are in my apartment in New

York, my home in France, or my safe-deposit box. This letter is your permission to enter my homes in New York and France and to access my safe-deposit box to gather any information you need to authenticate the manuscript. Again, don't hesitate to call on Arthur for anything you need. He is most dependable.

Dear children, please be careful. I sense danger in what I have asked you to do, and I would be very distressed should anything happen to you.

With warmest regards,
Sally

I was flummoxed. "Why, if she knew she wasn't well, would she be so adamant about tackling this Arnold Black character? The stress would be a killer in itself."

Mr. Babcock sat there for a moment and looked thoughtful. Finally, he said, "I've been Sally's lawyer for almost forty years. I think I know—or, rather, knew—her better than almost anyone else. Nick's disappearance left a void. Not knowing what happened to him was unfinished business she was determined to finish. From day one of Nick's disappearance, she had a visceral belief that his disappearance was the result of foul play, but there was no evidence of foul play. When she left in the morning that day, he was there, and when she came back in the evening, he was gone, along with the original manuscript. The police went over the place and the surrounding countryside with a fine-toothed comb, so to speak, and there was nothing to suggest foul play. The few bits of singed paper she found didn't count for anything or have any meaning.

"Quite frankly, I believe the police thought she was one of those eccentric foreigners—slightly off balance, reliving her wartime past. The police treated her with disdain and dismissed the whole episode as a case of a man who planned his own disappearance. The trail was cold, and then this." He pulled out a copy of the Arnold Black book. "I have always known about the carbon copy of the manuscript but had never seen it. There was no reason until this year, when this book came out. Sally had the manuscript, and she told me what she was about to do. She said she knew exactly whom she was going to retain to do the authentication—the two of you."

"Why us?" Maggie asked.

Mr. Babcock shrugged. "She never told me."

"How ill was she?" I asked.

"Physically, she had a weak heart—a result of a bout of rheumatic fever when she was young, which was worsened by her wartime service. What kept her going was her determination to uncover the truth of what really happened that day. Not for one minute did she believe Nick had planned his own disappearance. I tried to convince her she was like Don Quixote, tilting at windmills, but like the ever-faithful Pancho Sanchez, I did my best to pursue whatever line she wanted me to pursue, and here I am.

"In the interest of full disclosure, as the media types like to say, I must tell you that I have been in love with Sally since she first walked into my office over forty years ago. It was unrequited love, I'm afraid. I feel in many ways I failed her. I did not do enough either to help her uncover the truth or to dissuade her from pursuing her goal. My attempts to aid her were feeble at best. Perhaps my motive was selfish—that I hoped she would give it up and make a place for me in her life. But now in death, I feel I cannot desert her."

We averted our eyes.

"I know you have no obligation, either legal or moral, to continue on, but I hope you will."

And so here we were at the crossroad of choice and chance. Chance had brought Sally to us, and now we faced a choice: delve into the authorship of the manuscript, with all the pitfalls that choice presented, or let sleeping dogs lie. After all, what could be gained? Sally and Nick were both deceased. We had no one's word but Sally's that the manuscript was Nick's, and of course, the dead could not speak. So why bother?

Because something was gnawing at me, and more to the point, I believed Sally.

I felt a soft hand tap on my shoulder. Maggie and I looked each other in the eye, and I knew we were on the same page.

Maggie put her hand in mine, and I said, "All right, we'll look into it."

Mr. Babcock grasped our hands. "Thank you."

I asked, "But what about other relatives, the executor of her estate—shouldn't we get their permission to root around?"

A momentary look of consternation crossed his face. "There are no relatives. The bulk of her estate will go into a charitable trust to be administered per her wishes. I am the executor. I hope you won't be offended, but as her attorney, I am only authorized to speak to you about this specific direction. I'm sure you understand."

"In my previous life I was an attorney, so I understand the need to maintain client confidentiality."

"Thank you. You have a key for her apartment, and you may call on me at any time to get the keys to her home in France if you feel that is necessary and to the safe-deposit box."

I explained to him our impending travel plans.

"That is not a problem. Sadly, it doesn't have the same urgency as yesterday. I expect you will conduct your investigation as you see fit based on your availability. I know you have a business to run. I would appreciate it if you could send me regular reports together with your expense accounts."

He stood up, closed his briefcase, and snapped the locks, signaling that the meeting was at an end. We helped him on with his overcoat. As he opened the door, he turned and said, "Thank you for carrying on. I know this is what Sally would have wanted."

Then he was gone.

13

A few days later, shortly after closing time, Maggie and I were rummaging through our closets, retrieving the necessary summer attire for our sojourn in Saint Barth, when Astrid, who was making a valiant attempt to clean the bookstore, rang up to inform us that a cop was downstairs requesting the honor of our presence.

"What's his name?" I asked.

"Didn't ask."

"What does he want?"

"Didn't ask."

Sometimes it was exasperating that Astrid's curiosity did not extend beyond the mop and pail. I said I'd send Maggie down right away.

"He was quite emphatic that he wanted to see both of you," Astrid said.

Packing was one of my least loved chores but a necessary evil if I wanted to find myself on an airplane, so when I got a full head of steam up, I didn't like to be interrupted. Annoyed, I followed Maggie downstairs.

There, browsing the Dashiell Hammett collection

in Mysteries and Thrillers, was one of New York's finest, Detective Mike Farmer, my occasional tennis partner and a sort of friend in a wary kind of way.

I came up behind him and gave him a light tap on the shoulder. "Don't you see enough of this in real life?"

Without missing a beat, he replied, "Naw, my kid transferred to film school at NYU, and he's doing a paper on the films of Humphrey Bogart. It happens that the last one was *The Maltese Falcon.* I liked it, so I thought I might read it."

I plucked the book from his hands, opened the free endpaper, and pointed to the price.

"Well, I'm not that anxious to read it," he said.

"Go to Barnes and Noble, and get the paperback version," I suggested. I put the volume back in its place. "So to what do we owe the pleasure of this visit? Judging by the look on your face, I'd hazard a guess that it's not about tennis."

Mike looked at Maggie and then at me. "You'd be right; this is business."

Maggie came over, concerned. "Is it about Bill?" Bill was Maggie's father. As Sally had been, he was an active nonagenarian.

He gave us a blank look. "I thought Bill was in France."

Maggie exhaled audibly. "Let's go to the office," she said.

Our office wasn't the tidiest of places since it also doubled as a storage room for orphan books, papers, and all other manner of detritus that followed bookmen around. Mike shoved a few tomes to the side of one chair and sank into it. Maggie and I managed to find a couple of unoccupied spaces on the couch. Mike took out his notebook and flipped pages. We waited. He flipped a few more pages with his pencil.

I leaned forward. "So what's going on?"

He didn't look up from his notes. "I understand the two of you were acquainted with a Sally Bedford."

We nodded. Maggie asked, "You knew Sally?"

He looked up. "Nope, never had the pleasure of meeting her." He was silent again. The tap tap of his pencil against his notebook was the only sound in the room. "Your names appeared in a report in connection with her death. It said you discovered her body."

"That's right," I said.

"Mind telling me what you were doing there?"

"Mind telling me what this is all about?"

Unruffled by my rudeness, he answered, "Whenever any-one dies unexpectedly or in unusual circumstances—"

Maggie interrupted. "Hardly unusual. She had a serious heart condition and suffered a heart attack."

I felt a nervous twitch coming on.

Mike twirled the pencil around his fingers a few times and then asked, "What was your connection to Sally Bedford?"

The bluntness of the inquiry made me cautious. "She brought in a manuscript for evaluation, and we agreed to look at it."

The tapping resumed. "That's it?"

I knew what he was referring to. In a previous life, I'd gotten caught up in locating the owner of a baseball scorecard, who'd turned out to be Maggie's father, which had led to the uncovering of a major internet scam and theft from brokerage accounts, perpetrated by Maggie's ex-husband and his cousin. I had gone to Mike with the information I had gathered, and he'd had me wired. What he hadn't told me was that I had stumbled into a sting operation concerning the same two men and that Maggie's father and uncle had been involved all along, helping Mike set up the operation. Mike had seen an oppor-tunity in my stupidity and included me in the sting without my ever being aware that I was a participant.

In light of all that, I didn't feel too bad about being less than forthcoming with him about Sally, since I never knew where imparting any information to him might lead me. Needless to say, a certain tension had entered our relationship, which found its relief valve in our occasional tennis matches. Well, maybe it was just a release valve for my tension, since he seemed oblivious to it.

I gave him a bland smile. "That's it. Now it's your turn. Mrs. Bedford died of a heart attack, so why is her death of such interest to you?"

"Murder is always of interest to me."

14

"I beg your pardon?"

"Murder, Harry. Murder is always of interest to me," he repeated. He extracted a crushed package of cigarettes from his breast pocket, plucked out one that sagged precariously at its midsection, and tapped it against the packet, dislodging most of its cancer-causing contents onto his lap.

Maggie stood up abruptly. "You can't smoke in here, Mike. In case you've forgotten, this is a bookstore, and this is New York, where all manner of vice, including smoking, is forbidden in public places."

He peered at the cigarette and then at Maggie. "Don't worry; I quit. I just carry them around for something to occupy my hands. And no, I haven't forgotten where I am, and as far as I know, murder is still one of those vices prohibited by law, even in New York City."

I threw up my arms. "For heaven's sake, Mike, whose murder are we talking about?"

"Sally Bedford's murder—that's whose," Mike snapped.

"Are you suggesting Sally Bedford was murdered?"

"Oh, I'm not suggesting. I'm telling you as a fact she was," he replied.

"But how?" Maggie blurted out.

"Somebody gave her a nice big shot of epinephrine." Seeing the blank looks on our faces, he added, "Adrenaline is its more common name. Stopped her heart dead in its tracks."

"But how?" Maggie's voice faltered.

"How did we find out? Except for a very observant paramedic, we wouldn't have. When they brought her to the morgue, he pointed out a smallish, unusual white blister on the inside of her left arm to the medical examiner on duty. The examiner took a closer look, didn't like what he saw, and decided to examine a bit of the subcutaneous tissue around the blister. He found adrenaline in the sample, which was unusual, and decided to do a full autopsy. Whoever stuck it in her must have gone through the vein, pulled back to get the needle into the vein, and not realized he was leaving a calling card. You can guess the rest. They discovered excessive amounts of the stuff in her. That's when I entered the picture. The perpetrator obviously didn't know she had a weak heart. It was the equivalent of using a sledgehammer to knock off an ant."

"So it was murder," I muttered.

"I believe we have nicely squared the circle," Mike said dryly.

"But who?" Maggie asked.

"That is the sixty-four-dollar question, isn't it? I was hoping you might be able to shed some light on the matter."

"How would we know?"

His eyebrows ascended skyward. "I believe you found Mrs. Bedford dead, didn't you?"

We nodded.

Mike threw up his arms. "For crying out loud, Harry. You

and Maggie found her dead! What did you see? What did you hear? Who did you see? Before I head over to her apartment, I want to hear it from you."

I repeated what I had told him earlier—that Sally had asked us to evaluate a manuscript. "There was no name attached to it. She wanted us to ferret out and confirm the identity of the author."

Mike interrupted. "Why was that so important?"

Maggie and I glanced at each other. Maggie shrugged and said, "The manuscript was in a safe. Her husband disappeared over forty years ago. At the time of his disappearance, he was writing a book. Mrs. Bedford thought this was the book. She simply asked us to look at the manuscript and decide whether it was possible it was written by her husband."

"And?" Mike asked.

Suddenly, a water stain on the ceiling demanded my full attention.

"We have no idea who wrote it," Maggie said. "We haven't even looked at it yet."

I stared even more intently at the water stain to drown out the niggling little inner voice that kept repeating, *No good can come of this.*

Mike gave both of us a long look. "Let's put the manuscript aside for the time being, and assuming Harry has finished his examination of that fascinating water stain on the ceiling, maybe you could tell me about your visit to her apartment the day she died."

I started. "The doorman was expecting us. Sally had left instructions with him to let us up. She had given us a key the day before, when we first came to her apartment."

At the mention of a previous visit, Mike's pencil hovered slightly over his ever-present notebook, but he said nothing.

I went through the whole sequence of events, including

the arrival of the paramedics and our conversation with the doorman.

At the mention of the delivery boy, the pencil took a temporary rest in the palm of Mike's hand. "What did the doorman say about the delivery boy?"

Maggie shrugged. "Not much. He didn't see him come in but saw him leave. We assumed it was the same kid who almost bowled Harry over the day previous."

Mike tapped his pen against his nose. "So I take it you still have a key."

"Yes, we do, and the answer is no, I won't," I answered.

"I can always get a warrant," he said mildly.

"It's sticky for me," I said.

"How so?"

"The estate has retained us to complete the manuscript evaluation for estate valuation purposes. The attorney in charge is Arthur Babcock. If he says it's okay, then I'm fine with taking you over."

"She has an—"

I handed him Arthur Babcock's business card.

He looked at it and shrugged. "I suggest you give Mr. Babcock a call." He handed the card back to me. "Harry, this is for your own protection. I want you to accompany me when we go to the apartment, so you can tell me if it appears to be exactly as you left it." His voice was calm, but the message was clear, he was not going to take no for an answer.

I hesitated again.

Mike grabbed the phone off the cradle and thrust it at me. "I don't want to be a jerk, Harry, but now would be a good time."

Reluctantly, I took the proffered phone and keyed in Mr. Babcock's number.

"I didn't expect to hear from you so soon," Mr. Babcock said upon answering. "Has something turned up?"

That is an understatement, I thought to myself. "Actually, yes, something has turned up, and it's not good." I felt a catch in my throat. "Detective Farmer from the NYPD is in the bookstore right now. He has informed me that Sally was, er, the victim of foul play." A grunt emanated from the other end of the line. I continued. "He wants us to go to Sally's apartment with him, but I don't want to do that without your permission."

For a moment, I thought we had been disconnected. Finally, Mr. Babcock said that was fine and that he would meet us there in an hour.

I pressed the end key and handed the phone to Maggie, who placed the receiver back on the console. "He'll meet us there in an hour," I said.

15

Maggie and I made arrangements for our part-time bookkeeper to come in to manage the bookstore while we were out, and shortly after that, Mike shepherded a pair of stunned booksellers into a taxi for the short hop to Sally's apartment. Our riding together ensured Maggie and I could not engage in any private chitchat, which I was sure was exactly what Mike wanted to prevent. He had an uncanny sixth sense that told him when something wasn't quite right, and I knew it must have been in overdrive at that moment. Mike was not known to be loquacious at the best of times, but that day, he was positively taciturn.

Robbie was the doorman on duty when we arrived, so I explained to him that we were meeting Mr. Babcock at Sally's apartment. "This is Detective Farmer of the NYPD." At the look of alarm on Robbie's face, I quickly added, "Whenever someone dies unexpectedly, the NYPD conducts an investigation." The explanation seemed to assuage any concerns he had about the presence of one of New York's finest in the building.

A few moments later, we stepped off the elevator and into the foyer. Mike gave a low whistle. "Not bad."

"We should wait here for Babcock," said Maggie. Mike merely nodded.

I flicked away some lint on one of the sleeves of my coat and then examined the other one to make sure there were no errant bits on it. Maggie checked herself out in the hallway mirror and smoothed her hair. Mike took in his surroundings.

After what seemed like an eternity, the door opened, and out popped Mr. Babcock. He walked right up to Mike, stuck out his hand, and, without introducing himself, said, "You must be Detective Farmer. I'm Arthur Babcock, Mrs. Bedford's attorney. What is this all about?"

Mike shook his hand, handed him his card, and explained what had led the medical examiner to suspect foul play. "I know Harry, so when I saw his name on the report as having found her body, I decided to start there."

"Well, shall we proceed?" Mr. Babcock gestured for us to enter the apartment.

The four of us did a walk-through. Maggie and I pointed out where we had found Sally. Mike made notes from time to time.

At the end of our tour, I turned to Mike and said, "Other than a tidied-up bed, everything looks just as we left it."

Mike turned to Maggie, who nodded in agreement, and then asked, "How 'bout you, Mr. Babcock? Notice anything out of the ordinary, based on your visits here?"

Mr. Babcock shrugged. "It all seems pretty much as I remember it from my last visit with Sally."

"And when would that have been?"

"The day she gave me her instructions to engage Mr. Kramer and Ms. Parker in evaluating a manuscript in her possession." He paused for a moment and tapped his lips. "Hmm, maybe a week ago."

He must be mistaken, I thought to myself. The letter he

gave to us after Sally's death was dated the day of our first meeting, which had been just five days before. I started to open my mouth to correct him, but Maggie gave me a vicious jab in the ribs. I looked at her in annoyance; she just frowned back.

"I hope you appreciate, Detective, that there is very little I can disclose about our dealings, as she was, and now her estate is, my client," said Mr. Babcock.

Mike gave him a cold look. "And I am sure you are aware that, this being a murder investigation, your full cooperation will be expected."

I interrupted. "Have I missed something here?"

"I was just telling Mr. Babcock that I will need to meet with him to discuss this manuscript business," Mike said.

"And I was just saying that I wasn't sure what possible relevance that manuscript could have to her death," Mr. Babcock said. "The doorman mentioned to me that she had had several deliveries in the last few days and that it was always the same delivery person. Shouldn't you be focusing on that person?"

"And what might his motive be?" Without waiting for an answer from Babcock, Mike said, "Oh yes, maybe she didn't give him a big enough tip."

Looking offended, Mr. Babcock said, "On the contrary, she was very generous to service people. Maybe he thought he could find some more cash around the apartment."

My head felt as if a nail were being hammered right between my eyes.

Maggie intervened. "I think there is nothing more we can do here today, Mike. If we think of anything that might be important, we'll give you a call. In the meantime, what do you want us to do about the apartment? As Mr. Babcock will confirm, we have been retained by the estate to continue with the evaluation of the manuscript, and as you already know, Mrs. Bedford entrusted us with a key to her apartment. We also have the estate's authority to enter the apartment at any time to do our work. We will need to access the apartment from time to time to complete our evaluation."

"I have a CSI team arriving in about half an hour. I'll let you know when their work is done." Mike turned to Arthur Babcock. "I'll have my office phone you to make arrangements to meet again." With that, he pointed to the door and motioned for us to leave, which we were only too glad to do.

No one spoke a word on the way down.

Once we were outside, Mr. Babcock turned to us and asked, "Is he always so disagreeable?"

Maggie gave him a sour smile. "He's from Brooklyn," she said, as if that explained everything.

"We'll keep you up to date on our assessment of the manuscript," I said.

"Mr. Babcock—"

He gave Maggie a tired brush of his hand. "Please, call me Arthur. I have a feeling we're going to be seeing a lot of each other, so we might as well get comfortable."

"All right, Arthur it is, and it's Maggie and Harry to you. I was just going to say"—she paused, and I waited with bated breath to see what new nugget would escape her lips—"we haven't mentioned the possible Black connection to Detective Farmer."

He peered at her over his spectacles. "I thought as much, and quite frankly, at this stage, I think that's just as well. The last thing I need is to find Sally's estate embroiled in litigation."

Before I had a chance to discuss the matter further, he was striding down Gracie Square in search of a cab.

Benjamin Franklin once had said, "We must all hang together, or most assuredly we will hang separately." I was not sure I derived any comfort from the knowledge that the three of us might hang together.

16

When Mr. Babcock's figure had receded into the distance, I hissed at Maggie, "Exactly what was that all about?"

"Why, Harry, darling, I have no idea what you are talking about, but if you are about to launch into a lecture that has moral and legal overtones, at least find me a bar, where I can get a drink to sustain me."

She could be so damned annoying, but I found a bar on York Avenue, and we ordered our usual. We didn't exchange a word until our martinis had arrived and the waiter had left.

"We could just return the manuscript," I said.

Maggie twirled her olives in her martini, appearing to be in deep thought about my suggestion. Then she let the olives rest in peace and said, "We could, but we won't."

"Why didn't you tell Mike about the possible Black connection?"

"Why didn't you?"

She had a point.

She slid her hand across the table and grasped mine. "Listen, my darling, we have absolutely nothing to connect

Arnold Black to either Sally or Nick, other than Sally's allegation that the two books bear a striking resemblance to each other. We have nothing to prove Nick wrote it or to disprove that Black wrote it, yet—"

"Yet it's just too coincidental that Sally arrived with the manuscript, sent a mysterious email to Black, and then was murdered," I said. "Speaking of which, why didn't you tell Mike about that email?"

"Why didn't you tell Mike about the missing photograph?"

"I don't know. I don't know why I didn't mention it, except—"

"Except you had the same suspicion I did—that it's no coincidence Mike is handling this case."

I didn't want to admit the truth of what she was saying, but I was suspicious of his sudden appearance in our bookstore. I rubbed my eyes and ran my hands over my face. I looked up. "By the way, what was that jab in the ribs all about?"

She sat back in her chair and laughed. "So I did get your attention. I wasn't sure for a moment."

"Well, you've really got it now."

"Harry, if the last time Babcock saw Sally was seven days ago, how did he come into possession of a letter written by her to us supposedly after the first time we met her just a few days ago?"

"I thought Babcock might have been mistaken about the date."

She shook her head. "No way. My take on Babcock is that he is meticulous. He's a lawyer, Harry. What do lawyers do?"

It was another rhetorical question that I knew required no answer since she would supply one.

"They keep track of time, appointments, and so forth. He knew precisely when he met Sally last. So the only question is, why fudge dates like that?"

I was too tired and feeling too stupid to think of a response.

"And by the way, did you notice his reaction when I told him we hadn't mentioned the Black connection?"

"He thought it was just as well we hadn't at this stage."

"I found that very odd. I'm not sure what's going on here, Harry, but until we get a clearer picture, I think we should be guarded about what we say to whom."

"Maggie, I don't need to remind you that there is a thin line between exercising caution and obstruction of justice."

17

We opted for takeout pizza and a good bottle of wine for dinner that evening. There was nothing quite like a New York pizza to stir up the intellectual juices and fortify one for any battles that might lie ahead. Our friends from other parts of the country—indeed, all around the world—had a hard time understanding New Yorkers' passion for pizza. Whenever I waxed eloquent about the perfect slice of pizza, they just stared in disbelief at me.

How can I tell if I'm getting a great slice of pizza? If I pick up a nice hot slice of pizza with a thin crispy crust and it droops at the end from the weight of the cheese and sauce, folds nicely in the middle and cracks at the top of the crust, I know I am going to have a great slice.

As we demolished the pizza, we considered our alternatives.

"We could just forget the whole thing and return the manuscript," I said, repeating my earlier suggestion.

"We could, but we won't," replied Maggie, repeating her earlier answer.

I reached over and, with my napkin, dabbed at a bit of

tomato sauce perched precariously at the end of her chin. I was rewarded with a great big kiss for my efforts.

"By the way," I said, "do you remember Sally told us she had noted some discrepancies between Black's book and the manuscript?"

"I remember her telling us that, but I don't recall seeing a copy of the book anywhere in the apartment, and we did a pretty thorough check before we left."

"I don't remember seeing a copy either, but I have to admit I wasn't really focused on it."

"It must be there. I mean, who would remove it?"

"Perhaps the murderer."

"Looking for the missing pages?"

I rose to clear our plates. "It would have really helped to have it as a starting point."

Maggie looked thoughtful. "I agree, but I think at this point in time, we have no option but to start our own comparison. If we work diligently at it, taking into consideration that we do have a business to run, we should be able to form a preliminary assessment within about ten days."

I nodded in agreement. "Hopefully we will be able to get back into the apartment to see if we can find that book and whatever comments she noted."

"Assuming there is any need for us to go back into the apartment."

18

It was a good thing Harriet agreed to work full-time that week, as the manuscript took over our lives, leaving us little time to deal with the myriad of distractions inherent in running a bookstore, such as customers. We agreed to speed-read the book and manuscript and then trade observations.

I tackled the manuscript first and soon found myself absorbed in the perils of being a member of a resistance group in World War II. But for once, it wasn't my propensity to get lost in the minutiae of whatever subject caught my fancy that held me up. The manuscript did not lend itself to speed-reading, in part because it didn't scan well, and I spent a lot of time poring over faint typewriting and trying to decipher the handwritten scribbles in the margins. The book proved easier to wade through.

It didn't take a rocket scientist to observe the strong resemblance between the book and the manuscript, but the bookman in me knew that wasn't really conclusive of anything. It just made it more probable that the same person had written them.

After two days of almost nonstop reading, we sat down

and traded notes. After a few moments had elapsed, Maggie shuffled my notes into a neat pile. "Well, contrary to popular belief, we do agree on some things."

"There are striking similarities."

She flipped through my notes again and quoted one of my notations. "What do you mean by this reference: 'Although the two bear a striking resemblance to each other, I sense a different tone in Black's book'?"

I rubbed my eyes. "It's hard to put my finger on it, but when I came across some passages in Black's book, I got the sense he was writing from the perspective of a historian, a dispassionate observer, but when I read the manuscript, I got the sense it was intended to be a memoir, more personal. I don't know why, since they were so identical in many respects."

"I think I know what you mean."

"I made some notes about what I thought were anomalies between the two, but it was a superficial read, so there might be more."

"The bottom line is, even if there are a few or no anomalies, we have no conclusive evidence that points to one or the other as the author."

I nodded. "We may have to call on the services of our favorite literary archaeologist."

"If only we could get our hands on Sally's copy of the book to see what she found. I thought we might have heard from Mike by now."

"Well, for the time being, there's not much we can do about it, so we'll just keep going with what we have. If we haven't heard from Mike by tomorrow, we'll call in Syd sooner rather than later."

The next morning, while Maggie was soothing a customer having a hissy fit over a valuation George had sent her for an unexceptional copy of *A Farewell to Arms*, I decided to have another crack at trying to identify specific pages with apparent differences in the text. I looked at Maggie's notes and compared them to mine and then looked at the pages we had already noted. Most of the manuscript's pages were identical to the pages in the book, down to the last comma. After a long and tedious exercise, I discovered several nonmatching pages.

Maggie wandered in around noon. "So how goes the battle?" she asked sympathetically.

I slouched in my chair and closed my eyes, which felt as if they were about to drop out of their sockets.

She came over and started to give me a shoulder massage. "Anything startling?"

"I'm not sure," I said. "I just can't shake this feeling that I'm missing something."

"Tell me what you found; maybe another set of ears will help out."

"I went back and looked at the various pages we had made notations about. Most of them were identical, down to the commas. But I found several pages in the book that textually bore no resemblance to the pages in the manuscript."

She shrugged. "It's not that unusual, really, to see the final book form differ from the copy that initially went to the publisher."

"That's true," I said, "but think about what we are comparing. If Sally was telling the truth, the manuscript is over forty years old. Black's book was just published."

"And?"

"Why change some pages, and why make such wholesale changes? The history of that period hasn't changed that much."

Maggie's tongue made a circuit around her lips. "Maybe because he didn't have the original pages."

"Or he had something to hide."

19

"What are you getting at, Harry?"

"Remember the email Sally sent to Black and forwarded to us?"

She nodded. "'I have the missing pages.' But what does that mean? Sally told us she had noted differences, but she never told us what those differences were."

"Perhaps this was Sally's way of letting Black know she had an entire version of the manuscript, and ..."

"And?"

"Maybe he's had the original manuscript all along. Maybe there was something in those pages he didn't want anyone to know about, or ..."

"Or?"

"Or maybe his vanity got in the way, and he felt the need to put his own stamp on the book."

"Should we call Mike and see if we can get back into her apartment? Maybe we can find the book she was reading and look for her notations."

I shook my head. "No, the less we see of Mike right now the better."

She studied me for a moment. "Why?"

"Maggie, if Sally was telling Black that she had a copy of the entire manuscript, what might follow from that?"

She took a deep breath. "That she was in a position to expose him as a fraud."

"Is that motive for murder? Who knows? We don't know this man or what he might have to hide from the world aside from having copied someone else's work. I can't believe anyone would be desperate enough to kill someone over a possible copyright suit based on a manuscript with no name attached, especially when the supposed author has been dead for over forty years. Until we have some evidence as to who really wrote this book, we are not in any position to make accusations or possibly subject someone to a criminal investigation."

She sighed. "I agree, but I do feel a little uneasy about it."

"Me too, but I still think it is better to be prudent at this stage and continue with our own investigation. Speaking of which, yesterday I mentioned that I sensed there was a disconnect between the manuscript and the book, but I couldn't put my finger on it."

"You said you thought the tone or the voice was different."

At moments like those, I really appreciated having a mate in life. "Exactly. I want you to go over the work I did yesterday with a fresh set of eyes to make sure I am not imagining things."

Later that afternoon, while I tended the shop, Maggie set about reading the pages and reviewing the notes I had made. She was still hard at it when I came upstairs after closing up, so I started dinner. I had just finished applying a cleaver to some onions, when she wandered into the kitchen. She sat down at the counter. Without a word, I pushed a martini over to her. She took a sip and sat back.

"Well?" I said.

"I agree with you, Harry, that there is something decidedly odd about the book's pages that don't match the pages from our copy of the manuscript."

"So where do you think we should go from here?"

"I think we should have dinner. I'm starved. Maybe taking a break from it will spring something loose up here," she said, tapping the top of her head. "Besides, I promised George that before he returned, I would look at some of that collection of World War II literature Mrs. Peabody brought in."

"Not relishing the job?"

She wrinkled her nose and grimaced.

After dinner, we settled ourselves in front of the fireplace. Maggie sat in her armchair, surrounded by a pile of books that smelled as if they hadn't seen the light of day since World War II, and I sprawled across the couch with the day's sports section from the *New York Times*. I was absorbed in the latest compensation antics or, rather, demands of some second-rate baseball players, until a peal of laughter erupted from the chair opposite me.

"Who would have thought World War II history tomes would tickle your funny bone?" I said in jest.

She laughed and flipped the cover over. The book was an obscure social history of the upper classes of England in the early part of the twentieth century. "It's just a funny anecdote about Churchill and Nancy Astor. Apparently, they despised each other, so one night at a dinner party, some hostess with a perverse sense of humor sat them opposite each other at the dinner table. Let me read this exchange. I only wish I was as quick off the mark as Churchill was. This is Lady Astor speaking: 'Honestly, Mr. Churchill, if you were my husband, I would poison your tea.' To which Churchill replied, 'Madam, if I were your husband, I should drink it.'"

We both cracked up. Then I stopped laughing. "That's it."

I got up and ran to the study, leaving a bewildered Maggie behind, and returned a moment later with a fistful of manuscript sheets.

"What is it, Harry?"

I leafed through the pages of Nick's manuscript, found the page I was looking for, and then found the differing page in Black's book. I tapped the sheets with a pencil and then looked at Maggie, who was waiting for an explanation of my bizarre behavior.

"Listen to this," I said. "This is a line from Nick's manuscript: 'It was dangerous, but I knew I would go, regardless of the danger, to ensure that nothing compromised Operation Dragoon.'"

Maggie shrugged. "So?"

"Look here." I laid out the pages in front of her. "The words 'It was dangerous' are at the bottom of one page, and the rest are at the top of the next. This is what the corresponding page from Black's manuscript says: 'It was dangerous, but it was imperative I should continue on to determine the exact status of Operation Anvil.'"

She waited.

"Maggie, there are a couple of things out of sync here. First of all, Nick was American and, as expected, used the word *would* in this context, but in Black's book—"

"He used the word *should*, as is common in British usage," she said, unable to keep the excitement from her voice. "But you said there were two things, Harry."

"Operation Dragoon was the final code name assigned to the invasion of southern France; Operation Anvil was the first name. I remember that throughout the manuscript, the operation was consistently referred to as Dragoon. If the manuscript was authored by Black, why would he refer to the operation by different names in different parts of the manuscript?"

"And the manuscript refers to a person on the team as a Frenchman by the name of Jean Marcoux, who spoke perfect English in the British sense, and he was the person killed in the ambush. Sally confirmed that name."

We had our first glimpse at the truth.

20

Manuscript attribution was not a subject we had any expertise in, so the next morning, I put in a call to Syd, who did have the requisite knowledge. Maggie and I agreed we had to get a definitive opinion on whether the same author had written both the manuscript and the book and, if so, who had written it: Black, Bedford, or neither. Syd was the only person we trusted to do the evaluation.

We had no idea what we would do if, in fact, we found out that Nick Bedford was the author and Arnold Black had appropriated the work. After all, a plagiarizer did not a murderer make.

It was no surprise to me that my call to Syd went right to voice mail. Although Syd was one of the most technologically savvy people I knew, she had a dislike bordering on the pathological for telephones and suffered them only as a necessity of her business. I figured she'd get back to me by the end of the day.

Maggie was off to an estate sale, which left Harriet and me in the bookstore. Harriet was busy cataloging the books from a box that a book scout had dropped off. As I wandered by, she said casually, "I happened to be talking to my friend who works in Arnold Black's office."

A pirouette worthy of the New York City Ballet found me almost nose to nose with my favorite PhD candidate. "Really?"

"Really."

"And?"

She looked up and motioned for me to pull up a chair. She then leaned over and murmured, "She says there is something peculiar going on over at that office."

"Like?" I said.

"Only his executive assistant is now allowed into his office."

"That's not really strange," I said.

"My friend is a friend of his former secretary. She was also allowed into his office but he abruptly fired her about a month ago, just before the book came out. No one has seen or heard from her since. Also, no one has ever seen the original manuscript, except for that secretary."

"And presumably Arnold Black."

She looked at me as if trying to decide whether I was being a wiseass.

I sighed. "How do you know no one else has ever seen the manuscript?"

She gave me a patient smile. "My friend was delivering some research to his office. The door to the reception area was open, so my friend didn't bother to knock. Black was in the reception area with his back to my friend, castigating his former secretary, saying things like 'Who gave you the authority to poke around my office? Next time you have questions, you come to me first.' When my friend made her presence known, he glared at her, snatched the papers she was delivering from her hands, and went into his office. Talk about awkward.

"Naturally, my friend was concerned and asked her friend what was going on. She said she had been working on the manuscript for Black's book, doing some minor editorial changes. She came to a part that didn't make sense and thought something had been missed in the version she was working on. She knew Black kept an original paper copy in his office, so she retrieved it, and she was in the process of locating the section in question to compare it to hers, when he walked in and saw what she was doing. I guess he exploded and ripped the pages out of her hand. My friend was puzzled and asked, 'Why would he care? I mean, after all, you did the original transcription.' She said no, the version she was working on was given to her by his executive assistant. They both shrugged it off as just a bad-tempered moment and didn't think much about it. Then she was fired."

I considered the possible implications of that information. Before I could say anything, Harriet continued. "That's not all. After her friend was fired, my friend phoned her to find out what had happened. In the course of the conversation, her friend said, 'Isn't it ironic that the section I was looking for wasn't even there?'"

I have the missing pages rattled around in my head, bouncing from one side to the other. While I was trying to digest that new bit of information, my cell phone rang. Thinking it was Syd, I answered and said, "What kind of working hours do you keep?"

There was silence for a moment.

"And good morning to you too," growled Mike.

"Sorry, Mike. I was expecting someone else."

"I gathered that."

I waited.

"We're finished at Mrs. Bedford's apartment, so you and Maggie can go back in to do your *research*."

I detected a slight hint of sarcasm in his voice but said only "Thanks, Mike. Did you let Babcock know?" I heard a slow intake of air. "I thought you weren't supposed to smoke in your office, and more to the point, I thought you said you gave it up."

"What makes you think I'm in my office? And more to the point, I have—mostly. As for your first question, I keep cops' hours, so my office isn't my usual place of abode. As for the second question, yes, I did give Babcock the green light."

I hesitated and then asked, "Has anything turned up—any indication of who the murderer might be?"

"Nope, not yet, but I'll keep in touch."

I was about to hang up, when he added, seemingly as an afterthought, "Oh, by the way, I'd be interested to hear the results of your manuscript research, especially who the author might be."

He'd caught me off guard. "Why would you be interested in that?" I stammered.

"One never knows where one will find a motive for murder, so like I said, call me when you figure out who wrote this manuscript you were talking about."

The click of the receiver told me in no uncertain terms that he expected I would do just that.

Before I finished berating myself for being so cursedly transparent, the phone rang again. Having learned my lesson from the previous call, I picked up the phone and said, "Used and Rare Books. Harry Kramer speaking."

There was a slight pause, and then I heard, "My, my, aren't we formal today? Expecting a well-heeled customer, are we?"

I rolled my eyes heavenward. "Hi, Syd. And the answer is no, but I have been waiting for your call."

"And we're testy to boot. Really, Harry, you only called an hour ago. What's up?"

"Sorry, Syd. I just got off the phone with Mike Farmer."

"Ah. Say no more."

"Actually, he's part of a literary problem I have right now, which is why I'm calling you. We are definitely in need of your services."

"Can we talk about it by phone?"

"No, I think you should come over—it's going to take a while to go over everything. Could you join us here for dinner tonight?"

"Hang on a second while I grab the calendar."

I heard the shuffling of the mounds of papers that habitually occupied her desk and then a little squeak. She obviously had found the wayward calendar.

I heard the sound of the phone being picked up, and then she said, "I'm supposed to have dinner with a collector tonight, but he's so obnoxious that I'll be happy to plead illness. What time should I come over?"

"Let's say seven."

"Are you going to give me any clue as to what this is about?"

"We have been asked to do a manuscript attribution, but it's really a lot more complicated than we thought."

"Sounds interesting. See you later. I have to go tell a little white lie."

Just as I hit the end button, Maggie walked in. She filled me in on the estate sale, and I filled her in on the two conversations.

"The plot thickens," she said.

"So it seems."

"Do you think we should head over to Sally's?"

I shook my head. "Not today. I don't think there is a big rush now. Let's talk to Syd first in case she wants us to look for other information that might be in the apartment. Besides, my gut tells me Sally probably came across some of the same discrepancies we did."

The doorbell rang promptly at seven. I opened the door and handed Syd an ice-cold martini. She took it without a word, handed me her briefcase-sized handbag, and turned around, and I helped her off with her overcoat. She gave me a peck on the cheek and headed for the kitchen. "Good evening to you too!" I called after her. She just waved a hand in response.

By the time I got to the kitchen, she and Maggie were engaged in a serious discussion regarding the whereabouts of the latest sample sales. Since that was a topic utterly foreign to me, I decided it would be wise to sip my martini and remain silent.

As soon as Maggie put the eggplant towers in the oven to finish, we retired to the living room. I was dying to get to the topic at hand, but alas, Maggie got in first, and her question had nothing to do with what I considered to be the pressing business at hand.

"So, Syd, how's the English count?"

I moaned. "Why are women so fascinated by other women's love lives?"

They both stared at me as if I were an alien creature, which, as a male, I guessed I was if one looked at the world from the female side of the fence.

"Oh, he's a duke, not a count," Syd said. "God, what a colossal bore. I mean, there has to be more to life than the number of hunting dogs and horses that make for a good hunt. Besides, I don't approve of fox hunting, so I dumped him about a month ago. Actually, I've been seeing your friend Harold. He's quite adorable and very entertaining and has been a great help in some of my research."

I nearly fell off my chair. "Harold!" I blurted out. "Harold the librarian?"

They both turned to me and rolled their eyes. I had perceived Harold as my rival for Maggie's affections at one time, and she had said the same thing. I didn't get it. *What does the man have that attracts these incredibly beautiful women? He's fat and wears glasses with lenses as thick as Coke bottle glass, and he's, well, a librarian.*

As if she read my thoughts, Maggie said, "Harry just can't get over the fact that not all women pine after a pretty-boy face. That some of us actually consider intelligence to be sexy."

Syd grinned. "Well, speaking of intelligence, perhaps we should talk about your new mysterious assignment for me. I hope I'm not going to get shot at this time."

I lowered my eyes. Maggie studied the olive in her martini with the same intensity as one would have studied a lab specimen. The last time Syd had done some literary sleuthing for us, she'd ended up being the object of the bad guy's ire, which had resulted in her being shot at. However, she had wounded the bad guy more than he had wounded her, by stomping on his foot with a four-inch stiletto heel.

She raised her martini glass and then stopped in midair, looking first at Maggie and then at me.

I started. "Well—"

"There is a murder involved," Maggie said.

Syd carefully returned her glass to the table. "You're joking, right?"

We shook our heads.

Syd looked to Maggie and then to me. "Perhaps we should start at the beginning."

I went to the office to get our file and a copy of Black's book. I told Syd the whole story, including Babcock's visit, Sally's visit, our visits to her apartment, and her murder. I then showed her Black's book and the copy of Nick's manuscript. Maggie filled her in on the work we had done.

"It's hard to put your finger on anything specific; rather, it's more of a slight difference in tone and use of language," Maggie said.

I told her about the email Sally had sent to Black about the missing pages and the conversation Harriet had had with her friend at the institute where Black was employed as some sort of specialist.

"We also know Sally noted some discrepancies, but we haven't been able to locate either her copy of the book or whatever notes she may have made," I said.

"We need you to compare these two versions and tell us whether they were written by the same author, two authors, or otherwise and, if possible, try to identify who the real author is," Maggie said.

Syd sat there with her hands clasped in a steeple, tapping her index fingers on her lips, looking thoughtful. "Why do you think this is in any way connected to the murder of Sally Bedford? I am assuming this is the reason the ever-present Mike Farmer has been on your doorstep."

I nodded. "All we have told him is that we were retained by Sally and, subsequently, her estate to provide a definitive attribution of a manuscript that is part of her estate."

Syd looked skeptical. "Do you honestly think plagiarism is a sufficient motive for murder?"

"Sally was also certain that somehow, Black was connected with Nick's disappearance. If he was connected to Nick's disappearance and Sally uncovered something, that something might have been a motive for murder. Besides, why is Mike so interested in the outcome of our research all of a sudden?"

"So," said Maggie, "are you interested?"

Syd let out a big sigh. "Murder and manuscripts—does it get any more interesting?"

"I'll take that as a yes," Maggie said. "Let's eat dinner, and then we'll pack up all the material we have."

Over dinner, Syd filled us in on her schedule. She was doing a significant piece of work for an unnamed billionaire client who, in an effort to acquire a veneer of old-money respectability, had bought a library lock, stock, and bindings from a minor nobleman in England. The client had paid a fortune for it and, after the fact, decided he should have a valuation done by an independent appraiser.

Talk about putting the cart before the horse, I thought.

"It's a headache and time consuming," Syd said, "not to mention the fact that it's taxing my diplomatic skills to the limit. Ninety percent of the stuff is junk. He keeps hovering anxiously over my shoulder, and I can hardly tell him he would have been better off hiring an interior decorator and stuffing the shelves with shell books. The bottom line is, I'm looking for a few gems so he doesn't feel too bad."

"How soon do you think you could start on our project?" Now I was the overanxious client.

"I have to go to Paris on a job within the next two weeks. I'll try to get a preliminary report to you before I leave."

After dinner, we packed up all the material we had. I helped Syd into her coat. At the door, she turned to us and said, "This guy Black does not sound like a nice guy, so tread lightly."

21

Late the next day, Syd called.

"Harry, I've been examining the yellow carbon copy and noticed there are some handwritten notes in some of the margins. They are faint, but it's possible I can enlarge them digitally. If we had a sample of Bedford's handwriting to compare with the handwritten comments, it would support Sally Bedford's contention that her husband was the author."

"Sally never gave us a sample, so I'm not sure what I can come up with. I'll get back to you."

When Maggie came down, I told her about Syd's request.

"We could go over to the apartment to see if there's anything there," she said. "If not, maybe there is something in her safe-deposit box."

"Or maybe Arthur has some samples," I said.

"Good idea," she said.

I phoned Babcock's office and, after a short wait, was put through to Arthur. "What can I do for you, Harry?" he asked.

I told him the nature of my call.

"Unfortunately, I don't think I'm going to be of much help

to you," he said. "Sally and Nick never wrote many letters to each other. You have to remember they were in the OSS, and discretion was important, so as far as I know, there is no correspondence from that period. After the war, they married almost immediately, and they never spent more than a few days apart, so there was no need to write to each other. I have a lot of correspondence from Sally but none from Nick—Nick disappeared years before I became Sally's attorney. If any correspondence exists, it is in Sally's belongings, either here or in France. By the way, Detective Farmer phoned me to authorize your entry into the apartment again."

"Yes, I know, and it looks like this will be a good reason to go back in."

"I'm sorry I'm not of more assistance in this, Harry. Good luck. Let me know if you find anything."

I relayed to Maggie the results of my call. As soon as Harriet showed up, Maggie and I bundled up and headed to Sally's.

It was odd and downright unnerving to be back there. We went through every nook and cranny in the office and repeated the process throughout the rest of the apartment, but the search proved fruitless. We found no Black book and no paperwork bearing Nick's name, let alone his signature in his own hand. We found nothing, not even correspondence from a friend, just canceled checks with Sally's signature on them. We paused on the landing to discuss where we might look next.

"I just can't believe she didn't keep a single piece of correspondence or card or something from Nick. I mean, he must have written something to someone," I said.

"I think I know someone who might be able to help us," Maggie said.

The slight catch in her voice caught my attention. I turned to face her. In her hands, she held the picture of Sally and

Nick that had been resting on the console table at the top of the landing.

"What are you talking about?"

She looked at me and tapped the picture. "Don't you recognize him?"

I shrugged. "It's Nick."

"No, not Nick. I'm talking about the man in the background."

I looked. "What about him?"

She gently replaced the picture. "That man is your father-in-law."

22

snatched the picture from its resting place and cursed myself for neglecting to bring my reading glasses with me, not that my specs would have made much difference. The figure in the background was out of focus—to my eyes, a blur. "How can you tell?"

She gave me an impatient look. "For heaven's sake, I think I can recognize my own father."

I looked again. I still wasn't sure if I saw a faint resemblance or if I just thought I saw one because Maggie said so. "I'm just not sure I see it."

"Well, I am sure, and I think it's time to have a chat with him."

"How exactly do you plan to do that? He's away on a river cruise in France and not due to return for at least another week."

She glowered at me. She hated it when my practical side came out.

"Besides," I added, "for all you know, he might have been just passing by when the photo was taken, with no connection whatsoever to the event in that photo."

"I know, I know, and you are probably right, but you know what we say about coincidences."

Neither of us believed in coincidences.

"I have this nagging feeling that there is something more here, something larger, than resolving a copyright issue or solving a decades-old disappearance," she said, "but what?"

"I never underestimate your instincts, Maggie, but your father is away for the next week, so in the meantime, let's gather all the information we can. Hopefully the contents of the safe-deposit box will shed some light on the manuscript. Perhaps there will be some photos in there that can shed some light on whom Nick and Sally knew or associated with."

She gave me a reluctant nod. "You're right. And maybe by then, we will have Syd's comments back."

"And don't forget: we might have to go to France ourselves to check out Sally's farmhouse."

"The big question is, do we tell Babcock about any of this?"

"I'm not sure. On the off chance Sally did know Bill, she would most certainly have told Babcock, who would have had no trouble finding out that his daughter was a partner in a rare bookstore. The big question is, why not just tell us?"

"And did Dad know that Sally was going to approach us?"

"Let's get Babcock on the phone and arrange to pick up the safe-deposit box key. For the time being, we'll act as if everything is proceeding and say nothing about what we have found."

After a short conversation with Mr. Babcock's assistant, we made a quick detour to his office in Midtown. His assistant apologized. Mr. Babcock had left for the day but had left an envelope for us. Inside was the address for Sally's bank, which happened to be a US subsidiary of a French bank, and an envelope marked, "Keys." Luck was on our side. We managed to squeeze through the bank doors just before closing time.

We stated our business to the receptionist, who was *très française* and exuded the je ne sais quoi attitude that seemed to have been perfected by all French women regardless of age, station in life, or location. She tapped out a number on her desk set, spoke rapid-fire French, and then politely requested that we have a seat, as someone, who remained unnamed, would be out shortly to assist us.

Never one to do as I was told, I wandered around the reception area, staring with blank eyes at whatever hung on the walls. Startled by a tap on my shoulder, I swung around to face a gaunt man of medium height with a face that was all sharp angles and a forehead notable for the receding hairline at its peak. His skin pallor was winter gray. He peered at me over half glasses resting on the bridge of his nose. Extending his hand, he said, "Monsieur Parker and Madame Kramer."

I took his hand. Although it was warm in the room, his hand was damp and soft, leaving me to wonder if perhaps there was a sponge concealed within it. Maggie brushed her hand across her lips in an attempt to hide her amusement.

"No, I'm Harry Kramer." I turned to Maggie. "This is my wife, Maggie Parker."

Maggie stepped forward, gave him her thousand-watt smile, and took his hand. He flushed a furious red and sputtered an apology.

"And you are?" Maggie asked.

Gathering his wits about him, he said in clipped, accented English, "I am Henri Rousseau, senior wealth manager. I am—or, rather, was—Mrs. Bedford's account representative in the United States. Please follow me."

He turned on his heel and led us to a metal door that, when opened, revealed a small but luxuriously appointed office. He waved us inside, closed the door, pointed to two leather chairs, and then went around and positioned himself behind his desk. Placing his arms and elbows on the desk, he leaned forward, removed his glasses, and said, "I understand you wish to examine the contents of Mrs. Bedford's safe-deposit box."

"That's correct," Maggie said. "Mrs. Bedford retained us to do some work for her. After her death, the estate asked us to continue with the work." She produced the letter of authorization from Arthur Babcock.

"And what work would that be?" Mr. Rousseau asked.

My immediate impulse was to say, "None of your business," but before I could utter the words, Maggie interjected smoothly.

"I am afraid that is confidential. Suffice it to say we have been asked to provide an opinion on a particular estate asset. I believe Mr. Babcock's letter makes it clear that we are to have unimpeded access to the safe-deposit box." She fished out the envelope from Babcock's office marked, "Keys," and produced a key with a number on it. "And I believe this is the key to the safe-deposit box. Is there a problem?"

Mr. Rousseau gave her a long, hard stare. "No, it's just unusual that in the space of two days, I have 'ad two separate requests to look at Mrs. Bedford's safe-deposit box."

I felt the hair on the back of my neck stand to attention.

Maggie moved forward to the edge of her chair and stared directly into Mr. Rousseau's eyes. "Our understanding is that only my husband and I and Mr. Babcock have access to this safe-deposit box."

I felt a horrible lurch of the contents in my stomach.

He gave her a thin smile. "That is correct. That is why I find your visit so unusual. Mr. Babcock didn't mention that you too would also be arriving to look at the contents of the box. In fact, he never mentioned you at all."

"Are you saying Mr. Babcock was here yesterday?" Maggie asked.

"Yes, that is precisely what I am saying."

"Why?"

Mr. Rousseau shrugged. "He said he needed to retrieve a will, and in the meantime, as the lawyer for her estate, he was doing an inventory of the safe-deposit box. I am surprised he did not mention it to you."

Maggie gave a wave of her hand. "Not unusual. As the estate attorney, he has to do his due diligence. I hope he found what he was looking for."

He shrugged. "I really don't know. He was only in the vault a short time. In fact, I didn't see him leave."

"He was in the room alone?" I said.

Mr. Rousseau rewarded my stupidity with a patient smile. "Of course. It is bank privacy policy that customers be permitted the privacy of the vault as they examine the contents of their safe-deposit boxes. Just as you will be," he added pointedly.

Maggie rose. Mr. Rousseau hastened to his feet. I looked up in surprise. She jabbed me and said tersely, "Harry, I really think we should get on with our own examination of the box and let Mr. Rousseau get on with his day." She turned and made for the door, leaving him no further opportunity to quiz us about the nature of our visit.

Mr. Rousseau hurried to open the door and pointed to the end of the hallway. "Please follow me."

A massive steel door occupied the entire width of the hallway, ensuring there was only one way in and one way out. Mr. Rousseau swiped a card and stood up to an optical scanner. A moment later, the door swung open. A cool rush of air met us, and we stepped inside. A diminutive young man sat behind a desk. Mr. Rousseau presented us to him, made a copy of our identifications and the letter of authorization, and then turned us over to the young man.

The young man led us into a small room containing rows and rows of metal boxes, checked the key, consulted his sheet of paper, and withdrew a large rectangular steel box about two inches in height. I noted the presence of at least three CCTV cameras. After placing the box on the table, the young man had us sign the sheet and then left. The door closed without a sound behind him.

I motioned for Maggie to sit opposite me, nodding toward the cameras.

She sighed. "They are in every bank, Harry. It's not a nefarious plot to spy on us. What I'm curious about is what Babcock was really after and why he didn't mention to us that he had just examined the safe-deposit box."

"To answer your first question, according to Mr. Rousseau, he was looking for a will, probably the original. It's not unusual for someone to keep the original of his or her will. And he was doing an inventory. As to your second question, it's a logical thing for an attorney to do for probate purposes. He is, after all, responsible for the administration of the estate. Thirdly, we only spoke to his assistant, who, being the professional she is, would not discuss with us Babcock's every movement, since it is none of our business."

"Why are you whispering, Harry? Who is here to listen in on us?"

"I agree it seems odd, but let's leave Arthur Babcock for another day and see what we have here."

Maggie flipped the lid up and proceeded to empty the box's contents, which consisted of several large brown envelopes. She opened them one at a time, describing the contents as she went through them, and then laid them aside next to the appropriate envelope. The items had the musty smell that came from being cooped up in a metal box for too long, I was starting to feel that way myself.

"Well, this is interesting," said Maggie.

I looked up. "What is?"

She waved a snapshot in the air. "It's a photo that was stuck between two of the sheets of paper in this pile. It must have gotten damp, and some of the coating stuck to the paper. I wonder if this is one of the pictures Sally was referring to." She flipped it over. "Oh dear."

My eyes shot up. "That doesn't sound good."

She shoved the photograph at me, and I echoed her sentiment.

"So you recognize him?" she said.

"I don't recognize anyone in the photo, but I recognize the photo."

"You do?"

"Yes. It's the one I saw in Sally's apartment. Remember when I told you I was sure a photo was missing from the console table on the landing? Well, this is the photo I saw. The first time I saw it, I thought there was something familiar about one of the men in the photo."

"Well, you should see something familiar about one of them." She took the photo from my hand, placed it on the table, and tapped on one of the figures.

I took a closer look. The picture was faded and old, but there was no mistaking the eyes and the thick thatch of hair, which, in the photo, was very dark.

"Well, it seems to bear out your suspicion that Bill and Sally knew each other," I said.

"If she knew him, why didn't she go directly to him for help?"

I sighed. "Well, I guess we will just have to ask him when he comes home." I put the photo to the side, and we carried on sorting through the remaining papers in the safe.

I wasn't sure what I hoped to find in the box, but there wasn't anything that touched on the manuscript or had any handwriting on it that might have belonged to anyone other than Sally. Disappointed, we started to put the papers back in their envelopes.

I picked up the photograph. "I wonder why Sally decided to put this one photograph in the safe-deposit box. She left me with the impression there would be several. Unless, of course, someone removed them and didn't realize this one was here."

Maggie nodded in agreement as she ran her hand inside the safe-deposit box to make sure we hadn't missed anything. She paused with her hand still in the box.

I eyed her curiously. "Is there something else in there?"

She frowned. "I'm not sure. I thought I felt something on the top of the box, just behind the hinged section." She ran her fingers over the inside top again. "There is something there, but it's taped to the top of the box." She took her hand out and tried to peer inside. "It feels like a piece of tape or plastic, but I can't be sure. Here—see if you can see anything."

I put down the photo and turned the box toward me. I ran my fingers inside. She was right. There was something there. My fingers were too big to dislodge it, so I turned the box toward her again. By that time, she had discreetly retrieved a small pair of tweezers from her handbag. I stood up and bent over the table toward her. Carefully, she ran the tweezers along the top inside surface. The pointed ends of the tweezers made a sound like nails on a chalkboard that reverberated in the small confines of the room. She felt inside again, and I could hear the sound of her nail scratching at something. A few moments later, she withdrew a slender piece of plastic about three inches by three inches, taped on all four sides. Inside the plastic cover was a piece of faded yellow paper.

Maggie turned it over. "It appears to be a blank piece of paper," she muttered.

"Can you get it out of the plastic?"

She used the tweezers to open one side of the plastic and slid the piece of paper out of its protective cover. It was neatly folded in half. She carefully unfolded it.

"There are some markings or numbers on this side, but I have no idea what they could mean." She handed the paper to me.

I shrugged. "Just random numbers." I handed the paper back to her, and she slipped it back into its cover. "Why would Sally tape this to the top of the box?"

"Maybe she didn't; maybe Nick did, and she didn't know it was there."

"Hmm. Nick told Sally on the last day she saw him alive that he had some new information he was going to share with her, remember?"

She nodded.

"Well, maybe this had something to do with the new information. Maybe Sally came across it, and she concealed it in the box this way. Maybe she didn't understand the meaning of the numbers but sensed they might be important and decided to keep the paper just in case."

"Harry, someone thought this was important enough to deliberately conceal it in a safe-deposit box that very few people had access to. If it was Nick, why didn't he tell Sally what the numbers meant? If Sally knew it was here, why didn't she tell us? Babcock obviously didn't know it was here, because the plastic casing appears to be yellowed, with the tape never removed."

For a moment, we stared at the paper in silence. I looked at Maggie. She rested her hands over the plastic. I put my hand over hers and slid it toward me. She gently withdrew her hand

and accidentally knocked a stack of the loose papers off the table. She bent over, hastily retrieved the papers, and put them in their envelope.

"Well," I said, "I don't think there is anything else of interest here, do you?"

She shook her head. "I think we've found all we need." She closed the box and locked it.

We pushed our chairs away from the table and pressed the buzzer. In walked Mr. Rousseau. I wished I could say I was surprised, but I wasn't.

"You are *fini*?" he asked.

"*Oui*," Maggie said.

"Did you find anything that might help you?"

"Regrettably, no, but thank you for your trouble," I said.

His hawklike eyes followed our every move as Maggie placed the box back in its place.

He escorted us to the door, bowed, and said, "If there is anything else I can do for you, please call."

Once we were outside the door, I took Maggie's hand and started walking briskly.

"Do you have in your pocket what I think you have in your pocket?" I asked.

"Do you have in your pocket what I think you have in your pocket?" she said.

I felt my phone vibrate. I checked the screen. "Message from Syd."

23

Syd's message was terse: "On my way to the airport. Sent memo via email. Should be in your inbox. Will call when I return to NYC."

"Check your email," Maggie said.

I did, and sure enough, there it was. "Let's head back to the store and have a look."

Back at the store, I printed a couple of copies of the memo, and we left Harriet to close up.

"By the way, George is back and said he'd be in tomorrow," Harriet told us.

That was a relief.

The memo was straightforward and succinct.

Harry, Maggie,

I completed an initial comparison of the manuscript and book you gave me and wanted to give you my preliminary observations before I left town. Sorry I could not do a more complete investigation, but I have had an urgent request from my client in Paris to look at a manuscript bound for auction, so I've left earlier than expected.

The problem presented is one of manuscript attribution. You have provided me with a manuscript to be compared to the text of a published book. The manuscript is a typewritten second copy on yellow carbon paper. The title is *Stealth Victory: A History of the French Resistance in Occupied France, 1940–1944.* No author name is attached. For the purposes of this email, I will refer to it as the Bedford Ms. The text is a copy of a published book whose author is identified as Arnold Black. It bears the title *Secret Victory: French Resistance in Occupied France, 1940–1944.* For the purposes of this email, I will refer to it as the Black Book. The Bedford Ms. was provided to you by a Mrs. Sally Bedford, now deceased, who alleges that her husband, also deceased, was the author of the manuscript. Mrs. Bedford contends that Mr. Black copied, without authorization, some, if not all, of the Bedford Ms.

My preliminary observations are based on my examination of both the physical evidence and the lexical, grammatical, and orthographical evidence found in the text of each manuscript.

The Bedford Ms.

Paper
The Bedford Ms. is typewritten on yellow paper of a kind commonly used for second

carbon copies. It is considerably faded. Throughout the manuscript, there appear many smudged letters, indicating the use of carbon paper. This suggests that erasures were made to the original top copy without the use of an erasure shield, thus resulting in smudges. The use of carbon paper started to die out after 1954, when carbonless paper was introduced, but continued in use until the proliferation of word processors and computers in the latter part of the 1970s. No paper dating was attempted.

Hardware and Mechanical
The mechanical means to create the Bedford Ms. was most certainly a manual typewriter. The font is typical of a manual typewriter. I noted throughout the use of the lowercase *l* for the number one, which was common in typewriters manufactured pre-1956. The use of carbon paper and the absence of specific keys suggest the Bedford Ms. was created sometime earlier than the mid-1950s.

Type
There are both vertical and horizontal misalignments present. There are also typeface defects in evidence. The lowercase *a* is slightly higher relative to the other characters, and the lowercase *y* is too far to the right relative to the other characters. In addition, the top of the uppercase *B* is

completely solid, probably the result of a
defect in the manufacture of the machine.

Handwriting
Several handwritten notes in pencil appear in
the margins. They are faded to the point of
being almost indistinct.

The Black Book
The copy I examined shows a copyright date
of two months ago. It was published by a
company called Hareprint Inc. I have not
heard of this particular publishing house.
There is a paucity of information about the
author on the dust jacket and elsewhere.
A search on the internet yielded little more
information than what appeared on the dust
jacket. The author seems to be a person with
no past and not a lot of history.

Comparison of the Texts
My comparison confirmed what you earlier
suspected. Except for thirty pages, the
manuscript and the book are identical in
every respect, down to the last comma and
period. The pages that differ are interspersed
throughout various chapters of the Black
Book. I will refer to them from time to time
as the differing pages. The following are
general observations about the orthography,
grammar, and punctuation of the texts.

Orthography
The Bedford Ms. employs traditional American spelling throughout. See, for example, on page 10, the word *colored*; on page 35, the word *labored*; and on page 100, the word *center*. This is consistent with someone who was educated in the United States. By contrast, the Black Book employs English spelling usage in the pages that differ from the Bedford Ms. See, for example, on page 25, the word *analyse*; on page 75, the word *recognise*; and on page 125, the word *manoeuvre*. This leads me to speculate that whoever wrote these pages was educated either in England or at a school on the continent that taught English as a second language using the English system. I deliberately picked these examples because they appear in chapters in close proximity to Bedford Ms. pages in which these same words appear but are spelled in the American way.

Grammar
There are a couple of points of grammar that caught my eye. I followed up on your observation of the use of the words *should* and *would*. I analyzed and compared the use of the two words in the manuscripts. Again, throughout the Bedford Ms., the words are consistently used per American usage. This usage is again followed in the Black Book, except for the differing pages, when the author reverts to typical English usage.

Curious is the inappropriate use of capitalization in the Black Ms. See, for example, on page 26, the words *english Newspapers*; on page 77, the words *french Automobile*; and on page 130, the words *american Vehicles*. It could be an editing oversight, but it merits further investigation.

Punctuation

Throughout the Bedford Ms., I noted that when using abbreviations, the author used periods between letters—for example, O. S. S. or S. O. E.—whereas wherever abbreviations were required in the differing pages, no punctuation appeared.

Lexical Analysis

Thus far, I have only noted one curious anomaly in the Black Book, and that relates to the use of the word *telecommunications*. In the Bedford Ms., the words *communication*, *intercommunications*, and *wireless communication* are used to describe the methods of communicating with London. In the Black Book, the word *wireless* is used throughout, except in three instances, when reference is made to the inadequacies of the telecommunications systems. These references appear in the differing pages. The use of the word *telecommunications* is very modern and in contrast to similar words used in the rest of the text.

Style

This area was problematic because the t
were essentially similar except for the thir,
pages I referred to. Furthermore, there are no
other available texts by either author against
which I can compare these manuscripts. On a
more ephemeral level, I detect a difference in
tone between the similar and differing pages
within the Black Book. It is as if there was a
blank to be filled in, and Black was having a
hard time figuring out what to fill it with.

Preliminary Conclusions

Except for the differing pages I described, it is
obvious that the same person wrote both the
Bedford Ms. and the Black Book. The question
is, who is that person, and who wrote the
differing pages? To definitively exclude Black
as the author of the Bedford Ms., further
research will need to be undertaken.

1. It would be useful if we had a sample of
Nick Bedford's handwriting and a sample of
Arnold Black's to compare to the handwritten
notes on the yellow manuscript. The writing
on the Bedford Ms. is faint but can be
enhanced by the use of hyperspectral imaging
technology. With your approval, I will submit
samples of the Bedford Ms. to a colleague
who has access to such an imaging system. I
think I know how to get a sample of Black's
handwriting, but it may have to wait until I
return from Paris.

2. It would be beneficial if we could locate the typewriter that generated the Bedford Ms., but that possibility seems to be remote considering the passage of time and the death of both Mr. and Mrs. Bedford.

3. It would be helpful if there were samples of other published or unpublished work by each author to compare to the Bedford Ms. and to the differing pages in the Black Book. I am not sure how feasible this will be since from what you have told me, neither of these authors has previous works in print. I have done a preliminary search on Black based on his association with the think tank but so far have not come up with any published work. Is it possible he wrote memos in the course of his employment at the institute? That would require access to the institute's database. Should I be getting help on this front?

4. I also want to pursue the capitalization issue I referred to earlier.

I'll call you from Paris.
Syd

"What do you think?" I asked.

"We have our work cut out for us."

"Comparative samples of writing are nonexistent for Nick as far as we know and will be almost impossible to come by for Black."

"If she can enhance the writing on the yellow copy, maybe she could use the same technique to see if there is any writing on those charred bits of paper Sally gave us. If they are the same, that would be definitive proof of authorship."

I looked doubtful. "I wouldn't count on it. Those papers were really charred. I think there's a better chance we'll find something at Sally's farmhouse. I mean, Nick must have left something behind. Should we call Babcock for keys?"

Maggie grinned. "I don't think we need to." She rummaged around in the large envelope Mr. Babcock had given us; pulled out the smaller one marked, "Keys"; and removed a large Baldwin key. "Voilà! And the exact address is written on a piece of paper in there."

"By the way, what is hyperspectral imaging?"

"Beats me."

True to Harriet's word, George reappeared the next morning. After a long gabfest and catch-up, we mentioned to George that we were planning a weekend getaway.

"Go, go," he said. "You know I always say you two spend too much time cooped up in this bookstore. There are more important things to do in life."

"Too late for those important things, George. Need we show you our driver's licenses as proof of age?" Maggie teased.

But we can always keep trying, I thought to myself.

"Where are you going?" George asked.

"We're meeting our friend Syd in Paris," I lied.

George looked puzzled. "This is a getaway?"

"Oh, she's promised to introduce us to her duke friend," Maggie said.

Oh, what a web we weave …

24

Red-eye flights did not bring out the best in me. Having to sleep in a metal tube traveling through time and space was bad enough, but the run-up to the flight meant navigating your way through some godforsaken airport—in our case, JFK. Its overseers seemed determined to strip it of all traces of humanity. Your dignity, not to mention your sanity, was under constant assault by importunate requests to take off your belt and shoes and remove electronic equipment and laptops from their cases before you got to the head of the line.

"Have your passports and boarding cards ready for inspection," demanded a security guard.

Grumpy adults, sullen children—what more could add to my misery? I thought. I soon found out.

Having somehow neglected to remove some change from a pocket, I set bells and whistles off and was sent off for a secondary screening.

Having run the security gauntlet, I found Maggie on the other side, tapping her boot impatiently on the floor. She made a point of checking her watch. "What on earth happened to you? I thought you were right behind me."

I shrugged helplessly. "Don't ask."

Once we were safely ensconced in the business-class lounge, we puzzled over the numbers on the paper we had found in the safe-deposit box: 57°20725, 61°21741.

"Any ideas?" I asked.

Maggie shook her head. "Not a clue. Maybe Syd will have some ideas. Speaking of whom, I left her a message telling her what we were up to."

"What did she say?"

"She wished she were with us and then told me what we should be looking for."

"I suppose she hopes that miraculously, we will find a typewriter with all the defects she mentioned."

"Pretty much, but also anything with handwriting on it or maybe those missing pages Sally's email referred to."

I groaned. "Not asking for much, is she?"

Maggie laughed. "Nothing more than what we would like to find."

"When does she get back to the States?"

Before she could answer, our flight was called.

I was not the best of sleepers on an airplane, unlike my lovely wife, who was fast asleep before the plane left the ground. I tossed and turned, trying to get comfortable, but the unknown that lay ahead of us kept running through my head. *Should we have turned all this over to Mike?* I wondered. *Too late now.*

Bleary-eyed, I managed to clear immigration without someone questioning whether I was, in fact, the person pictured on my passport. Maggie, on the other hand, looked as if she had slept on a feather bed. Charles de Gaulle was not a user-friendly airport, so by the time we located our gate, they were already boarding our flight to Toulouse.

The flight was just long enough to allow us to pore over

a French road map to figure out the shortest, or what we thought would be the shortest, route to Sally's farmhouse. The plane shuddered slightly; the seat-belt sign came on; and an unpleasant robotic voice warned that we were about to begin our initial descent into Toulouse, and therefore, passengers were to stow all of their carry-on luggage. Like obedient children, Maggie and I did as we were told, although our fellow passengers seemed unconcerned with the request and ignored it.

After a few lost-in-translation moments, I found myself behind the wheel of a minuscule Renault, jousting with manic French drivers trying to escape to the country. Maggie navigated, and after a couple of navigational mishaps, by midafternoon, we were on our way north to an unknown and uncertain destination.

Navigating the back roads of France proved to be thornier than we anticipated. Narrow lanes hemmed in by hedges and junctions with no directional signs meant that dusk was settling in as we crawled along a narrow, rutted path that led to a graveled driveway. I mentally crossed my fingers that we had finally arrived.

"This must be it," said Maggie.

I looked around and shook my head. "Can't be. There are lights in the window."

She groaned. "I can't believe it. I was sure I had us on the right track."

Track was the operative word, I thought.

"We have to be close," I said. "Maybe whoever lives here is familiar with the area and can point us in the right direction."

We clamored out of the car, leaving the motor running and headlights on so we could pick our way to some stone stairs that led to a terrace. Dusk had morphed to dark, so I was barely able to make out the shape of the door in front of me.

A huge metal knocker occupied dead center. I reached for it. At the same time, the door swung open, flooding the terrace with near-blinding light. A male figure engulfed in shadow stood in the middle of the doorway.

"You're late. I was just about to start dinner without you."

We stood anchored in place.

"Well, don't just stand there. Shut the car off, and get inside before the whole place gets cold."

25

"What are you doing here?" Maggie asked.

"I might ask you the same," Bill said.

Into the verbal sparring match between father and daughter, I tiptoed timidly. "Is there any possibility of a thirsty man getting a drink in this house?"

They both turned and looked at me as though they'd just realized they had a surprise guest at the door.

"I forget myself," Bill said. "Of course there is." After waving us into the warm comfort of a fireplace, he started mixing drinks at a nearby sideboard.

"How did you know we were coming?" I asked.

"Arthur Babcock alerted me to the fact that you might. Arthur and I are old friends. At first, he didn't make the connection between Maggie and me, but when he met her, he was almost certain she was my daughter. He said the resemblance was striking, and then it made sense why Sally was so insistent on retaining the bookstore to work on her project. I wasn't overly concerned, but then again, I didn't know what the project was, for reasons of attorney-client privilege."

"He is a stickler for that all right," Maggie said.

"He also phoned to let me know what happened to Sally," Bill said.

"Why did it make sense to him that Sally was retaining us? We were never really certain why she retained us."

"Because Sally, Nick, and I knew each other from the war years."

The silence in the room hovered.

Bill rubbed his eyes and leaned forward in his chair. "It was a part of my life that I could not and did not share with anyone, not because I didn't want to but because I was constrained legally from doing so. I shouldn't even be discussing it with you now, although your uncle James knows most of the story." He shrugged and slumped back in his chair. "At my age, it makes very little difference who knows what I did during the war."

He paused again, rubbing his hand over his forehead, and then continued. "When World War II broke out, I was a Rhodes scholar at Oxford. Nick Bedford was my roommate. The US, of course, wasn't in the war, and we had no idea whether it would ever enter the war. Youth hangs like a cloak of invincibility on your shoulders, and we were convinced that if we didn't get in with the Brits, we would miss out on the action. Callow youth that we were, after the fall of France, we went to London to see if we could make contact with anyone who could get us into the action. Needless to say, no one would speak to us. Everyone viewed us with suspicion.

"Then serendipity struck. One evening, Nick and I were sitting in the bar at the Connaught, when the air raid sirens sounded. Everyone was herded into the underground shelters. We were chatting—or, rather, Nick, as was his wont, was chatting up a young woman, also American, who had just gotten out of France ahead of the invading German army. That woman was Sally Bedford, or, as she was then, Sally Reed."

That answered one or two questions.

"To make a very long story somewhat shorter, we mentioned that we were trying to sign up and would join anything to get into the war. She said she knew a few people at the American embassy and would check to see if she could find someone to talk to us about working there.

"A few days went by, and we heard nothing. We thought we had been given the brush-off, so we decided to head back to Oxford. We were checking out of our hotel, when she reappeared. She told us that she had been invited to a dinner party that night and asked us if we would be her escorts. So much for Oxford—we were prepared to find any excuse to stay in London. There was no mention of embassy jobs, so we let it go.

"That evening, we picked her up at her flat, and off we went to this dinner party at the home of Sir Someone. Nick was seated between Sally and a woman by the name of Penelope Gaitskell, and I was on the other side of Mrs. Gaitskell. She was extremely charming. The fact that I was studying linguistics and history at Oxford and was proficient in French and Spanish seemed to be of great interest to her. The fact that I had lived in the south of France for a semester and was familiar with the terrain gave us something in common, as she had lived there as well. We talked politics and the course of the war. When I mentioned how frustrated Nick and I were at being on the sidelines when it was imperative to defeat the Germans, she merely gave me an empathetic smile and said she was sure something would come along. Then the courses changed."

He grimaced. "Well, actually, we went from a Spam appetizer to a Spam main course."

We couldn't help but laugh. Bill's dislike of Spam was legendary, and now we understood why.

"Anyway, dinner party etiquette at the time required that at each change of course, you turn your attention to the person on the other side of you, so that was the end of my conversation with Mrs. Gaitskell. At the end of the evening, we thanked Sally profusely for the invite and then went our own way, thinking how lucky we were to have met all these interesting people that evening. We were so naive it's a wonder they even gave us a second glance."

"So what happened?" I asked.

He shifted in his seat and took a sip of his brandy. "A few days later, a note from the Honorable Penelope Gaitskell arrived at our rooms, inviting us both to lunch at the Savoy. All I could think was that the British nobility must get more ration coupons than American commoners. She left a phone number to RSVP, and of course, we did. Who would turn down an invitation to eat? But what really intrigued us was her closing line: 'I may have a lead on some work you might find interesting.'"

He paused to stoke the fire. I rose to stretch my limbs and refresh our drinks. When we were all settled again, Bill resumed.

"So we met Mrs. Gaitskell for lunch the following day. It was a pleasant lunch. She mentioned that we each had some assets that might prove useful in war work, especially our command of the French language and knowledge of the French countryside, not to mention that we were Americans. We were puzzled as to how that would be useful for war work in England. She admitted to being curious about our desire to engage in war work, when we could retreat to the safety of America. Nick and I went off on a rant about how disgusted we were that our country had not come to the aid of Britain and declared war immediately. We said Nazism was a peril to be beaten back by everyone."

He shook his head. "As I said, we were naive in the extreme. Anyway, at the end of lunch, she stood rather abruptly, handed me a piece of paper, and said if we were really interested in pursuing war work, we should present ourselves at three o'clock the next day at the address on the piece of paper.

"We were intrigued. We spent half the night speculating on what she had in mind. We presented ourselves promptly at the address on the paper only to find ourselves standing in front of the Three Crowns pub. We thought there had to be some mistake, or worse yet, she had just given us the royal heave-ho.

"We went inside, showed the bartender the piece of paper Penelope had given us, and asked if that was the address on the card. He looked at the paper and then at us. He told us to have a seat and disappeared. Obedient little pups that we were, we did what we were told. Back came the bartender. He motioned for us to follow him through a side door and up a flight of stairs and then through another door. We almost tripped over our own feet: there were Sally and Penelope. It turned out that was a recruiting office for the Special Operations Executive, or SOE, the precursor to Britain's modern intelligence-gathering agencies.

"Penelope was *the* recruiting officer. The SOE really were interested in us because we were American. Our American citizenship meant we were still able to travel relatively freely in France, since the US was still officially neutral. She told us that if we were really interested in working for the organization, we would need to get the embassy's approval and show up for training at a specified site by the end of the week."

He paused to have a sip of wine. By then, Maggie and I were sitting on the edge of the sofa, wholly engrossed in his saga.

"Sally already had her permission and coached us on the

procedure. It wasn't so hard, and by the end of the week, we started training. We did all the usual stuff: use of the wireless, code work, language and political assets, and who was who. As Americans, we were given plausible cover stories: journalists covering the action in France. In early 1941, we were sent off to France at separate times to separate places but with instructions on how to meet up with each other. Our task was to assess the strength of the resistance, the views of the local population, and the presence of Germans in occupied territory. We had some contact names." He buried his head in his hands.

Maggie stood up, but he waved her off.

"God rest their souls," he murmured. He fell silent for a moment and then continued. "The information we gathered was invaluable. Until late in 1941, things went smoothly. The three of us would meet informally at embassy functions and so on. We tried to be careful, knowing that one misstep, one negative word or opinion about the regime, would be cause for deportation or worse.

"Then Pearl Harbor happened. All of a sudden, it wasn't so safe to be an American in France. We were ordered to return to Britain, so we made our way back to London via Spain and Portugal. As soon as we got back to London, we headed to the embassy to sign up. By that time, Wild Bill Donovan was in the picture and had heard about us. We signed up to do intelligence work again, only this time with Wild Bill and the US, the only difference being that the degree of urgency had just increased by a power of ten. Initially, we were sent back to the US for a debriefing on our work in France and further training; then we were sent back into the field for intelligence gathering in various posts around the world. Sally was sent to France with a French counterpart to scout and make contact with French resistance groups in the Lot and Dordogne regions.

"In 1943, we were called back to London, and just after D-Day in June '44, Nick and I parachuted into the Lozère region. The Allies were planning a landing in Southern France in August 1944, Operation Dragoon. We were to link up with the French Resistance in the area, gather as much intelligence as possible on German troop movements, and engage in sabotage to weaken German supply lines and keep them bottled up and distracted so they couldn't rush north to undo the work of Overlord.

"That was when we crossed paths with Sally again. She acted as a liaison between other groups and us. She told us she had received a message that a French SOE agent who could speak German and English as well as French would join our team. That in itself wasn't unusual, but Sally was uneasy. The message hadn't come from her customary contact, so she had no way to verify who the addition was. It was a very tense time for her. Several resistance members connected with other teams had been caught in a roundup, and she was concerned that we were all close to being exposed. She left us with the details for the rendezvous with the third person.

"So it was that we met the agent we knew as Jean Marcoux. He did speak flawless French, German, and English—almost too flawless. For some reason—perhaps it was Sally's uneasiness—neither Nick nor I completely trusted the man. As much as possible, we tried to make sure one of us was with him at all times, and we never disclosed the location of the wireless set. But there was only so much we could do. After all, his whole point to being there was to move freely in towns and villages to assess the location and strength of German troops, so by necessity, he had to go off on his own. He always produced reports, but we had no way to confirm his information. As I said, we tried to build information firewalls between him and the resistance, but from time to time, it was necessary to include him in sensitive operational meetings."

He paused to take a sip of his drink. "His arrival coincided with a sharp rise in resistance losses. We expected a certain amount of attrition, but this was far more than what we had been used to. One day Nick pointed out to me that the team members who were rounded up came only from teams whose meetings Marcoux had been allowed to attend. Now we were nervous. The invasion was only days off. We had to assume that some of the team members who had been rounded up had broken and might have revealed aspects of our mission.

"Our fears were intensified one evening when Marcoux made a casual comment about Anvil. That was the original name given to the idea of Dragoon in 1942. The name Dragoon had only just been assigned, and we had never used it in front of him, and we had definitely never discussed or described the operation as Anvil. How did he know about it? His mission, according to the papers he'd given us, was just to gather intelligence on German troop strength and movements. His orders did not reveal why this intelligence was needed. We guessed he had probably picked up hints of the operation during his training in England and was pumping for information. We just shrugged and brushed it off.

"A few nights later, we were due to carry out an operation to sabotage a French railway switching station with a group of French partisans. About an hour into it, we were ambushed. The first person hit by sniper fire was Marcoux. We managed to take cover behind a stone fence enclosing a pasture, where we were pinned down by intermittent sniper fire for hours. Just before dawn, we got our first look at the road. It was empty—nobody. No Germans. No sign of life. Marcoux was the only person we lost. We weren't sure what to think, but we were not going to hang around trying to figure it out. That was the last we saw or heard of Marcoux other than to report his loss to SOE."

He flicked his sleeve up and tapped his watch. "After the war, Nick decided to write a personal memoir-cum-history about our adventures with SOE and OSS in France. We had kept in touch after the war, so from time to time, he would contact me to discuss various points of his recollections. He told me he had been looking into the fate of Jean Marcoux but had hit a dead end. At that time, the Brits were not prepared to discuss anything about anyone who had been involved in the SOE. The last time I talked to Nick before he disappeared, he was very excited about some new information he had found out about a Jean Marcoux. He was following up with an old acquaintance from our resistance days and thought it might prove our theory that there had been a traitor in our midst and that the traitor was Jean Marcoux. Then he disappeared."

"Did he mention what he had found out?" I asked.

"No, just that it would confirm that Marcoux was not who he appeared to be."

"I'm curious," Maggie said, "as to why everything had to be classified. I mean, the war was over, and the man was dead."

Bill turned to her with a fond smile. "For the same reason my fingerprints were classified: to protect not only the dead but also the living."

Maggie blushed. "You knew!"

During our last caper Syd or rather her contact tried to access a federal database to identify some fingerprints on a vintage baseball scorecard but was blocked when the file came up classified.

Bill allowed himself a weak smile. "Of course I did. Did you think for a moment that when trying to break into a classified database, one wouldn't attract some attention? If you had waited awhile, you could have accessed the name of anyone who ever had anything to do with the OSS."

"Hindsight is always twenty-twenty," I grumbled.

"Do you have a picture of this guy?" Maggie asked.

He shrugged. "I don't, but I thought Sally had one. I remember we were at a farmhouse in the Lot, and one of the French Resistance guys took a picture of the three of us. I thought Nick gave it to Sally."

Maggie picked up her handbag and took out the picture we had taken from the safe-deposit box. She went over and sat on the arm of Bill's chair and showed him the picture. "Could this be the picture?"

"Oh yes, that's the three of us. Marcoux is the one standing with his face tilted down in shadow."

"We really need a clearer picture of Marcoux to compare to Black's photo on the dust jacket."

"Believe me, if I saw him again, I would remember him."

"How so?"

"His eyes. His eyes were the eyes of a snake, vacant and cold."

I shot forward on the couch. "What did you say?"

Bill looked at me. "I said he had the eyes of a snake."

"Maggie, where did we hear that description before?"

She looked at me in surprise and shrugged.

I stood up and started pacing the room. "That's it. I knew I had heard that description before. Maggie, do you remember the morning after Sally dropped off the manuscript?"

"Who could forget? We were having a debate about whether to take on the project. So what?"

"What was the plan?"

"We asked Harriet to make a copy of the manuscript. She thought it was a manuscript by Arnold Black."

"And?" I said.

"Oh!" she said. "Harriet said, 'I get the feeling from looking at his photograph that he is a snake in the grass.'"

"Do you have a copy of the book with you?" asked Bill.

Unfortunately, that was one thing we hadn't packed. We shook our heads. "But we should be able to find it online," I said.

"Not here," Bill said. "Look around. Do you see anything remotely like it could be connected to anything? According to Arthur, this place has been closed up since Sally left for New York. I was grateful the water and electricity were still on. There's no central heating, but I guess the people who look after the property thought she was coming back, because there is a pile of wood in the woodshed."

"We'll be back in the States in a day or so. You can check it out then," Maggie said.

Somewhere behind us, a timer went off. Bill pushed himself out of his chair, tapped his watch again, and said, "And on that note, I think we should enjoy the very rustic dinner I have prepared before it's too late."

Rustic was a misnomer for the luxurious boeuf bourguignon we enjoyed, along with a superior red Bordeaux.

Fortified by food and the excellent cognac we treated ourselves to after dinner, I screwed up my courage and said, "We thought you were on a river cruise. Why did you decide to come to Sally's place?"

He held up his glass and swirled the liquid around the balloon a few times. "I was devastated by Arthur's news of Sally's death. I had always planned to drop in on Sally after the cruise and didn't realize she had gone to New York. I spoke with her before I left, and she merely said she would be here. After Arthur gave me the news, I suppose I came in part to say goodbye to an old friend and colleague and in part to make sense of what this was all about. And if Arthur was correct about your possible appearance here in connection with the project you were working on for her, I felt I should be here to offer assistance if that was required. And now it's your turn. What is this project, who is this Arnold Black character, and why are you pursuing it now that Sally is gone?"

Maggie took a deep breath and recounted the events leading up to the discovery of Sally's body, followed by the visit by Mike Farmer to inform us that her death was not natural but a homicide.

"Homicide?" Bill said.

Maggie was taken aback. "Yes, homicide. I thought Arthur told you that."

Bill was visibly shaken and shook his head rapidly. "No, he only said Sally had died unexpectedly. Why would anyone want to harm Sally?"

"We aren't sure, but we believe it has something to do with her allegation that this Black person appropriated Nick's work. That was our project: to prove Nick was the true author of the work claimed by Black," I said.

Maggie added, "We came here hoping to find some clues or evidence that would point to Nick as the author."

"But if Sally is dead, how can you continue?"

"Because she left us a letter asking us to do so and authorizing the estate to pay us. We thought about it, and after we found out she had been murdered, we were convinced her death had something to do with Black, so we agreed to keep going," Maggie replied.

"And what does Mike say about this?"

We glanced at each other and then looked down.

"Don't tell me you haven't told him about your suspicions."

I shrugged. "What were we supposed to tell him? That Black possibly appropriated a dead man's work and therefore may have killed Sally?"

"Well, when you put it like that ..." His voice trailed off.

"We felt there had to be something more to it. Syd has done a preliminary analysis of the manuscript and the book and believes the same person wrote both. The question is, who is that person? That's why we need to go through the house to see if there are any samples of handwriting or an old typewriter or anything to point to Nick."

"But what do you hope to get out of this, even if you prove Nick is the author?"

"Vindication for Sally and Nick and possibly something that points toward who her murderer is."

26

A cloudburst during the night left in its wake sludge-colored clouds and a stiff breeze blowing out of the east. The wind roiled the dead vegetation, mounting it in piles against the cottage. The fire had died out during the night, leaving the room frigid. If I wanted to be warm again, I knew what had to be done. I crept out of bed, pulled on a pair of jeans, fished out an old wool sweater from my suitcase, and, without disturbing any of the ancient floorboards, tiptoed to the back door. I grabbed a firewood basket and headed to the woodpile. There I found Bill swinging an ax with a vigor that would have made Paul Bunyan proud.

He caught sight of me and teased, "Good to see at least one of you gets up at a reasonable hour. You're just in time. The chopping part is great exercise, but the carrying part kills my knees."

I saluted. "Happy to be of assistance." I started filling my basket and his.

"You know, Harry, it's okay to say no to some of my beautiful daughter's plans, especially those that find you treading a fine line between investigating a theft of intellectual property and obstructing justice."

"Easy for you to say. Not everyone gets to sleep with her every night. I do, and I want to keep it that way."

He slapped me on the back and gave me a friendly shoulder hug. "You have a point there, but tread carefully. It might be something of an embarrassment if both of us were disbarred. Here—if you can hand me one basket, I can manage it."

I waved him off. "No problem. I can do it. I'll help you get the fires going."

I pondered his concern about our treading into dicey legal territory while I lit the fire in our bedroom and then wandered over to the bed. I peeled back the duvet amid protestations from my loved one, bent over her supine body, and briefly stroked the back of her neck, which had the desired effect of making her turn over to look at me. She put her arms around my neck and gave me a sleepy grin. I brushed aside a stray hair and kissed the tip of her upturned nose.

"You're going to have to do better than that if you want me to forsake this warm and cozy nest," she said.

I bent over her again; gave her a big, smothering smooch; rose up; and tore back the bedcovers. "Time to rise and shine, princess. Bill is downstairs waiting for us."

She groaned.

I headed for the door. "I'm on breakfast detail—gotta go." I had just enough time to slam the door before the thud of a pillow reminded me of her accurate aim.

I found Bill carefully tending a skillet full of bacon with one hand and flipping eggs with the other.

He handed me the tongs to move the bacon around and then asked, "Any further thoughts after last night?"

"Not really. How much did you know about this guy Jean Marcoux?"

"Nothing other than what I told you last night, although he suggested he was a linguist and scholar of languages. I think he mentioned that he had taught at a university in Strasbourg."

"By the way, I meant to tell you last night that we found a small sheet of paper in the safe-deposit box with a string of numbers printed on it. We want you to have a look at it later to see if the numbers make any sense to you."

For a time, we stood over the stove in companionable silence broken only by the sounds of sizzling, sputtering fat. Bill handed me plates and utensils.

"So do you use Sally's place often?" I asked.

He walked over to the coffeepot and poured more coffee. "Whenever I come to France. Sally and Nick always said, 'Our house is your house,' so I would use it from time to time. Why do you ask?"

From behind us a very familiar voice answered. "It's just that you never mentioned you knew Sally."

"You really shouldn't sneak up on people like that," I griped.

Bill smiled and accepted a peck on the cheek from Maggie. "I never thought about it, to be truthful. After Nick disappeared, I tried to help in the investigation, but to no avail. Sally and I kept in touch after that but saw each other only intermittently. It was that kind of friendship, born out of the hardships of war and nurtured by shared experiences and shared grief over the loss of a friend. Whenever we saw each other, we just picked up where we'd left off. And, I might add, you never mentioned you knew Sally."

"We probably wouldn't have made the connection except for a photo in Sally's apartment," Maggie said. "You were in the background. It was taken at some festive event."

"Ah, that must have been at their wedding. Harry, where is that piece of paper you told me about?"

I retrieved the paper from our bedroom and handed it over to Bill to have a look.

He shook his head, puzzled. "Maybe it's a safe combination or maybe directions. Look at these smudges—it could be the degree sign. Or not." He sighed. "Well, I suppose as soon as we finish breakfast, we'd better get on with this search and see what we can find. How do you suggest we go about this?"

I understood his reluctance. Now that the task was at hand, I felt a certain degree of discomfort. I hated the idea of prying and rifling through a dead woman's belongings. But Maggie seemingly had no such qualms.

"Why don't I tackle the basement and her bedroom, and you two search the rest of the rooms?" Without waiting for an answer, she headed downstairs.

Bill stared into the distance with a grim expression tightening his lips.

"You don't have to do this if you don't want to," I said gently.

He gave me a grim smile. "She was one of my oldest and dearest friends. I owe it to her and Nick to get to the bottom of this." He paused and then, with a catch in his voice, said, "I feel like a vulture poking around in what remains of her presence."

At a loss for words to comfort him, I said briskly, "It looks like this cabinet would be the most likely place to have stored papers and other memorabilia."

We poked around, opening doors and drawers, sifting through file folders, and checking for any loose or stray bits of paper, but Sally was nothing if not neat, and each drawer was tidier than the last.

Finally, Bill looked up. "Did you find anything?"

"Just some old receipts, credit card bills—that sort of thing. How about you?"

He flipped through a sheaf of papers. "Same sort of thing. There's a legal file with correspondence to and from Arthur with what appears to be instructions for the dispersal of her estate."

"What's the date on it?"

"All the correspondence was in the last few weeks before her death. The instructions pretty much confirm what Arthur told you. Did he confirm to you that the will had been signed?"

"To be honest, I didn't ask. I just assumed it had been, but now I'm not sure." I told him about our visit to the bank and the revelation that Arthur had been there the day before and examined the box, apparently in search of a will."

"He probably did so just out of an abundance of caution, wanting to make sure no subsequent will had been signed."

"Did he mention any specifics of the will when he phoned you?"

"Not really. He had been reviewing the provisions of Sally's will and wanted to let me know I had been appointed one of the trustees of her estate. As Arthur mentioned to you, most of her estate is going to her charitable foundation. He wanted to know when I would be returning, so we could meet." He closed the last drawer on his side of the cabinet and sighed. "Nothing of interest."

I nodded and finished poking through the bottom drawer on my side. Again, I saw only some old receipts and land documents but nothing with handwriting on it that could possibly have belonged to Nick. Disappointed, I shoved the drawer back into its slot—and it made a tiny click. When I looked down, the bottom of the drawer had pulled apart from the front and sides.

I looked at the drawer in dismay and then looked at Bill. "Please tell me this is not a priceless antique, the repair of which will bankrupt me."

He laughed. "No, this is just an old wardrobe that came with the farm. Sally converted it into an office cabinet." He squatted down in front of it, ran his hand along the edge, and then did it again. "Harry, get me a sharp kitchen knife."

Surprised by the urgency in his voice, I grabbed a knife from the knife block. I squatted down beside him and handed him the knife. He carefully ran the knife along the open edge. A moment later, I heard another click. The bottom section shot out just a fraction more. Reaching underneath, he carefully eased the lower panel forward, revealing a concealed drawer. Inside was a sheaf of papers.

For a moment, we just stared at the sheets of paper. Bill gestured to me. I removed the papers. I turned them over. Some old photographs dropped out and fluttered to the floor. My jaw went slack.

"So," I said to the sheets of paper in my hands, "this is where you have been hiding all these years."

Bill gave me a puzzled look. "What are they?"

"The missing pages."

27

"What are you talking about?" Bill asked.

"Just before Sally was murdered, she sent an email to Black that she separately forwarded to Maggie and me. The email simply said, 'I have the missing pages.' She had never mentioned missing pages before then, and by the time we saw the email, she was already dead. We assumed she meant the pages that matched the yellow carbon copy version but differed from the concurrent pages in the Black book. We searched everywhere in her apartment with no luck. The safe-deposit box yielded the same result. She apparently went to great lengths to ensure no one would find them easily. The million-dollar question is, where did they come from? Why weren't they with the manuscript that disappeared with Nick?" I looked up at the sound of footsteps approaching.

Maggie stood there looking dejected. "Nothing," she said.

I motioned to her to sit down on the floor with Bill and me. "Not to worry, because we found something you will find most interesting." I handed her the sheaf of papers.

She took one look and breathed slowly. "The missing pages. Where did you find them?"

Bill pointed toward the now fully extended hidden drawer. "There."

She took the sheets and slowly flipped through them, her expression going from excitement to disappointment. She shook her head. "These are not manuscript pages."

My euphoria of discovery was instantly crushed. "What do you mean?"

"These appear to be research notes. At least I think they are. Most of it is written in shorthand, although there seem to be references to interviews and books."

"Which means?" I asked.

"Whoever took the original manuscript from Nick wasn't aware of their existence; maybe Sally didn't even know they were here," Maggie said.

"When Sally sent that email about the missing pages to Black, he would naturally assume Sally knew which manuscript pages differed from the text in his book."

Bill tapped the pages. "It doesn't make any sense. Why would he panic over the discovery of a few missing pages? If he was bold enough to copy ninety percent of the manuscript, why would he be troubled by having to explain a few more pages?"

"Maybe he thought she was talking about photographs," I said.

"Could be," Maggie said. "She did say she had gone into Cahors that morning to deliver the film for processing. She forgot all about them in the aftermath of Nick's disappearance, until the film developer phoned her. She said that any photographs would either be in her safety deposit box or here."

"But there were no photographs in the box except for the one we showed to you earlier."

"This is getting us nowhere. Let's do one more search

of the house to make sure we haven't overlooked some spot where she might have left duplicates," said Maggie. "By the way, I did not find anything that even resembled a typewriter down there."

I did not feel optimistic but agreed. "I'll go through these cabinets again. Bill, why don't you have a final peek around the kitchen?"

I started going through the cabinet again, more thoroughly than the first time, searching for any nook or cranny that might reveal a concealed drawer. Nothing. I did a final search of the hidden drawer with the same result. I gave it a firm push to put it back in place and then got on my knees.

Sometimes one knew when he'd made the transition from late middle age to early older age, such as when one's knees refused to move from a kneeling to an upright position.

I got one knee up to the ninety-degree position and was about to push myself into the upright position, when I noticed the photographs that had fallen out of the drawer earlier. I reached down and flipped through them. Most were pictures of Sally and Nick. I smiled. In one of the photographs, Sally and Nick were seated on the patio in front of the farmhouse, raising glasses of wine to the camera, and in another, they were celebrating at the dinner table. I turned over the last photo. A man had his arm draped casually around the waist of a woman who was standing sideways and leaning into him with her face partially obscured. Between them, they cradled a baby. My smile disappeared.

"I think you should let me have that photograph, Harry."

Startled, I leaped up. I had been staring so intently at the photograph that I hadn't heard Bill come up behind me. His hand was extended. His eyes held mine. Without a word, I handed it to him. He tucked it in his pocket and turned away.

Maggie rejoined us. "I didn't find a thing. How about you two?"

Bill shook his head. "Nothing, my dear."

"Harry?" she said.

I shrugged. "Not much. Just a photo of Nick and Sally in front of the farmhouse."

"Well, at least it's something."

"God, I need a drink," said Bill.

I did not think one was going to be enough.

28

Three glum souls huddled around the dining room table that evening. Our investigative endeavors had not borne much fruit. The pages we'd found might as well have been in Greek, as none of us knew shorthand. *Does anyone know shorthand today?* I wondered. And we were no closer to uncovering the true identity of Jean Marcoux.

My gut told me Jean Marcoux and Arnold Black were the same person. However, proving it was going to be problematic, and even if he was, so what? Would those bits of paper we'd found in the safe-deposit box yield any further clues? And what about the photograph Bill had pocketed? What did it mean? All I knew was that it was going to prove to be a gigantic headache at some point.

"I still can't fathom that someone would commit two acts of murder to cover up a manuscript appropriation," I said. "What are we missing?"

Maggie twirled her spoon between her index finger and thumb. "There must be something in those pages that will shed some light. We need to find someone who knows shorthand."

"I agree," I said. "Once we get home, I'll check with Harriet

to see if she knows anyone who can help out in that department. Is there anything intelligible at all in those sheets?"

Maggie handed me the sheaf of papers. "Hmm. There
appears to be a woman's name. Does the name Roanne mean
anything to either of you?"

Bill turned to me. "How is it spelled?"

I spelled it for him.

He looked thoughtful. "I don't think that is the name of a
woman; I believe it's the name of a place in the Rhône-Alpes
region of France, just to the northwest of Lyon. During the
war, it was a hotbed of resistance fighters. After the war, it
became a staging area for refugees. Anything else?"

"Just some scribbles in pencil. I think it says, 'Interview
with MJM.' That's about all I can make out."

"I don't think it's a coincidence that the initials include
JM, which are the initials of Jean Marcoux," I said.

"Until we find someone to decipher these shorthand notes
we are just shooting bullets in the dark," Bill said.

"Harry," Maggie said, "do you think it would be a good
idea to have Harriet approach her friend who used to work
at the International Institute for Conservative Values to see
if she would be willing to meet with us? Maybe she can shed
some light on Black and where the original manuscript for his
book is now."

"For sure."

"I also think we need to have Syd go over, in minute detail,
the text in the manuscript that differs from the book and determine if there is anything else of significance in the differences."

"Agreed."

"What are you going to do about Mike Farmer?" Bill
asked.

There was that one-ton gorilla in the room.

I fidgeted with one of the cuffs on my shirt for a moment.

"I don't know what we should do. He specifically asked me for a report on our attribution project, but since we haven't reached a conclusion on who wrote what, what have I got to report? At some point, we have to go to him with what we have, but what do we really have?"

"Nothing but speculation," Bill said. "But for now, I think we should all go to bed."

The next morning, not a word was spoken as we packed up the house and put all our belongings in the car. Bill locked the door and put the key back in its hiding place. For a long moment, he stood by the car, staring at the house, and then he quietly bowed his head and got in the car.

29

Our plan to catch an early flight back to the United States was almost foiled by a protest on the part of thousands of indignant French farmers objecting to the end of one agricultural subsidy or another and using their tractors as their primary weapons to block the main arteries into Toulouse. My intrepid wife was not about to let a little thing like a strike stand between our own bed and us and managed to maneuver our little Renault down back alleys and byways until eventually, we found ourselves in a parking lot at the airport, where we promptly abandoned our car. We made it onto the plane, and finally, at some godforsaken hour of the following morning, we crashed into our own bed. I blissfully floated along in my dreams to the strains of the "William Tell Overture," until a jab in my ribs jolted me awake.

"Answer your phone," a voice groggy with sleep admonished.

I groaned, grabbed my cell phone, hit the accept button, and said, "Harry Kramer."

"What's wrong with you, Harry? You sound like you just woke up."

"Thanks to you, Syd, I did just wake up. By the way, why are you calling at this hour of the morning? I thought you were on some job."

"It's almost ten o'clock, Harry. Please tell me—what would be an appropriate time of day to phone you so as not to interfere with your beauty sleep?"

"Sarcasm will get you nowhere, Syd," I said crossly. "Our flight didn't arrive until well after midnight, thanks to a bunch of disgruntled French farmers, and we were tired, hence the late start."

"What on earth did French farmers have to do with your flight?"

Before I could answer, a thwack on the side of my arm reminded me there was another person in the bed.

"Who on earth is it?" Maggie asked.

I put my hand over the receiver and hissed, "Syd."

A mane of red hair rose from the depths, and there was Ms. Parker at full attention. How she could rise from the sleep of the dead to full throttle was beyond me. "Well, for heaven's sake, what has she found out?"

"I don't know; I haven't had time to ask her, because you are so busy asking me questions." I put Syd on speaker and said, "So what's up?"

"Well, not you two—that's for sure. Anyway, to answer your question, quite a bit, not the least of which is that we are now the proud possessors of a sample of Mr. Black's handwriting."

"Really? How?"

"I'll tell you all about it when you come downstairs."

I stared at the phone for a minute. "Where are you, Syd?"

"Downstairs."

I hung up and turned to Maggie. "She's downstairs. Apparently, she has a handwriting sample from Black's very own hand."

"For heaven's sake, Harry, I am not deaf," Maggie said. "I heard her, as you had her on speaker."

We stumbled out of bed. Forty minutes later, after we'd showered and dressed and I'd shaved, we made our way downstairs, where we found Syd and George engaged in an intense discussion about whether there was an English author with the breadth of knowledge and interests to make up a troika with Goethe and Voltaire. At least I thought that was what it was about.

"I hate to interrupt this scintillating conversation," I said, "but I believe you pried us out of our nice, warm, cozy bed for a reason unrelated to either Goethe or Voltaire."

They both gave us looks that said, "Philistines."

I signaled for them to follow me to the office and asked Harriet to man the front counter. Once we were in the office, I brought George up to date on the events of the past month and summarized for both of them our trip to France and what we had found there.

"Tsk, tsk, did I not tell you this would be time consuming?" George said.

I rolled my eyes. "Not to mention frustrating."

Maggie turned to Syd. "Your turn. How did you manage to get a sample of Black's handwriting?"

She grinned. "I went to his book signing and talk at Barnes and Noble. I lined up with the rest of the crowd. When my turn came, he asked me if I wanted any inscription. I told him I was an avid history buff, so he inscribed it, 'To Syd. From one history buff to another. Best wishes. Arnold Black.'" With a flourish, she pulled the book out of her tote bag and handed it to us.

We oohed and aahed and complimented her on her ingenuity.

"At least I can attempt to make a comparison with the notes on the yellow copy," Syd said.

"How long will that take?" I asked.

She thought for a moment. "Probably a good week."

"Anything else?" I asked.

"That's it so far."

"Maybe the shorthand notes we found at the farmhouse will help us out."

George tapped his pencil lightly on the table. "Hmm. Teasing information out of seemingly disparate words will test the mettle and patience of any literary archaeologist, but sometimes the answer is right there under our noses. This is a case of not seeing the trees for the forest. By the way, what did you think of the man?"

"It was a brief encounter, so my impressions may be totally out of whack. The thing that struck me was his eyes. I actually felt a shiver when he looked at me, but I couldn't look away. The man was smiling at me, but his eyes were cold." Syd grimaced. "I'm probably just being oversensitive. Did you have any further thoughts on that string of numbers?"

Seeing the puzzled look on George's face, I explained about the piece of paper that had been taped to the top of the safe-deposit box.

"May I see it?" he asked.

Maggie retrieved the envelope. George carefully withdrew the paper, let his half glasses slide halfway down his nose, and examined the numbers.

"We thought it might be some kind of safe combination, and Dad thought maybe it was a directional clue because of the degree signs," Maggie said.

George looked up. "My dear child, would you be good enough to get my magnifying glass from the top drawer of my desk?"

Maggie did as asked.

George bent the desk lamp over the piece of paper. He

placed the magnifying glass over the paper and then peered intently at the numbers. "Hmm, just as I suspected."

"Is there something you recognize about the numbers?" I asked, unable to conceal my excitement.

George looked up. "Not the numbers. It's this tiny smudge I was curious about."

"What about it?"

"If you look closely at the smudge under the magnifying glass, you will see it actually appears to be a lowercase *e*."

"And?" Syd asked.

"That is typically how ordinal numbers are abbreviated in French. Therefore 57e would be 'fifty-seventh.' I think it is more likely to be a volume number."

"But a volume of what, and what are the other numbers?" asked Maggie.

He rose, went over to the periodical rack, and picked up the *Times*. After spreading it out in front of us, he pointed to the top of the first page. We looked over his shoulder. It read, "Vol. CLXI. No. 55748."

"I believe it is the number of the edition of a newspaper," George said. "Fifty-seven is the equivalent of a volume number, and the numbers represent the number of the edition."

"But which newspaper? There must be hundreds of newspapers in France," Maggie said.

George shrugged. "I would hazard a guess that if Mr. Bedford was doing research in connection with the resistance movement, it was most likely a newspaper that was in existence during the war. But of course, that's just speculation on my part. Why don't you ask your friend Truman what the library has for newspaper databases?"

I sighed. Was I never to be rid of this albatross? It drove me crazy that both Maggie and Syd found Truman so attractive. *What is it about that guy?* A sharp jab in the ribs reminded me in no uncertain terms that jealousy was attractive to no one.

"What a good idea," I said, unable to keep the sarcasm from my tongue.

Maggie gave me one more warning look and then went to the office. A few minutes later, she emerged and said, "Truman can meet with us at three o'clock this afternoon." Turning to Syd, she added, "Do you want to join us?"

"I can't. I have a meeting at lunch."

George turned to Syd. "It's not like you, my dear, to take such a long lunch hour. It must be a very important client."

Two little dots of crimson flowered on Syd's cheeks. "Actually, the duke mentioned my name to a friend of his, who called and asked if I'd like to meet over lunch."

George looked puzzled. "I didn't realize you were on speaking terms with the duke since—"

"Since I dumped him," Syd said. Seeing the look of mortification on George's face, she laughed amiably and gave him a hug. "Just because I don't sleep with him doesn't mean I don't talk to him. One never knows when a duke will come in handy."

A speck of dust on the table captured my eye. I brushed it off with my sleeve.

"Truman will be so disappointed." Maggie smoothly interjected as she turned to pluck a renegade volume of twentieth-century beat poets perched precipitously on the edge of the table.

"Got to go," Syd said, unfolding herself to her full nearly six-foot height. Flinging on her coat, she turned to me and said, "I'll check in with you later."

Why she was addressing me, when my dearly beloved wife had made the crack, I had no idea, but the slightly malicious thought that Truman would yet again be a bridesmaid elicited a tiny smirk on my lips, for which I was rewarded with a jab in the side, this time courtesy of Syd.

George shook his head. "I will never understand American dating rituals."

Maggie gave him an affectionate peck on his pudgy cheek and said, "Nor do we, at least as far as Syd is concerned. Come, Harry. Let's go see what we can find out at the library."

30

The New York Public Library, in all its beaux arts splendor, presided over a two-block stretch of Fifth Avenue between Fortieth and Forty-Second Streets. Supplicants to that temple of knowledge had to pass under the watchful eyes of two leonine paragons of virtue, Patience and Fortitude. We found Truman behind the reference desk in the Great Reading Room. He motioned to us through a side gate and led us to a cubicle at the rear of the reference desk.

"This," he said with an apologetic grimace, "is my office."

There were closets in the smallest New York studio apartments that were roomier than the space Truman ushered us into. It offered two back-to-back desks, which were entirely obscured by the presence of numerous journals, reference books, and other clutter. The desktop monitor was the only visible sign of technology. Above the desks were shelves that, unless great care was taken, had the ability to cause serious damage to your forehead. Backpacks were perched on each chair. How in the name of heaven two people ever managed to work in there simultaneously was beyond me. If the occupants decided to swivel around at the same time, they would find their knees locked in a painful embrace.

"How on earth do you work in here?" Maggie asked, horrified.

"Most of the time, I'm not in here," he answered cheerfully. "Now, what is this project you mentioned over the phone?"

On the way to the library, Maggie and I had discussed how much information we should share with Truman. We'd agreed it was best to share the minimal amount so as not to implicate him in our investigation and, where necessary, to tell little white lies.

"We've been retained to do a manuscript attribution. The manuscript had some numerical markings on it. We're hoping the markings will provide us with some evidence to support our theory of who the author is," Maggie said.

"And why do you think I might be able to help you?"

"George thinks they might be references to newspaper editions," I answered. "If you concur, then perhaps you can suggest how we go about determining which newspaper it is and locating the editions."

Truman looked doubtful. "There are so many newspapers in this country. More than a few use the same volume and edition numbering system."

Maggie coughed. "It's a little more complicated than that."

"How so?"

"We believe the newspaper or newspapers are French," I answered.

Truman removed his spectacles, rubbed his eyes, and replaced them in precisely the same ridge on his nose he had removed them from. "Tell me you're joking."

We shook our heads.

He sighed. "It's like looking for a needle in a haystack. Why does George think they are French newspapers?"

I pulled out the slip of paper with the numbers on it: 57°20725, 61°21741. Underneath, I had printed what George had seen under the magnifying glass: 57ᵉ20725, 61ᵉ21741.

"Ah, I see," said Truman. "In French, ordinal numbers are abbreviated using the *e* symbol."

Okay, I have to give Truman his due, I thought.

"But again, you have the same problem. There are so many newspapers in France, some of which date back to the nineteenth century and earlier."

It was time to dribble out a little more information.

"The manuscript we have been asked to look at concerns the French Resistance in World War II," I said, "so we are pretty sure, based on what we know of the supposed author, that his research would have focused on the war years."

"So assuming we are right," Maggie said, "we've compiled a list of French newspapers past and present that published in France during the war years." She produced the list.

Truman looked at us incredulously. "Even if we had the full archive for all of these newspapers, which we don't, it would take until the next millennium to check each one by the volume and edition method."

"Do you have any French newspapers?" Maggie's voice registered disappointment.

"We have a database of foreign newspapers in our microfilm library that we can consult, but it's not that extensive." He pulled up a database of foreign newspapers and went to the French section. "See what I mean?" He pointed randomly at one listing. The only years the library had in house were the 1882–1884 editions.

"Any other suggestions?" I asked.

"We can check the WorldCat database, but I think a better bet is to check BnF's digital website, Gallica, which can be accessed from anywhere."

"BnF?"

"Bibliothéque nationale de France," answered Maggie.
She's been hanging around librarians for way too long, I
thought.

A few keystrokes brought up the Gallica website.

"Now what?" I asked.

"Let's browse periodicals," Truman said. One key-
stroke later, a page listing the French newspapers available
to be searched popped up. There were twenty-three digitized
possibilities.

"Where to begin?" I said, pondering out loud.

"The list isn't that long," Truman said. "I would suggest
we access each database until we find one that numbers each
edition in the fashion in which these numbers appear. If each
of us takes a third of the list, it probably won't take us very
long to narrow down the candidates. If we do find a match,
the hard part will be to figure out the date of each edition."

"One thing at a time," Maggie said.

I had a laptop with me, and Truman commandeered the
other workstation for Maggie. We divided up the list and
started to scan each newspaper. The task was not as daunting
as I had feared. Each paper had its own system for recording year, volume, and number for each day of publication.
However, although the process was easy, the results were
elusive. I came to the end of my list without any luck.

"Eureka!"

I looked up to witness a triumphant smile fill Truman's
face.

Maggie rolled over on her chair and peered at the screen.
"It looks like we may have our newspaper," she said, unable
to keep the excitement from her voice.

"Which one is it?" I asked.

"The now defunct *Le Matin*," answered Truman. "And

better yet, it shouldn't be hard to find the two editions that these numbers refer to." He pointed to the first number and then at the page he had displayed on his workstation. "It says, '58ᵉ année.'"

"Meaning the fifty-eighth year, so therefore, 61ᵉ would be three years forward, and 57ᵉ would be one year prior," I said.

"Once we have a baseline edition number, we can work forward from that in each of the years," Maggie said.

Truman checked his watch. "We'll have to resume tomorrow, I'm afraid. It's almost time for closing."

I checked my watch: 5:45 p.m. Where had the afternoon gone?

"That's okay, Truman. Why don't you come to the shop, and we can work from there?" Maggie said.

I had hoped we would leave Truman behind, but apparently, my beloved wife felt a need for his further assistance.

"Really, Maggie, maybe Truman has better things to do with his evenings than spend them in our shop, tracking down French newspapers."

"No, not really," said Truman. "In fact, I'm kind of fascinated by the whole exercise."

"Well, that's that then. Why don't we regroup at the shop around seven thirty?" I said.

"Nonsense," said Maggie. "Truman may as well come with us. We can have a drink, do some work, and then have dinner upstairs."

"Suits me," said a delighted Truman.

I knew when I was defeated.

31

I didn't know why I got so futzed about Truman. He actually was a really decent guy. But as a guy, I just couldn't figure out what women saw in him. Maggie insisted Truman was a great friend and companion. So did Syd. Even I had to admit that seeing sexual attraction behind every exchanged glance was irrational.

As it turned out, we had a productive, convivial evening that left more open questions than we anticipated.

We started with the 1940 editions. It didn't take long to find the one we were looking for: December 23, 1940. In its digital state, it was four pages of cramped, small type—all in French, of course.

"Who among us is fluent in French?" I asked, knowing full well what the answer was.

"Well, if Syd wasn't so busy trying to line up a date, she might be able to help us."

I glared at Maggie. Truman looked at me for elucidation. For once, I felt sorry for him. "Syd's ex-boyfriend, the duke, asked her to meet a friend of his. It's not really a date. And Maggie really shouldn't be so catty."

"Oh, that's right. She asked me whether I thought it was

a good idea," Truman said. "You know, she thought the duke was a perfect bore and thought she might be wasting her time. I told her, 'Nothing ventured, nothing gained.'"

Now it was our turn to look surprised.

"Well, maybe we could try a different tack," he said. "Are there any names or place words we might look for? At least if you find some keywords, Syd could hone in on that article in particular."

I was starting to appreciate Truman a bit more.

"As a matter of fact," Maggie answered, "we do know that one of the resistance fighters mentioned in the manuscript is a Jean Marcoux. Let's scan the newspaper and see if we can spot his name. Truman, do you think we can enlarge this enough to make it a little easier to look through? If we could make a couple of copies, it would speed up the process."

"I think we should try to search for the name first to see if it is even in this edition," he said. "Let's convert to the English mode and see what we can find."

Don't you just love technology? I thought.

"Now that we can read the screens, let's go to full-screen mode and see if it will allow us to do a word search." Truman clicked, and sure enough, up came a screen that allowed us to do a word search. He input the name Jean and clicked again.

"Oh my God!" exclaimed Maggie.

Three references popped up for Jean, but only one had any relevance to us. Tucked on the second page was a four-line article that announced the *"mort de* Jean Marcoux," which even I, a dolt at languages, knew announced the death of Jean Marcoux.

"I believe we can convert the file to PDF, and if so, that will allow us to enlarge the print," Truman said. A few keystrokes later, the December 23, 1940, edition of *Le Matin* appeared before us in PDF. We enlarged the print size to 100 percent and located the article we were looking for.

Maggie grabbed a French-to-English dictionary from the language section, and word for word, we translated the text: "The death of Jean Marcoux, renowned linguist and professor of languages, on December 22, 1940, at Roanne is announced."

"Isn't Roanne the name of the city mentioned in those research notes?" I said.

Truman gave me a blank stare. Maggie quickly filled him in on the research notes that dated from the time of the manuscript.

I glanced at my watch and rubbed my eyes. It was almost midnight. Where had the evening gone?

Truman stifled a yawn and stood up, arching and stretching his back. "I have to go. I have a staff meeting at eight o'clock tomorrow morning. You can probably figure out the second edition with Syd's help, assuming she is available."

"That's the sixty-four-dollar question, isn't it?" I said.

We saw Truman out the door, locked up, and headed upstairs. On the way up, Maggie grabbed a world atlas.

I groaned. "Not tonight, Mags."

"It'll only take a minute, Harry. I just want to get a sense of Roanne's proximity to Sally's farmhouse."

We hopped into bed. Maggie opened up a detailed map of France. "Dad was right; it is just a hop, skip, and a jump from Sally's place. Coincidence?"

"Could be, but you know me; I don't believe in coincidences. Obviously, the Jean Marcoux whom Bill knew could not have been the Jean Marcoux mentioned in this article. If the deceased Jean Marcoux was actually from that area, why would someone working in the area during the latter part of the war assume the name and run the risk that someone might recognize the name?"

"Maybe someone did."

32

It didn't take long the following day to locate the second referenced edition, thanks to Truman's sleuthing the previous night. The problem was that once we found it, we could see no references to a Jean Marcoux, even though we used the broadest possible search term, as we had the previous day.

We were poring over the pages of the paper, when George arrived. We filled him in on what we had found and, more to the point, what we had not found, which was an obvious connection between the death notice in the one edition and anything in the second.

"Why don't you let me look at those pages? My French is a little rusty, but I'm pretty sure I can read most of it." Seeing the surprised looks on our faces, he waggled his finger at us and said, "You forget that in Europe, knowing two, three, or more languages is not uncommon."

We handed the pages to him and then went off to find Harriet to brief her on her assignment. We showed her the research notes, but like us, she had no knowledge of shorthand.

"What about your friend who was Black's assistant? Would she know shorthand?" Maggie asked.

"Maybe," replied Harriet. "I'll ask her. I'm sure if there is any way she can help out, she will. She thinks the man is evil."

"Well, see what you can do. If not, we'll have to find someone, maybe a retired secretary."

Just then, George reappeared.

"Did you find anything?" I asked.

"No."

I felt depression settling in.

"But I did come across something else that may be interesting," he said.

Now he had our attention.

"There is an article about high-ranking Nazi officers visiting Paris. The article listed some names, but nothing caught my eye until I looked at the picture accompanying the article. In the picture, there is listed a German officer by the name of Arnholdt von Bloch. Then I remembered that the article had mentioned that von Bloch was accompanying the general as a translator. Didn't Bill say that Marcoux had come to them because of his proficiency in languages?"

We nodded.

"I was intrigued. If you say Arnholdt Bloch in an American accent—"

"It sounds identical to Arnold Black," I said.

Maggie peered closely at the grainy photograph.

On a hunch, I grabbed the magnifying glass and took a closer look at the features. "Maggie, would you bring me a copy of Black's book? I want to look at the photograph of Arnold Black on the book jacket."

She brought the book jacket over and laid it out with Black's photograph faceup.

I ran the magnifying glass over the picture again and then over the photograph on the book jacket.

Maggie looked puzzled. "What are you looking for, Harry?"

I shook my head. "I was hoping the man in that photograph had some resemblance to Arnold Black, but the photo is so grainy I can't be sure."

33

The following afternoon, Harriet arrived at the store with her friend in tow. Mila Zilke was tall and thin to the point of being spectral, with no seeming definition between her lower and upper body. A black turtleneck sweater only accentuated her giraffe-like neck. Her square face was framed by a thick fringe of silvery hair, and she wore a pair of large, round red-framed eyeglasses. Hazel eyes glanced at us from behind the glasses—or, more accurately, darted from side to side as she tried to take in all three of us. Her mouth seemed to be beset by a permanent tic. I motioned for her to have a seat.

She folded her long torso onto a chair, leaned forward, and clasped her hands tightly in her lap. "What is it about Black you would like to know?" Her brusqueness left us momentarily speechless.

Maggie looked at me. I looked at Harriet. She shrugged as if to say, "I told you she was a no-nonsense kind of person."

I said, "I'm not sure what Harriet has told you—"

Mila raised her hand and cut me off. "Just that you are working on an issue of manuscript attribution that might be

166

related to Black's work and that you have some shorthand notes you need to have deciphered."

"Yes, quite so. We have been asked to review a manuscript that bears a remarkable similarity to Black's book. Our client insists the manuscript was written by her deceased husband."

"You mean your client is accusing Mr. Black of plagiarism."

"Yes. You can understand that we can't just go around accusing a man of Black's reputed stature of appropriating someone else's material without substantive proof; otherwise, we open ourselves to all sorts of legal claims."

"Well, nothing would surprise me when it comes to Black," she said gruffly.

"And why would that be?" Maggie asked.

Mila turned to Maggie and fixed her gaze on her as if seeing her for the first time. "He wasn't exactly scrupulous about giving credit to others who did research on his various projects at the institute. In fact, he never gave credit to anyone. To the world, it appeared as if he were the creator of all his papers."

"And that wasn't the case, I take it," I said.

"Far from it."

"So what can you tell us about the manuscript for his book?" I asked.

She shrugged. "Not much. I only worked at the institute for about six months. A friend of mine, Leah Bernstein, was his junior assistant, until he fired her. I understand Harriet has told you all about that."

We nodded.

She took a deep breath. "I haven't talked to her since my last call, which was about a week or so after she left when she told me that when she was looking at the original manuscript she couldn't find the pages she was looking for. I went to her home in Brooklyn, in the Gowanus area. She owns a little row house there. No one answered when I rang the bell. I saw mail piled up and newspapers scattered about. I was heading back to the subway, when a neighbor came out. I asked him if he had seen Leah lately. He hadn't seen her since the week before, when he'd noticed her having an intense discussion with a man who got out of a dark sedan. According to the neighbor, she turned to walk away, when the man grabbed her arm. The area she lives in is a bit on the seedy side. The neighbor became alarmed and started to approach them, but Leah waved him off. The guy hopped into the car and took off. The neighbor asked her if she was okay. He offered to call the police, but Leah declined and walked into her house. That was the last time anyone saw her."

"Did you go to the police?" asked Maggie.

"I did. I filed a missing person report, but I don't know if anyone followed up. I was told they get a multitude of missing person reports. They said they would let me know when they received any information. After that, I was transferred into Black's area temporarily. After a few days, I quit the institute altogether and decided to do freelance editing."

"Why did you quit?" I asked.

"One day I was sitting at my desk, when Black walked in. He had his cell phone to his ear and just nodded at me as he walked into his office. His office door was open, so I could hear his end of the conversation. I don't know who he was talking to, but I heard him say quite distinctly, 'I got rid of that Jewish bitch.' There was a pause, and then he said, 'No one will miss her. She only associated with one person in the office.' Just then, his executive assistant walked in, glared at me, and closed the door. That was it for me. I knew I was the other person, and I wasn't about to take any chances."

"Do you know where Black lives?"

She shook her head. "I believe he has a home out on Long

Island. Leah said something about going out to his home on the island to do some work. I just assumed she meant Long Island."

"And you haven't heard from Leah at all?"

She shook her head. "Before I left the institute, I went to human resources and pretended I didn't know where Leah lived and asked for a forwarding address. I just wanted to check to make sure that was the only address they had for her. They said for privacy reasons, they could not share that information." She shuddered. "I could hardly wait to get out of there."

"What do you think has become of her?" Maggie asked.

"I think she is dead."

34

"What on earth makes you think that?" I asked.

"Just before Leah was fired, I called her to confirm a meeting we had arranged for the next day. She sounded agitated. I asked her what was up. She was whispering—said she had come across some interesting information. Then I heard Black in the background, barking at her to come take dictation, and the line went dead. I didn't think much about it, to be honest.

"The next day, I showed up for our meeting, which was off-site, but she didn't show. When I went back to work, I headed upstairs to her desk, but she wasn't there. I asked Black's executive assistant where she was and was curtly informed that she had resigned. It didn't make any sense. Leah never gave any indication she was leaving. As I mentioned I phoned her several times after the call about the manuscript, but her phone went right to voice mail. I waited a few days, and then, as I told Harriet, I went to Leah's house and had the discussion with her neighbor and asked him to ask her to call me. Nothing.

"By that time, I was really alarmed, so a few days later,

I went back to her place one more time. The yard was over-grown, but the mail and newspapers were gone. I walked around to the back of the house and came face-to-face with two men in suits. They glared at me and asked me what I was doing there. I told them I was a friend of Leah's and came by to have a visit. One of the men walked up to me and said, 'Well, she's not here; she's gone to visit her parents.' I asked him who he was. He said he was her uncle. I asked when she would be returning. He said, 'I have no idea, Miss Zilke.' So I left."

"I'm not sure why that makes you so sure she has come to harm," said Maggie.

Mila looked up. "For one thing, I know for a fact that Leah's parents are dead. For another, she has no uncles on either side. Her parents were the only survivors in her family of the concentration camps. Finally, the man addressed me by my name, but I had never told him my name, and I had never seen him before."

I felt as if all the oxygen had been sucked out of the room.

"Anyway," she said, "I will help you in any way I can, but I will only do so if you agree to help me find out what has happened to Leah."

"Of course we will," I answered.

We sat silently for a moment. Finally, I said, "Right now, we really need someone who can try to decipher these short-hand notes." I tapped the sheets I had placed on the table.

"Well, we had better get to it."

A few hours later, Mila reappeared with a bundle of paper in her hands. "This is about all I could transcribe from the notes you gave me. There were sections where the marks were just too faint to be comprehensible." She handed copies of the transcriptions to Maggie and me.

Our initial impression that the papers were research notes had been incorrect. They appeared to be a written record of a verbatim interview with a Madame Marcoux. There were also notes in brackets.

> Interview with M? Marcoux on September 14, 1952. Husband Jean Marcoux, linguistics professor, DOD 12/40. (Transcribed from ...)
>
> Q: Are you the wife of the Jean Marcoux named in this notice of death [showed her a clipping from *Le Matin* dated December 23, 1940]?
>
> A: Yes, I placed that notice.
>
> Q: What was your husband's profession?
>
> A: He was a linguistics professor at the University of Strasbourg. Before 1939, we offered language-immersion courses during the summer at our farm near Roanne to supplement our income. After the war began in September 1939, we fled Northern France because my husband was Jewish [Mme. Marcoux informed me that she is French Huguenot], and we had heard about the treatment of Jews in Germany. We came to the farm and decided to offer language courses year-round, as we had no other source of income. Jean was quite a well-known linguistics scholar, so word got out, and we had no trouble attracting students. After the invasion of France in May 1940, we even had students from Germany, primarily

Jewish refugees who had fled south. Then, in early December of 1940, he disappeared.

Q: Disappeared?

A: Yes. One day he received a telephone call. He told me he had to go to town on urgent business but would be back by dark. He never returned. [Interview paused so Mrs. Marcoux could collect herself.] I reported his disappearance to the local police, but nothing happened. They knew he was Jewish, so they made no effort. I went back to the farmhouse and walked the path I thought he had taken but could find nothing. A few weeks later, a hunter stumbled over a body at the foot of a cliff about halfway between our farm and Roanne. It was Jean. That's when I placed the notice in *Le Matin*. Jean had many friends and colleagues—it was the easiest way to notify them.

Q: What happened to the school?

A: At the time Jean disappeared, we had ten students. They all initially stayed on to see whether Jean would reappear, but after ten days, they went home. It was a disaster—we had to return all the tuition they had paid. So we shut the school down.

Q: *We?*

A: My son, Jacques, and I. Shortly after that, my son disappeared into the French Resistance. He never returned. I have no one.

Q: I have another article from *Le Matin*, dated March 14, 1944, to show you. It is an article that concerns the visit of a high-ranking

Nazi officer to Paris. [Showed her the article.]
Do you recognize anyone in the picture
accompanying the article?

A: [She studied the picture and adjusted
her glasses.] Who is this man [pointing at a
man standing slightly in the background]?

Q: This is a man who resembles a man
from our resistance unit who went by the
name Jean Marcoux.

A: [She peered closely at the picture
and shook her head.] No, no, no. This is not
my Jean or my son. [She studied the photo
again.] I think I recognize that man. I think
he is Arnholdt von Bloch, one of the students
living with us at the time Jean disappeared.

Q: Yes, that is how he is identified in the
caption, but who is Arnholdt von Bloch?

A: He told us he came from Strasbourg,
where he had been teaching German.
When the war started, he thought it best to
disappear because he had been involved in
some political movements in Germany. He
decided to come to our school in part to hide
and in part to improve his English and French.
He thought he could make his way to Spain
and then to England.

Q: How did he find out about the school?

A: He said he knew of Jean's reputation
from Strasbourg.

Q: What was he like?

A: Very quiet. No trouble to speak of. He
kept to himself. [She looked troubled.] He had
a certain froideur—a coldness—about him,

but perhaps it was just his eyes that were so cold.

Q: Did your husband get along with him?

A: [Looked troubled.] For the most part, but Jean and my son both were uncomfortable around him because he was German. Well, as I said before, our sympathies were not with Germany. Herr von Bloch professed to be anti-Nazi, but we were suspicious. After all, who in occupied France would be so bold as to state he was anti-Nazi, when he had no way of knowing if we were? Surely only someone who had no fear of the occupying authorities could say such a thing. How would he know we wouldn't report him? But we needed the money, and we had several Jewish students, so we kept silent. [Long pause.] He seemed particularly interested in the Jewish students—where they came from, who their families were, and where they lived.

Q: Was that so unusual? Don't most students exchange this sort of information?

A: You must remember the times we lived in. Everyone was frightened. People learned not to ask questions. But Jean only became genuinely alarmed after overhearing a telephone conversation. You see, all of our students were permitted one call per week. Jean heard Herr von Bloch talking in rapid German while relaying to someone all the information he had collected about the students and their families, but it was only the

Jewish students he was talking about. He did
not know Jean was present. When he realized
Jean had heard everything, he brushed it off
as a conversation with his mother, saying she
wanted to know every detail of his life. Jean
asked if that included their religion, to which
he replied, "Yes, my mother is Jewish, and she
worries about me being corrupted by gentiles.
She is very reassured that I have members
of my own religion here." Jean let it go but
didn't believe for one minute that von Bloch
was Jewish.

    Q: What did your husband do?

    A: He started to make discreet inquiries.
He wrote a letter to the school that von Bloch
said he had attended. He went to the post to
mail it. When Jean returned, von Bloch was in
his office, which was strictly prohibited unless
Jean was there. Jean demanded to know what
he was doing there. He said he'd dropped
by to get help with an unusually complex
passage of *Les Fleurs du Mal* and showed
him the page. He said he assumed Jean had
stepped out momentarily, as the door was
open, so he'd decided to wait. There wasn't
much to do but carry on. After von Bloch left
the room, Jean examined his desk. Nothing
seemed to be disturbed, except the copy of
the letter he had written was now facing the
side where von Bloch had been seated.

    Q: Were there any more incidents like this?

    A: No, the next day Jean received the call I
told you about earlier, and that was it.

Q: What happened to von Bloch?

A: A few days after Jean disappeared, he disappeared.

Q: I don't understand.

A: One morning a few days after Jean's disappearance, I called all the students to breakfast. When von Bloch didn't show up, we checked his room. Completely clean. Nothing remained of him.

Q: Did you ever see him again?

A: [In a halting voice] I'm not sure. After the students had left, my son disappeared into the resistance. I was on my own. I couldn't manage the farm, so I moved into the town of Roanne. I kept very much to myself and rarely ventured out all those years, except to go to the market every Wednesday. In the late autumn of 1944, I was following my regular routine. It was a very chaotic, dangerous time. Everyone was expecting the liberation of that part of France to happen at any time. There were German troop movements everywhere, and nothing seemed to deter them from carrying out roundups of Jews and young men for slave labor or shooting anyone they suspected of being part of the resistance. As I came around the corner of the church on the market square, I saw some men in German uniforms standing next to a truck. I hung back in the shadows. Sometimes you just don't want to see things, and sometimes you do not want to be seen. But even from my vantage point, it was clear they were rounding up locals and marching them into the truck. There was something familiar about the German officer in charge. I had the most dreadful feeling I had seen him before.

Q: Do you know what happened to the men they rounded up?

A: Yes. They were taken to the square and shot.

Q: Did you witness this?

A: Yes. I hung in the shadows and watched from the side of the church. The German was shouting in French, "This is what happens to those who oppose the führer, and it will happen to you!" Then he gave the order to fire. As soon as I saw what was happening, I ran in the side door of the church and crouched down behind an altar in a side chapel.

Q: What happened after that?

A: I waited for what seemed to be an eternity. I was about to leave my hiding space, when I heard the main church door open. At first, I just heard the sound of boots on the stone floor. I was terrified. From my hiding place, I could see a German soldier making his way up the center aisle, furtively checking his surroundings to make sure no one else was in the church. As he got closer, I realized he was the German officer, and as he glanced around the church, I understood why he was so familiar. I was sure it was von Bloch. He disappeared from my view when he went behind the main altar. When he came into my line of sight again, he was in farm worker's clothes. He took one last look around and then left the church. I waited for a few minutes and then went into the nave. I pulled my scarf tight and low on my face and made my way to the sanctuary. I checked behind the altar, and sure enough, there was the uniform. I am ashamed to say this, but I went through his pockets. There was nothing except a few pieces of paper. [She paused and went to a sideboard and returned with some small pieces of paper. She gave me the papers.] One was an address in Berlin. The other was a Nazi membership card identifying von Bloch as a member of the party.

Q: What did you do after you left the church?

A: I returned to the square. It was horrific. Blood was everywhere, and bodies were being stacked in carts for burial. There was no sign of any Germans. What they did was sheer cruelty—vengeance.

Q: I want to show you one more picture. [I showed her a picture of Bill Smith and myself with the person we thought was Jean Marcoux.] Do you recognize anyone in this picture?

A: Well, that's you, of course, seated. I don't know him [pointing at Bill], but the third man is most certainly von Bloch.

Once again, we were flirting with the truth. If Mrs. Marcoux had in fact seen von Bloch that day in 1944, then he was not only a Nazi spy but possibly a war criminal. Was this what Nick had stumbled onto? What had happened to the Nazi membership card? Was it included in the bits of ashes Sally had given us?

"What do you make of it?" Mila asked.

I looked up to find her eyes peering intently at me. "To be honest, I'm not quite sure."

"Is it possible that von Bloch and Black are the same person?" Maggie asked.

I looked at her and shrugged. "My gut feeling is yes, but how do we prove it?"

"There may be a way to prove he is one and the same person," Harriet said.

"And that would be?"

"If von Bloch was in the German army, then there must be a record somewhere. After the war, the Allied authorities were pretty thorough in the denazification process. There must be a way to get access to that sort of record."

We all stared at her.

She looked at us expectantly. "Wouldn't there?"

"To search records in Germany would require money and resources beyond our means," said Maggie.

"There may be another way." Mila tapped her pen on the desk, looking thoughtful. "I know Black is still looking for an assistant. He's never met Harriet, and I've never mentioned her. Why not have Harriet apply for the job? Who knows? Maybe over a couple of weeks, she might be able to glean some information. If nothing is coming up, she could just resign, and no one would be the wiser."

The idea was brilliant—a new twist on the old fox in the henhouse, except this time, it would be a hen in the fox's den.

"Too dangerous," I said.

"I can do it, Harry," said Harriet quietly. "And I will be

careful. My concern is that it might seem odd if, out of the clear blue, they get a résumé from me. What if they ask me how I found out about the job opening?"

"Not to worry," said Mila. "They outsource their HR function. All we have to do is go to that website, get you registered, and indicate you are interested in that job. So if anyone asks you, just say you found it through a web search."

Maggie turned to Harriet. "Are you sure you want to do this? It really could be dangerous."

"I'll be fine, and I will be careful."

"Two weeks—no more," Maggie said.

35

We met with Bill and Syd the next day to share our latest information and our plan to plant Harriet in Black's office.

Everyone thought the idea of placing Harriet was a good one and doable, but Bill was skeptical about the kind of information she would have access to and its usefulness. Once again, it was Harriet who settled the issue.

"Let's try it. Nothing ventured, nothing gained," she said, and with that, she strode off to work on that part of the plan with Mila.

While Harriet and Mila worked out a plan to insert Harriet into the institute, the rest of us compared notes.

Syd said, "I did manage to compare the sample of handwriting I obtained from Black with some of the notations on the copy of the manuscript. The work is not complete; however, I can say with ninety percent certainty that those notations were not made by Black. Unfortunately, the scribbles on the shorthand notes that were in longhand were not sufficient to compare, although I am doing more work on those as well."

"Bill, did you have a chance to contact your sources in London and Washington?" I asked.

"I'm afraid I have reached a dead end. There is no record anywhere of a Jean Marcoux, either as a nom de plume or as a real name, in the archives of the SOE. I had a friend run a name check on the name Arnold Black from the early 1940s to the end of the war. Black is a common surname, but the combination of Arnold and Black is not common. The only Arnold Black we came across was a teacher who was evacuated from France in 1940 and later presumed dead in the Blitz. If the Marcoux I knew was a spy, he was probably very adept at changing identities and probably did so many times."

Maggie filled them in on the work Mila had done. "So another layer has been added to the mystery. Who is von Bloch? The photo in the newspaper story is too grainy for us to say positively that von Bloch and Black are one and the same. Per the interview transcript, the third man in a picture shown to Madame Marcoux was identified as von Bloch, whom you knew as Marcoux. Even if all three names belong to the same person where does that get us."

"Why did von Bloch change his name, and when?" I said. "I mean, I suppose it could be perfectly innocent. Some people Anglicize their names because they believe the names are too long or too difficult to pronounce. Or maybe not so innocent. Maybe he has something to hide."

"Or is hiding from someone."

"Or maybe he entered the country illegally," Syd said.

Bill looked thoughtful. "Or perhaps he is in the country legally. What if someone or some agency cleared the way for his entry into the country?"

"Meaning?" I asked.

"After the war, the Allies imposed a denazification process on Germany. Every adult person in Germany was required to complete forms detailing his or her background. It was meant to root out any vestiges of the Nazi political culture in Germany. A few years after the end of the war, Communism and its spread became the perceived threat, and agencies of the US government recruited and employed numerous former Nazis as sources of information. Our people knew—or should have known—that many of these agents were former Nazis who had, in all probability, committed war crimes. If these notes are accurate and Black and von Bloch are the same person, then it is likely he was guilty on some level of some crime. If he was a German spy, then he would have been a valued source of information and quite possibly was recruited by some agency of our government. It was no secret these same agencies provided assistance to Nazi officials and collaborators via entry to the US as a reward for their work."

"But why change his name?" Syd asked.

"In the seventies, the Office of Special Investigations was tasked to fully investigate the presence of Nazi war criminals in the United States and to strip them of their citizenship. We don't know for certain when he changed his name, but in any event, von Bloch would not want his real name or Nazi past to be exposed. If von Bloch has a shady Nazi past, the real questions are, how did he get into the country, under whose auspices, and why wasn't he exposed during the OSI investigations of the seventies?"

"What do we really know about this fellow?" George asked.

"Not much," answered Maggie. "The book jacket has about three lines, all related to the fact that he is associated with the International Institute for Conservative Values. Mila told Harriet that according to her friend Leah, who was his junior assistant, before joining the institute, he worked with an intelligence agency of the US government and was quietly eased out when he was implicated in illegal arms deals."

"By the way," I added, "this Leah person supposedly re-signed and since then has disappeared. Mila thinks she is dead." I recounted to him Mila's encounter with the men in the backyard of Leah's house. "We promised her that in return for her help, we would attempt to find out what happened to Leah."

The revelation elicited a round of groans and hand wring-ing from everyone but Maggie.

"Well, what would you have us do?" Maggie said. "Ignore the fact that a young woman disappeared under mysterious circumstances after being fired by the man who said, 'I got rid of that Jewish bitch'?"

George put out a soothing hand. "Of course not. But per-haps you should consider consulting with the good Detective Farmer."

Now it was my turn to groan. At the mention of the name Mike Farmer, a wave of guilt washed over me. We had prom-ised to keep him up to date and, of course, had done no such thing.

"George has a point," said Bill. "We can't avoid him for-ever, and this might be a way to get him in the loop without revealing that you have been less than forthcoming about your little venture."

Before I could think of an answer, Maggie rushed in. "A missing person report has been filed and not acted on. What makes you think Mike can do anything more? And more to the point, how do we explain how we came across all of this?"

Before I could express my thoughts, Bill held up his hand to stop me. "Let's poke around a little more. If this man is the person we think he is, then he is hiding something, and I think we should attempt to find out what that something is."

Syd spoke up. "The most obvious thing is his identity. The only certain way to confirm that von Bloch and Black are one and the same is by fingerprints, but I don't know where we would find prints for von Bloch."

"Maybe you could try that friend of yours," Bill said.

Maggie giggled. I snorted. George looked mystified.

Never one to take a jab sitting down, Syd rose to her full six feet and jabbed back. "If you think you can do better, why don't you go back to your contacts in Washington? If you are as successful as you were in London ..." She let the sentence drift off.

That was our Syd; she could give as good as she got.

Bill turned serious. "We can try, but if Black is von Bloch, I am pretty sure any fingerprints are buried somewhere in the labyrinths of Washington never to be found."

"What about a Freedom of Information Act request?" George said.

Bill shrugged. "That would just alert him that someone was checking on him. I will try my contacts in Washington again, but I have to say, I have a very uneasy feeling about this."

Lashings of rain against the windows did nothing to dispel the gloom in the room.

"Why don't we let him tell us?" I asked.

Maggie put a hand on my shoulder. "Tell us what, Harry?"

"About his background. We own a bookstore, don't we? Why don't we stage a series called 'Conversations with Authors'? We could have a series on resistance movements of the twentieth century or some such thing. We'll invite him to read from his book and discuss the resistance movement in France during World War II. We could follow an interview format—that is, with one of us asking questions and then opening up the floor to readers' questions and comments. We could ask, 'How did you develop your style?' and other inane questions. Of course, we would have to introduce him, so we'll ask him to provide some background material."

George peered over his half glasses. "Excellent idea. We should have done this long ago. Why is it, Harry, that you only think of such things when we are all about to put our lives in danger?"

I couldn't tell whether he was joking or not.

"What do you hope to accomplish, Harry?" Bill asked.

"If he takes the bait, he will probably want to meet with us first to discuss the format. We could invite him to come to the bookstore to meet with us and look at the physical layout."

Bill looked skeptical. "I'm not sure that's a good idea, Harry. What if he knows of my connection to Maggie?"

"Why not let him know we know you?"

The protracted silence that followed was a clear indication that no one thought that was a good idea, but that had never stopped me before.

"I don't mean we'll walk up to him and say, 'We know Bill Smith.' It has to be a subtler approach. I plan to lure him to the bookstore. Judging from Mila's comments, it shouldn't take much to massage his ego. We'll stage the area as if we really were going to have a reading. Part of the staging will be photographs of resistance fighters, one of which will be the photograph of the three of you. It might provoke a reaction."

Bill sighed. "It's not perfect, but it's not a bad idea."

"I'll send a letter of invitation tomorrow," Maggie said. "If Harriet is hired by his office, she will be able to track his schedule and make sure he sees the invitation."

"And don't forget," I said, "she may be able to find a link to Leah's disappearance, so we'll have a decent reason for bringing Mike into the loop."

Little did I know my opportunity to do just that would happen sooner rather than later.

36

Mila confirmed the International Institute for Conservative Values outsourced its HR function to Ferguson and Wright HR Solutions Inc. It didn't take us long to peruse the listings and figure out which listing was for the administrative assistant at the institute. Harriet set to work drafting a résumé, omitting only her current position with us. She held a small part-time job with the main library at Columbia, so we figured if they checked her references, we were covered.

On Monday, Harriet uploaded her impressive, albeit somewhat sanitized, résumé to the agency. On Tuesday, she received a call asking her to come in for an interview. On Wednesday morning, she was interviewed by the agency. On Wednesday afternoon, she was interviewed by Black himself. On Thursday, she was hired.

Part one of plan A was in motion, although we had no clue what part two would be.

On Friday, she threatened to strangle each and every one of us with her own bare hands.

"But why?" I asked.

She turned toward me and hissed at me through clenched teeth, "Because he is the creepiest person I have ever been in the same room with—that's why." She was wound more tightly than the bun on top of her head.

"Creepy how?" Maggie asked cautiously.

She looked at both of us as if we had grown two heads. Enunciating each word for the benefit of our aging ears, she answered, "Have you ever met the man?"

"No, that is why you are there—to ensure he receives our invitation to speak at our bookstore so we *do* get to meet him," I replied with equal clarity.

"And anything else you can find out," added Maggie.

Harriet spun on her heel, alternately wringing her hands and flinging them in the air.

This is a bit melodramatic, I thought, but I said merely, "How bad can it be after only one day?"

She wilted into the nearest chair. "I'm not sure how much snooping I can safely do."

"You do have access to the files, don't you?"

Harriet looked at me and nodded. "In a minimal way. I can't turn around in that office without the dragon lady looking over my shoulder and constantly yipping, 'Oh, Mr. Black doesn't allow access to this or that.' So I ask, 'How am I to do my work?' The answer always is 'One of us brings the work to you. You do it. You return it to the one who gave it to you. We file it.'"

Maggie tapped her on the shoulder. "Who is the dragon lady?"

"His executive assistant."

"So what have you done for him so far?" I asked.

"Not much of anything. Sending a few letters to bookstores, making appointments, confirming dinner reservations—nothing significant."

I took a deep breath. "Try it for one week. If nothing turns up or if Black doesn't take our bait and you are still feeling uncomfortable, then quit—just say the position is not challenging enough."

She clasped her hands together and rested her head on them, appearing to be buried in prayer. A few moments later, she looked up. "Very well. One week. That's it."

"And, Harriet," I added, "it would be useful if you could give us a list of whom he is seeing and meeting, even if it appears to be an innocent dinner invitation."

"Okay." She stood up.

"By the way," said Maggie as Harriet put on her coat, "what is so creepy about him?"

"Apart from the eyes, he has this unnerving habit of appearing out of nowhere. You never hear him. I was copying a document, and when I turned around, he was standing right behind me. I didn't hear a thing. Then he insisted I show him what I was copying, which was the document he'd given me and told me to copy. I think the guy is paranoid."

A few days later, Harriet slipped in through the back door of the store to bring news from the far side. "Sorry to be so late," she puffed. "The man himself had a last-minute bit of typing to do, and wouldn't you know it? He went through half a dozen iterations."

"Anything interesting?" I asked.

"Not in that particular letter. Just a note to the telephone company complaining about a two-dollar overcharge."

"Apart from that," asked Maggie, "anything interesting?"

Harriet rummaged around in her knapsack and eventually pulled out a small square of paper. After carefully unfolding it, she put it on the desk and smoothed it out. It was all I could do not to snatch it from her hands. Harriet was a deliberate person, and I'd learned long ago that if one attempted to hurry her along, it only slowed the process down, as she then had to take the time to articulate in great detail why she was proceeding thus and such. Hence, I held my tongue and feigned patience and interest, unlike my wife, who could not resist the urge to roll her eyes several times around her sockets. Finally, the process of smoothing was done. We leaned over to have a look, and then we looked at Harriet, mystified.

"But, Harriet," I stuttered, barely able to conceal my annoyance, "this is not a calendar."

She looked at me, miffed that I was stating the obvious. "Well, of course not an actual calendar. At first, I thought I might get a chance to photocopy or photograph the pages from his calendar using my iPhone, but as I told you, the guy is always popping up out of nowhere, so I couldn't take a chance on him catching me. How would I explain that?"

Before I could offer an answer, she continued. "So I decided I would try to memorize a day with the names and times and then go to the bathroom, make notes on my iPhone, and email the notes to my home printer, after which I would delete the notes. It wasn't particularly hard," she said wryly. "He only has a few appointments on any given day."

I looked at the list. "A few" was an understatement. There were exactly three over two days.

03/04
S Johnson (Subject: Funding requirements)
Lunch: EG

03/05
EG: Meeting canceled

03/05
M. Smith: Meeting

"Is this it?" Maggie asked.

Harriet gave Maggie an exasperated look. "I have to be really careful about not drawing attention to myself or looking too nosy. If you want me to go back in time or forward for more than a couple of days in memorizing his calendar, I'm going to have to spend more time working there than I care to." Her voice dropped to a conspiratorial whisper. "However, I did luck out in one respect. The institute is supposedly a nonprofit. For whatever reason, the IRS is doing an audit covering the last twenty-four months. Believe it or not, there still needs to be a paper trail to satisfy the IRS. I was asked to make copies of, among other items, telephone billing statements for randomly selected telephone numbers, and guess whose number was randomly selected?"

I knew from long experience that her question was rhetorical, requiring no response on our part.

"Arnold Black, Esquire—that's who. I had to sign the originals out to make the copies. When I was making copies of the telephone statements related to his direct line, I inadvertently pressed the number two for the number of copies. Oops! I figured you had Sally's telephone number, so maybe you could cross-check to see if any calls were made to her from Black's number."

Harriet never ceased to surprise.

She pulled out a sheaf of papers and handed them to Maggie, who asked, "But how did you manage to copy these without Black seeing you?"

She gave Maggie a self-satisfied grin. "Because all of the copying for the audit is done on the floor where the audit is taking place, not on the floor where Black's office is located. I put a paper clip on each set and stuffed both of them in the file folder. I lucked out. Black had left for the day, and the dragon lady was busy talking on the phone. For once, paranoia worked in my favor. While pretending to wait for the dragon lady to finish her call, I placed the file folder on my lap. As I stood up to return the originals to her, I 'accidentally' dropped the file folder from my lap, scattering the contents conveniently under my desk. It was easy to bend over to retrieve the originals and, at the same time, stuff the copies into my knapsack that I keep under my desk. Once I picked up the originals, I merely put them on her desk. She waved me off, and a half hour later, I was out of there."

"How could you be so sure which ones were the copies?"

"Oh, that was easy. I just put a different-colored paper clip on the copies."

Maggie laughed. "Well done, Harriet."

I interjected. "Yes, but …"

"What?"

"What would you have done if she had just asked you to put the file on her desk?"

She brushed her hand through the air. "No problem. I would have explained that someone, probably one of the auditors, had set the copy number to two, so I thought the right thing to do was to return all the extras to her. I probably would have gotten a raise."

I just shook my head. Harriet was getting into this.

"Who are the people on that list of yours, and are they significant to our investigation for any reason?" I asked. "I mean, there must be a zillion M. Smiths in the world."

Harriet said she would try to do some research on the names and get back to us later tomorrow.

I must have been asleep at the switch, because it wasn't until our accountant called to remind us that we were under a deadline to submit certain information about the bookstore to the IRS concerning a tax year three years prior that I asked myself the obvious question: Why was the IRS auditing a private foundation?

Mid–tax season seemed an odd time of the year to start an audit. Tax returns for the previous year were not due yet, and tax season was just gearing up. More than that, if the IRS had only just raised red flags on a return we filed three years ago, why would they be doing an audit on books and records of a tax year for which returns were not yet due and, from what Harriet said, requesting information from that year as well? The IRS could pretty well audit anything or anyone it chose to audit, so I supposed it was possible this was just a random spot audit. Or perhaps, for some reason, the IRS suspected that the institute was offside the requirements for exempt status, so they were doing a compliance check. I sighed. Sometimes I wished I had never gone to law school.

I checked to make sure George was in the front, and off I went to do a little research into when and why the IRS might do an audit of a private foundation.

A few hours into my chore, George called me from the front desk.

"Miss Mila is here to see you," he said.

"Send her back."

A whoosh of air announced her arrival at the door. I turned to greet her, but before I could say anything, she slapped the *New York Post* in front of me and stabbed her finger on it.

"Whoa, calm down," I said. "Have a seat. What's happened?"

Instead of heeding my advice, she proceeded to pace the room and kept pointing at the newspaper. "That's what's wrong." She grabbed the paper and shook it in my face.

Fearing that she was working herself up to an imminent cardiac arrest, I grabbed the paper and opened it. The headline blared, "Body Washes Up in Gowanus." The picture

accompanying the headline showed three cops transferring
a body bag to a waiting ambulance. I glanced at Mila and
then read,

> The body of an unidentified young woman was
> found tangled in debris along the Gowanus
> Canal yesterday. The woman's remains were
> removed from the canal after a passing kayaker
> noticed an overturned kayak and, on investi-
> gating, found the body partially submerged
> nearby. Police sources said that based on the
> state of decomposition, the woman had not
> been in the water long. She had midlength dark
> brown hair and was fully clothed, with one
> boot missing. The same sources confirmed that
> the Mickey Mouse watch worn by the woman
> stopped at 2:30 p.m. Police are speculating
> that based on the proximity of the body to the
> overturned kayak, her death was an accidental
> drowning.

"And?" I said.

She wrung her hands. "Don't you see? That body is probably Leah."

I sat her down again. "What makes you think that?"

She stood up and paced some more. "It's the timing. It's
the location. Her row house backed on the Gowanus. And she
was a bird-watcher."

What bird-watching had to do with her disappearance
eluded me, but before I had a chance to ask her for enlightenment, she rushed on.

"She owned a kayak. Part of the reason she lived in such a
seedy section was to have enough space to store the darn thing.

She belonged to a club that took kayak trips to various parts of New York, specifically to watch birds. And"—she paused and inhaled some air—"she owned a Mickey Mouse watch. It had a huge face that lit up in the dark." She sat down, deflated.

I had to admit there seemed to be cause for thinking the woman in the article was her friend. Nevertheless, it was a stretch to come to the conclusion that Leah had been murdered, which was what I proceeded to tell Mila. "Well, even if we assume it is Leah's body that has washed up, it is possible she had an accident. Furthermore, they have yet to identify her. I am sure they will review all missing person reports as part of that process, and they are bound to contact you because you filed a missing person report. Or if you think it is her, you can go immediately to the police with your story."

She was silent for a moment. "I don't know what to do. I am afraid that if I go back to the police and ask about this, it may stir up the waters over at the institute, and everyone will know who stirred the water up. I guess I'm worried that if he got rid of Leah, the same might happen to me." She hunched over her knees and buried her face in her hands.

I pulled up a chair next to her and put my hand on her shoulder. "Look, I have a contact in the NYPD. I'll see what I can find out."

The suggestion seemed to calm her. "I suppose that's about all we can do for now." She looked at her watch and heaved herself out of her chair. "Have to go. Got a new client—thank goodness."

After her departure, I spent a good deal of the afternoon pondering the best way to approach Mike without letting on what we were doing. Enlightenment on that topic eluded me, but a martini did not, so in the hope that that most salubrious of cocktails would help open my pea brain to some brilliant idea, I headed to the kitchen to make one.

37

Happenstance was a much-overused word, in my opinion. However, I didn't know how else to describe what happened in the bookstore the next day. I was waiting for Harriet to arrive with her daily update, and while waiting for her, I decided to do a little administrative catch-up—my euphemism for cataloging new arrivals, which, although boring and mindless, was a necessary evil in our line of business. The doorbell gave off a tinkle, followed by a bang as the door was slammed shut. There was nothing more irritating to a shopkeeper than the sound of a slammed door. I was about to admonish Harriet for the umpteenth time that doors were meant to be gently closed, when I looked up and saw, standing before me, Mike Farmer.

"You should get a stopper put on that door."

"Good to see you too, Mike."

He stared at me, unblinking. Social pleasantries were not his long suit.

"So what brings you here?"

"Just a couple of small items."

I stared longingly at the front door in the hope that one

of those ever-elusive beings known as customers would save
me from what I was sure was not a social visit. It appeared my
prayers were to be answered, as I saw a figure approach the
front door. But then, just as quickly, it rushed away. I frowned.
I could have sworn it was Harriet.

Mike turned around to look at the door, and seeing nothing to speak of, since there was nothing to speak of, he turned
his attention to me. "I'm following up on the Bedford case."

"Any leads?" I asked cautiously.

"I was hoping you might help out on that front," he
answered.

"How so?"

His fingers, darkened by years of nicotine abuse, lingered
on a first-edition Washington Irving, making me visibly
cringe. "Oh yeah, I forgot. This is your livelihood. Anyway,
have you made progress on authenticating the manuscript
Mrs. Bedford left for you?"

"A little bit. Why? Is it important?"

"I believe it just might be."

"Well, actually, we are convinced the manuscript was
written by her husband," I said truthfully.

He looked at me sharply. "Her husband?"

I nodded.

"Well, if that were the case, wouldn't she have known it
was her husband's manuscript?"

So much for being truthful. Now what? I hesitated and then
plunged in. "Of course Mrs. Bedford knew that her husband
was the author, but to protect it from further copyright erosion,
because he had not signed the copy or in any way indicated he
was the author, she thought it best to establish with extrinsic
evidence that he was indisputably the author." I had to remind
myself that the more I prattled on, the more likely I was to dig
myself a deeper grave. I could tell he was having none of it.

"I will need to see a copy of the manuscript," he said abruptly.

That surprised me. "Why?" I sputtered.

He gave me an "Are you really such a simpleton?" look. "You never know—there may be clues. If not to the identity of the killer, then perhaps to a motive, which might lead to something else."

I shrugged. "As soon as my assistant comes in, I'll have her make you a copy."

"I'd like it on my desk by tomorrow, if that is not too inconvenient for you."

Without waiting for an answer, he was gone.

I stared at the empty spot where he had been, as if trying to conjure up a reason for the untimely request.

"What did that man want?"

I whirled around to find Harriet standing in the doorway to the back office area. "Don't you believe in knocking or quietly announcing yourself so that you don't precipitate a heart attack?"

"Sorry. I was just surprised to see him talking to you when I came up to the front door a while ago."

So it was Harriet I had seen.

"Why did you rush away, and why were you surprised to see him?" I asked.

"Because he is one of the auditors."

38

"That can't be," I said.

"I beg your pardon?"

I shook my head. "Are you absolutely positive he is one of the auditors?"

"Of course I am. I may be nearsighted, but I did have my glasses on. Why are you looking at me like I have lost my mind?"

"Because he is no auditor. He is Detective Mike Farmer, currently fully employed by the NYPD."

"What?"

"You heard me."

"How do you know him, and why is he pretending to be an auditor?"

"Why are you two whispering?"

Harriet almost did a backflip over the chair. I turned to find Maggie staring at me with a bemused grin on her face.

When my heart settled into its proper position, I said, "You won't believe this." I filled her in on Mike Farmer's visit and Harriet's previous encounter with him as part of the audit team at the institute.

Her eyebrows shot up. A frown creased her face. "What is he up to, do you suppose?"

"Whatever it is, it's not good news for us. The first question is, why does he want a copy of the manuscript, and the second is, how is that request related to his posing as an auditor at the institute?"

Harriet's lips pursed. "I wonder if it has anything to do with the fact that Black received your invitation today."

"If he only received it today, how could Mike possibly know about it?"

"Earlier today, he came up to see the dragon lady—something about wanting Black's correspondence logs for the last twelve months. The dragon lady keeps all that stuff electronically on her own PC, and no one else has access to it. She told him that her printer wasn't working. I thought that was very strange, since I'd used it earlier. So she sent it to print to Black's personal printer, which is in his office. She hit a few keys, went into Black's office, and closed the door. Now, a task that should have taken thirty seconds took a full five minutes. I suspect she was calling Black."

"How did she explain her absence?" I asked.

Harriet quit wringing her hands momentarily. "She said she had to reboot the printer. She handed him a file folder. That was the other odd thing: the folder was not very thick. I know he gets a lot of mail, but judging by the size of this folder, you'd think he'd only been at the institute a few months instead of years."

"Hmm. Anything else unusual?"

"Come to think of it, there was one other unusual thing. The minute the dragon lady left the room, your friend started casually circling the desk to see what he could see. He even shuffled papers for a better look. Your invitation was there. I can't say for sure, but if he's any kind of detective, he's probably already looked into Arnold Black and knows about his writing sideline."

"And the wheels started turning," Maggie said.

"So he figured maybe there's more than a coincidence here," I said.

"And he's obviously not investigating a theft of intellectual property," Maggie added.

"So what is he investigating?"

39

The next morning, while I was shelving new arrivals, a solution to the vexing problem of keeping my word to Mila and the equally vexing problem of Mike Farmer finally came to me. I grabbed the phone and, within minutes, was connected to Mike.

We exchanged the usual banalities before he finally asked me, "What's up?"

"Nothing much. Actually, I just wanted to make sure you received the copy of the manuscript you requested. We sent it by overnight yesterday afternoon."

I could hear the shuffle of papers in the background. "Yep, it's here."

"Good. Let me know if there is anything else you need."

"I will." Mike was not known for his use of complex sentences. "Now, if there is nothing else, I have work to do, Harry."

I bet you do, I thought to myself, *including a little "audit" work.* "Can't think of anything." I paused for a moment. "Oh, Mike, there is one thing."

"Shoot."

"One of our contract employees is concerned about a friend of hers who seems to have disappeared. She filed a missing person report but has had no follow-up. I know it's not exactly in your job description, but do you think you might poke around to see if there has been any action on it?"

"No problem. What's the name of the missing person?"

"Leah Bernstein."

The airwaves went disconcertingly silent. For a moment, I thought my call had been dropped. "Mi—"

"I'm here, Harry." His tone was brusque. "How do you spell that?"

I spelled the name.

"And who is the friend making the inquiry?"

I felt an odd tingling sensation creeping up my spine. "The same friend who filed the missing person report: Mila Zilke."

"And you say she works for you?"

"No, I said she is a contract employee who sporadically helps us out with orthography issues."

"Speak English, Harry."

"She looks into issues of correct spelling," I said, which was sort of true, depending on how one looked at shorthand.

There was another pause. "I'll look into it and get back to you," he said abruptly. "Now, if there is nothing else, I have to get to work." Without waiting for a reply, he hung up.

While I was pondering that conversation, the phone rang in my hand.

"Everything Used and Rare."

"I should like to speak to Mr. Kramer." The voice was clipped, and the diction was formal, with just a hint of an accent.

"That would be me," I answered.

"This is Arnold Black. I received your letter concerning the series you are offering at your bookstore."

"Oh yes, thank you for getting back to me. We are hoping you will be able to participate."

Ignoring my statement, he said, "I understood that your bookstore specialized in used and rare volumes. My book is rather current."

"Yes, that is the bulk of our business, but we do carry some current volumes, in particular if we are planning a theme-related set of readings."

"Who else might be participating in these conversations?"

Now I had to improvise. "We haven't put together the final lineup as of yet, but we have one scholar who has agreed to do a piece on the interwar years from a German and American perspective."

"And who might that scholar be?"

"That would be my partner, George Zoski, who is also an expert on that period."

George looked up and waggled his finger at me. I could only shrug.

There was a momentary silence on the other end of the line.

"How did you come to learn of my book?"

What an odd question. Did he not get the fact that we are a bookstore?

"As I mentioned, we stock current titles as well as used and rare books. An associate of ours who used to work at the International Institute for Conservative Values thought it might be a good fit for our series."

"Really. And who might that be?"

"Mila Zilke. Do you know her?"

There was another pause, this one slightly more pregnant than the last.

"Very well indeed. How is Miss Zilke?"

"She was fine the last time I saw her."

"I am somewhat surprised that Miss Zilke would recommend my book to you. When she resigned from the institute, she did not appear to be altogether happy with working for me."

I thought it interesting that he'd translated her saying his book was a good fit into her recommending the book, but I decided to ignore that and his last observation. "Perhaps you might like to come to the store to check us out, Mr. Black. We could show you our proposed setup, and you could decide if this is something that might interest you."

"Hmm. Perhaps that would be a good idea. I have another reading next weekend. Would it be possible to drop by early Saturday afternoon before my other reading?"

"That would be perfect." I gave him our address and hung up, collapsing into the nearest chair, with droplets of sweat beading on my forehead.

"Well?" said Maggie.

"He's coming here next Saturday early afternoon."

40

Talking to Black made my skin crawl. I couldn't put my finger on why; it just did. By the time Syd and Bill met us at the shop the next day, I was starting to have second thoughts about meeting the guy.

"Even if he is suspicious, what is he going to do to you in the store?" Syd asked, pooh-poohing my nervousness. That did nothing to alleviate my uneasiness.

"She's right, Harry," Bill said. "The store is about the safest place. Maggie and George will be here. Besides, if Harriet is willing to go into the lion's den—"

"And who knows? Maybe we'll even have a few customers hanging around," said Maggie.

"Ha-ha-ha" was all I could muster.

Maggie put her hand on my shoulder. "Let's do this and see where it goes. If it looks really bad, we'll call it a day and call in Mike."

What could I say? After all, it had been my plan to begin with.

"Fine, fine. George, will you help us stage that area? You know, put the authors' table out, stack the books, and get a poster ready. We'll comb our stacks for books on various resistance movements and put those out as well. We'll place the photographs around the room, ostensibly for atmosphere, but one of them will be the one of the three of you in France. I want to set it somewhere very visible so he can't miss it."

Maggie looked skeptical. "What kind of reaction do you think you'll get?"

"Not sure, but I want to try it."

"What if he gets spooked and decides not to go forward? We'll be back to square one," said Syd.

I conceded that was a weakness in the plan. "I'm really hoping he will go away and want to think about it and then try to set up another meeting to see what, if anything, we know."

41

Early Saturday morning, Black phoned to confirm he would be at the bookstore at two o'clock. At precisely 2:00 p.m., the doorbell chimed, and the door swung open. It was one thing to have pictured the man in the abstract and quite another to come face-to-face with the person we thought of as evil incarnate. His frame filled the doorway. His navy overcoat was tailored to perfection. He paused inside the door, removed his leather gloves, and tapped them lightly against the palm of his hand while taking in his surroundings. Then, almost as if he had just become aware of our presence, he strode toward the counter.

Soon an oblong face featuring high, sharp cheekbones stood before us. His high forehead was exacerbated by a receding hairline. His skin was the shade of parchment and stretched tight, leaving one with the impression of plastic surgery gone awry. His lips were so thin they almost appeared to form one straight line. But his eyes—I could not take my eyes off them. They were cold and empty.

"I am Arnold Black. I am here to meet with Mr. Kramer."

Again, I was struck by the odd accent and formal diction. Perhaps English was his second language.

I held out my hand. "I'm Harry Kramer, and this is my wife, Maggie. Thank you for coming over."

He took my hand. The handshake was limp and brief. Perhaps he didn't like physical contact. He nodded toward Maggie but didn't invite any further contact.

A mildly uncomfortable silence followed, broken finally by Maggie, who said, "Why don't we go into the office to discuss our proposed series, and then you can have a tour of the reading area to see if it suits you?" She gestured to the hallway and, without waiting for an answer, started down the hall, which gave Black no room to suggest otherwise. I motioned for him to follow her, and I took up the rear.

Just as we reached the door to the office, George emerged, carrying a stack of books.

"Oh, George, this is Mr. Black. He's here to consider participating in our history series," I said. "Mr. Black, this is our partner, George Zoski."

"How do you do, Mr. Black?" George said. "I apologize for not being able to shake your hand, but as you can see, mine are otherwise occupied."

I glanced at Black. Was that a slight grimace I saw?

"Quite all right," he answered coolly.

"I'll talk to you later, George," I said.

"I will finish setting up the reading area. I found some interesting photographs that I think will set the tone for the period."

I closed the door to the office.

"So tell me what you have in mind, Mr. Kramer," Black said.

"As I mentioned when I spoke to you earlier, we are planning a 'Conversations with Authors' series. The theme of the first conversations will be 'War and Peace.' One of the areas we want to highlight is the role resistance movements have played in both war and peace. As I mentioned, Mila Zilke knew of your book and suggested that perhaps it might be a useful starting point."

"I see. Is Miss Zilke in today? I should very much like to say hello to her."

"No, unfortunately, this is her day off."

"That is unfortunate. In any event, tell me more about this event."

"We want it to be more than a book signing and reading, although that will be a part of it. For example, we want to illuminate the obstacles resistance movements faced and whether there was communication between different resistance movements, like those of France and Germany in World War II."

He gave me an icy stare. "There was no resistance movement in Germany."

Well, there was a piece of revisionist history if ever I had heard one. Before I could think of anything to say, he brushed his hand through the air as if to swat a fly.

"Hmm, I see. What do you need from me?"

"We'd like to prepare a biographical piece to go with the book. Your biography is quite brief. We would like to include your background, what got you interested in this period of history, and so on. For instance, did you participate in any of the events you write about?"

The smallest smile appeared on his face. "I was rather too young to participate in the events I describe. No, it was just an interest—a hobby, if you will, that I picked up on my journey from English immigrant just on the cusp of adolescence in England at the outbreak of the war to my life as an American citizen. I will be pleased to write a bit of a biographical sketch for you for the event."

Did I hear him correctly? I wondered.

"That would be excellent," Maggie said smoothly. "We'll email you a copy of our standard author agreement. We'll just need your email address."

"Oh, I'm afraid I am from a generation who do not, as you young people say, do email, but you can just send it over to the institute's office in New York. My assistant will ensure I receive it."

"Very well. Shall we look at the reading area to see if it suits you?" She rose and made her way to the door. I beckoned to Black to follow.

George had just finished staging our little tableau as we emerged from the office. A stack of books was artfully arranged at one end of the table, with a mockup of the proposed poster featuring a blown-up version of the author photograph that appeared on the dust jacket and a photo of the book itself. On adjacent tables were a selection of books on the topic of resistance movements dating all the way back to the mid-nineteenth century, with photographs or drawings from the period. Black's book was placed front row center with photos of resistance fighters from various books, including, of course, the one of Bill, Nick, and the imposter Marcoux.

For a moment, I thought he wasn't going to show the slightest interest in the display, which would not have been according to our plan. But after he checked out the author table, his book on the adjacent table caught his eye, and the usual authorial vanity kicked in. He picked up the book, briefly leafed through it, and glanced over the photographs. He paused, replaced the book, leaned over to look more closely, and then picked up the picture we most wanted him to notice. He stared intently at it for a minute. That was Maggie's cue.

"Oh, I see you found my own personal resistance fighter," Maggie said lightly.

He looked at her, startled.

"That's my father," she said. "He was with the OSS during the war. This is one of the few photographs from the war that he's ever shared with me."

Regaining his composure, he asked Maggie, "Who is your father?"

How odd. He doesn't want to know which figure is her father, only who he is.

"Bill Smith. He's read your book and is anxious to come to your reading to meet you."

Black's body went rigid. For a moment, there was complete silence in the room. "Well, I must think about this. It seems it will involve some investment of time on my part, so I will have to check with the institute to determine what my schedule will be over the next few weeks. I will have to get back to you. How soon must you have an answer?"

Feigning disappointment, I said, "Well, we were hoping to do it very soon since you are doing several readings, and naturally, it would greatly facilitate the sale of your books in our store. Would you be able to give us a definitive answer by the end of this week?"

"Yes, yes, of course. Now I must leave, or I shall be late for my reading on the west side."

I accompanied him to the door. No hand was proffered. Just as his hand turned the door handle, I said, "By the way, I almost forgot. Mila asked me to inquire if you have heard from her friend Leah. Apparently, they worked together at the institute, and Mila hasn't heard from her since she left."

He turned to face me, his face an unattractive shade of ash. For the first time, I saw a crack in the veneer. "No, no," he stuttered. "I haven't heard anything, but then again, I didn't expect to. We did not part on good terms. Now, really, Mr. Kramer, I must go." With that, he walked out.

Well, the fat was undoubtedly in the fire now.

42

"Now what?"

I turned my gaze from the receding figure of Arnold Black to Maggie. "I think we should check out Leah Bernstein's place."

"And why would that be?" she asked.

"We know she found something, but no one seems to have an inkling of what that something is—that is, if you believe Mila Zilke. Maybe we'll notice something that will give us a clue as to what she found."

"And what, may I ask, has that to do with our manuscript attribution problem or, for that matter, with Sally's death?"

"I don't know that it does, but it might."

"And what about Mike Farmer?"

"Weren't you the one who didn't want to involve him yet? I believe you said we were pursuing a legitimate line of inquiry and implied it didn't require his participation yet."

She conceded the point.

It had occurred to me that we might be straying across an invisible, somewhat murky boundary separating our legitimate line of inquiry to establish authorship and our interfering in a murder investigation and placing ourselves squarely in a place that was Mike's territory.

I turned to Maggie. "Mike hasn't gotten back to me about the missing person request I made. I find that odd. I mean, how long can it take to check into a missing person report? He is also not being very forthcoming about the investigation into Sally's murder. He wanted that manuscript for a reason. We have no evidence that any murder or disappearance is related to our inquiry, so I see nothing wrong with pursuing our line of investigation, no matter where it leads us, and if it happens to lead us to Leah Bernstein's house, so be it. Besides, Mila has asked us to look a little further into Leah's disappearance or murder."

Raised eyebrows conveyed her lack of appreciation for my obfuscation.

"No harm, no foul, right?" I said.

"It will have to be on Sunday, when the shop is closed."

43

A gunmetal sky oozing drizzle made for a messy, slushy start to our little foray to the hinterlands of Brooklyn. I glanced over my shoulder, longing for the comfort of our Sunday routine: breakfast in bed, a leisurely read of the *Times*, and, of course—

A sharp finger in my ribs brought me back to the present moment, unwelcome though it was. Maggie poked me again but this time with a smile.

"There will be lots of time for all that when we get back. And might I remind you, this was your idea."

I hated it when she read my thoughts. I sighed, resigned myself to the inevitable, pushed a button, and popped the umbrella. She joined me, sliding her arm around my waist, and pointed me toward the subway. Sharing an umbrella with her was a small consolation but a nice one.

I freely confessed that I was directionally challenged, but fortunately, I was married to a woman who seemingly had some sort of built-in GPS system that never led us astray.

One hour and three subway lines later, we emerged from the Hades of the underground to the same dismal gray weather in what was a foreign land to me but was known to many New Yorkers as Gowanus. Like a homing pigeon, Maggie led us toward the canal—down desolate, trash-laden streets; past shuttered bars and convenience stores; and around down-at-the-heels motels—until we found ourselves in front of a shabby two-story row house where Leah Bernstein lived.

According to Mila, Leah owned the place. That fact intrigued me. How did she afford it on an administrative assistant's salary? Yes, the canal was a Superfund site, a toxic cesspool worthy of a setting in a horror movie, but for many techie and artistic types, it was a land of opportunity. In a city running short of developable lots, it had the added feature of being located between two desirable neighborhoods in Brooklyn, Carroll Gardens and Park Slope, and real estate prices were accordingly proceeding upward at a vertiginous rate, even for shabby properties like that one.

"She must have bought it long ago," Maggie said.

I stared sideways at her. "Do I have a transparent skull?"

She stared at me quizzically.

"Never mind. I was just thinking what you were thinking."

"We have known each other a rather long time, Harry."

"Maybe because it's close to a Superfund site, she got a deal. We should check into when she bought it. Harriet thought it was relatively recently, based on what Mila told her, and I know what they are paying Harriet. Based on that salary, she would have had to live at home until she was fifty."

Maggie shivered. "Well, let's see if we can find anything."

I unlatched the metal gate. It squealed as if in pain. "Needs WD-40."

A cracked and lifted concrete walkway littered with yellowed newspapers led us to what passed for a front door. The aluminum frame was bent and rusted, and the glass inserts were pockmarked with sunbursts of shattered glass. We tried the doorbell. No sound. We tried knocking, with the expected result. It was evident no one lived there.

Judging by the flyers sticking out of the peeling metal mailbox, no one had been there for some time. I opened the mailbox to inspect the contents—just a few flyers and a catalog from an outerwear company, addressed to "L. Burnley or resident."

"Just junk," I said.

"Stuff it back in the mailbox, and let's check the side of the house," Maggie said.

"Hey, what do you think you are doing? Stealing mail is a federal offense, you know."

Both of us wheeled around to face our accuser, who turned out to be a balding, scruffy-looking middle-aged guy.

"You scared the living daylights out of us," Maggie said.

"Well, that's what you get for snooping in other people's mailboxes."

I held out my hand. "Sorry. We were checking on a friend of ours. We've been trying to get a hold of her, but she's not answering her phone."

"Who's your friend?" he asked tersely.

Maggie, having recovered her wits, said coolly, "Leah—"

He interrupted. "Don't you bother to read the papers?"

We looked at each other. I did not have a good feeling about this.

"We've been out of the country for a while," Maggie said. "Why do you ask?"

"Because if you did, you'd know she is dead."

"You must be mistaken," I sputtered.

"Nope, saw it in the *Post*, and it's never wrong. Not to mention the fact that it was confirmed by one of New York's finest when they came to check her house."

A sudden gust of wind sent stray flyers and dead leaves

tumbling over the street in disarray until the chain-link fence captured and held them.

"That mustn't have been too pleasant," Maggie said.

"Yeah, it was a real traffic jam here for a while. First, the finest, followed by the *friends*."

The way he said the word *friends* told me he wasn't so sure they were friends.

"What did they want?" I asked.

"Said they were the executors of her will and were doing an inventory of her belongings."

"Well, I suppose since she didn't have close family, someone had to do it," I said.

"I just thought it was odd that, if they were good enough friends that she trusted them to handle her will, they didn't have access to a key."

"How do you know that?"

"Because they came to my door to ask me if I had a key. That's when I became a little suspicious. I mean, why would they think I had a key? I only had one because Lee locked herself out one time and asked me if she could leave a key with me. As far as I knew, no one else knew I had one. Not only that, but they were asking a bunch of questions about whether anybody had been around to visit her lately."

"So what did you do?"

"I told them I had talked to the cops about all of that. I asked them if they had anything from Lee authorizing them to have access to the key. The woman produced the will and her identification. It looked legit, so I gave them the key and asked them to return it when they were done, in case the cops needed it again."

"Did they?"

"Oh yes. After the friends left, I waited a couple of minutes and then went over to check that the door was locked. It was." He looked sheepish for a moment. "My curiosity got the better of me. I unlocked it and went in. Nothing appeared to have been moved."

"Maybe they were just seeing what needed to be moved."

"If that's the case, why haven't they come back?"

"How long ago was this?"

"About a week, I guess."

"Maybe the movers were busy."

"A moving company did come back. Went through the same routine, only this time, I pretended I didn't have the key any longer and told them they would have to go to the cops to get it. Haven't seen anyone since."

By that time, my feet felt as if they were frozen blocks of ice, and I feared if I didn't move now, I might never move again.

"Well, I guess there's not much we can do to help out now. By the way, we should have introduced ourselves earlier. I'm Harry Kramer, and this is my wife, Maggie." I took off my glove and extended my hand.

"Peter Graber." He shook my hand. "Listen, if you'd like, I'll open the house for you if you want a last look. Some of her photos are still there. You might see yourself in one."

Maggie took his hand with hers. "That's very kind. We would like to but not if it's going to be a bother for you."

"Come with me. I live right here." Peter picked up some stray papers and motioned toward the adjoining row house. "I told the kid who delivered the papers to cut them off, but who listens anymore?" he grumbled.

Peter's house looked shabby on the outside, but inside, it was toasty warm. He went to the rear of the house and returned carrying a key. "I'll take you over, and when you are done, just bring back the key."

"By the way," Maggie said, "would it be possible to get the

names of the friends who visited you? I'd like to contact them to see if there will be a memorial service."

"You can try, but I've left several messages, and no response. Hang on." He rummaged through a drawer in a small chest in the hallway and retrieved a piece of paper. "They said it was their family calling card."

He handed it to me. Engraved on it were the names Martha and Matthew Spratt. Below their names was a telephone number. I felt a tight knot take hold in my gut. *Not possible.* I looked again.

Nope, it was no mistake.

44

"Harry, are you okay?" Maggie said.

"Yes, of course." I handed back the card.

Peter waved me off. "Take it. I already made a copy, just in case."

He led us to the house, unlocked the door, and handed me the keys. He was about to leave, when I remembered the piece of mail in my pocket. I fumbled in my pocket, grabbed it, and handed it to him. "I think this came to Leah's house by mistake. Maybe you would know where it should be delivered."

He looked at it and then looked at me oddly.

"What is it?" Maggie asked.

"This is Lee's mail," he said.

I grabbed it from him and looked again. I shook my head. "Sorry. Without my glasses, I can't see well. I thought it was addressed to an L. Bernstein."

He looked at it again. "Nope, Burnley. Easy mistake. It's only junk mail. I'll throw it out."

The door closed. Maggie turned to me. "What is on that card?"

"Oh, nothing much, just Mike Farmer's personal cell phone number."

I rarely saw my wife rendered speechless, but in that case, it was understandable. I was feeling slightly discombobulated myself.

"Are you sure?" she asked.

"I've phoned that number so many times to set up tennis matches I could dial it blindfolded."

"Phone him."

I retrieved my cell phone and punched in the number. I put it on speaker. The brusque voice I knew so well came on, instructing the caller to leave a message.

"It's Harry. Just checking to see if you want to play any tennis. Give me a call," I said, and I hung up. "Well, that answers that question."

"But raises a whole lot more," she said quietly.

"Like who is Lee Burnley, and why was she using the name Leah Bernstein?"

"Is there a connection to Sally's murder?"

"And what is Mila Zilke's part in all of this?"

Maggie looked mystified. "What do you mean?"

"Well, if Mila and Leah were such great friends, how could she not have known her real name? Obviously, Lee never bothered to hide her real name while living here. Don't you think it's just a little odd, especially since Mila knew this is where Leah lived?" I shivered. A chill that no winter coat could keep out pervaded the room.

"Do you think there is some connection between Mila and Mike?"

I shook my head. "I don't know what to think. It's just that—"

"Something is very odd about all of this," she said.

I nodded. "What do we really know about Mila other than that Harriet knows her?"

"And how well does Harriet know Mila?"

We looked at each other. "I think it would be wise to call Harriet and make sure she doesn't mention to Mila that she knows that Mike the auditor is really Mike the cop," I said. "In the meantime, let's poke around to see if we can figure out what Lee Burnley came across at the institute."

Unlike the exterior of the house, the interior, although shabby, was spotless, with nary a dust bunny to be found. *We should have her cleaning lady.* No electronic equipment was in sight, but I couldn't say I was surprised. I was pretty sure the so-called Spratts would have taken care of that already. We rifled through drawers, poked into closets, and looked under carpets, but nothing was out of the ordinary.

"Whatever she discovered, she didn't leave any record of it here," I said.

"It would help if we had some idea what she came across."

Twilight closed in. The lights in Peter Graber's house cast a glow that illuminated shadowy movements behind the blinds.

Maggie looked at her watch. "It's getting late. We'd better finish up and return this key."

I followed her into the kitchen, a tiny space at the back of the house. The appliances were dated, and the linoleum floor was chipped. An open shelf above the stove housed an array of cookbooks. To the left of the stove was a cookbook holder with a battered copy of *Mastering the Art of French Cooking* propped up in it.

I looked over my shoulder at Maggie. "I guess she was interested in the culinary arts," I said, pointing at the book.

Maggie looked over at me and, knowing that any book older than twenty years could arouse my collecting libido, teased, "Is it a first edition?"

"I doubt it. Even if it were, it would be almost worthless, judging by its condition." But of course, my curiosity got the better of me, and I removed it from the holder to have a peek.

As I did so, the binding separated from the spine, sending loose pages flying everywhere.

Maggie gave me a poke in the ribs. "Well, if it was worth something before, it sure won't be now."

"Very funny." I gathered up the loose sheets. When I picked up the book, the loose binding separated some more, revealing some loose paper flattened to the interior of the spine. "I think I found what Lee discovered."

Maggie looked up. "What?"

"Take a look." I handed her the papers I'd found in the spine.

"Oh!"

One was a photocopy of a German passport page admitting one Arnholdt von Bloch to the United States in 1948. The second was a faded letter, signed by the director of the CIA, to the head of the then INS, directing the expedited entry and granting of permanent resident status in the United States to one Arnholdt von Bloch. The last was a photocopy of a picture of four German officers flanking Hitler in Paris. It was grainy, but there was no mistaking who was in the photograph. Just to the left of Hitler stood Arnholdt von Bloch, now known as Arnold Black. It was the same picture we had found in the French newspaper.

"Let me see that letter again, Harry."

I handed it to her.

She stared intently at the signature for a moment. "Well, this is certainly a new twist." She tapped the letter lightly. "Whoever signed this letter has the same last name as our current vice president, who happens to be the leading contender for his party's nomination in the next presidential election."

45

"Well?" Maggie said.

"Well what?" I asked.

After our unsettling visit to Lee Burnley's home, the warmth of our own home and hearth, along with a glass of wine, was a welcome relief as we puttered around the kitchen, making dinner.

"Harry, we can no longer avoid the fact that somehow, what we are doing is related to one, possibly two—"

I lifted a spoonful of tomato sauce to her lips to taste for seasoning. "Or three murders if you count Nick Bedford's disappearance as a murder," I said, finishing for her.

She licked her lips and nodded. I was not sure if she was agreeing with the murder count, the seasoning in the tomato sauce, or both.

"I'm having a hard time making all the connections," she said. "I can see how our work might be connected to Sally's murder and Nick's disappearance. After all, if we could prove that Black appropriated at least ninety percent of Nick's manuscript, exposing him as a literary thief, it would seem the threat of disgrace and ruin of his reputation might have been

226

sufficient motive to get rid of her, and if we did uncover how and from whom he acquired the manuscript, that might lead to uncomfortable questions surrounding the circumstances of Nick's disappearance."

I placed my stirring spoon on the spoon rest. "But what we are doing doesn't seem to be connected to the death of Lee, a.k.a. Leah. The only connecting fact is that Mike knew Lee Burnley, and both were involved with something at the institute, where they both used different names and—"

"And Mike is investigating Sally's death."

"It seems we have yet more questions than answers."

"Like why did he use a different name when talking to Peter Graber?"

"And what was he looking for in that house?"

"And did we find what he was looking for?"

"Well, if he was looking for something, the only way he would have known there was something to look for was if Mila told him. Don't forget: she was the one who told us that Lee, a.k.a. Leah, had phoned her while agitated about finding something. And Mila was working at the institute too. Which makes me think Mila was the woman accompanying Mike and posing as his wife and a friend of Lee."

Maggie looked thoughtful. "What doesn't make sense is, why did Mila leave the institute? I mean, if they were investigating Black, why would she leave?"

"The real question is, why was Mike looking for that something?"

"And what if he had come across the documents we found? How are they related to the work he is doing at the institute?"

"My guess is they are not, unless Mike is doing an investigation into possible Nazi war criminals living in the States, which isn't exactly within his jurisdiction. Even if he saw the picture, it is grainy enough that he might have passed right over it and made no connection to Black. Remember, the only reason we made the connection is because of the photograph of the three men together. We were looking for Black."

"Sometimes I think we'll never square the circle."

Before I could offer what I considered to be the only way to do just that, my cell phone rang.

"Harry Kramer," I said.

"Mr. Kramer, this is Arnold Black."

I mouthed the name to Maggie. "Mr. Black, how can I help you?"

He was brusque to the point of rudeness, with no apology for disturbing us so late on a Sunday. "I have a few questions about the author event. There are a few matters I would like clarification on."

"Ask away."

"If you don't mind, I would prefer to meet with you in person."

I thought about that for a minute.

"Of course. Please feel free to drop by the bookstore any time tomorrow. We'll be in all day."

"My days are rather busy. If you don't mind, I'd rather meet at my office tomorrow evening. It shouldn't take long."

"What time would suit you? We have a few items that we need to clarify with you as well."

"Shall we say six thirty? The institute is closed, and it is much quieter. I'll leave your name at the desk." He hung up without waiting for an answer.

46

Night was stalking dusk as Maggie and I made our way across town to Black's office. It was a typical gusty spring evening but, for the moment at least, was dry. The lobby to the building was cramped and was almost entirely taken up by a surly security guard whose name tag identified him as Victor. We identified ourselves.

Victor glowered at Maggie. "You aren't on the list." He pointed at me. "Only he is."

Maggie stood directly in front of the desk; stared him squarely in the eyes; and, in a tone of voice that suggested she was reasoning with a recalcitrant child, said, "Victor, I am his wife, and after our meeting with Mr. Black, we are going to have dinner at a very expensive restaurant in the neighborhood." The emphasis she placed on the word *our* left no room for doubt that *we* would be seeing Mr. Black together.

She continued. "We naturally assumed that when Mr. Black requested the meeting, he understood that there would be two of us, since my husband clearly said to him that *we* had a few questions too. Mr. Black is well aware that I am one of the owners of the bookstore where he will be giving a reading. However, if you prefer, I can sit here with you until their meeting is over." She didn't move.

Victor blinked first. "Sign in."

With the formalities completed, he escorted us to the elevator, keyed in the floor, and stood there until the door closed. Maggie and I looked at each other. *So much for security.* He had not once asked to look in Maggie's oversized bag.

The elevator opened to what appeared to be the reception area. The glow of an exit sign and a glimmer of light from a door slightly ajar at the far end of the area were our only sources of illumination. We picked our way toward the door through an obstacle course of desks, chairs, and office equipment, guided only by that thin stream of light. I knocked.

"Enter."

I hesitated. Would it be better to just back off? It wasn't too late.

Maggie pushed the door open. It was too late. She stepped to the side.

I walked through the door, squinting into the gloom to locate the source of the voice. Black was seated in an armchair, his face obscured by the shadow cast by the floor lamp behind him.

At first, I thought he hadn't seen us. Then he glanced up, his pursed lips registering disapproval. He carefully tidied the papers he was reading and laid them on his lap.

"Mrs. Kramer, I was not expecting you."

"As I told your security guard, we do own the bookstore together, and I believe Harry made it clear that we too had need of some clarification."

He ignored her comment and pointed to the chairs. "I'll have to speak to the agency that mans our security desk. They are always supposed to check before admitting anyone whose name is not on the list. Nevertheless, you are here now, so let us first clear up any questions you may have."

Never one to mince words, Maggie got right to the point. "There are some blank spaces in your past."

His face remained expressionless.

I cleared my throat. "Issues of authorship have been raised with us."

"Really?"

"Yes, really. That, combined with the fact that you have never previously published anything on any aspect of World War II and the lack of any information about your career from the time you moved to this country until 1977, has caused us to take these claims seriously."

"And who, may I ask, is questioning my authorship?"

The room seemed suddenly airless, and I felt my chest constrict. The moment had come.

Maggie leaned forward. "One of our very good customers approached us after buying your book. She was under the impression her husband knew you."

"Really. And who might your customer be?"

"Sally Bedford."

47

The muffled roar of the street traffic below hung in the silence of the room. Staring the devil in the eyes was hard enough; trying not to blink was harder still.

"May I ask what makes you think I had anything to do with these people you mention?"

"Person, singular," I said.

He shrugged.

Maggie took a copy of the manuscript from her oversized bag and dropped it onto the desk. "This," she said.

He stared at it for a moment and shrugged. "What is it?"

"It's a manuscript that bears an uncanny resemblance to your book," I said.

His eyes shifted from one of us to the other. Still, he said nothing.

Maggie tapped her finger on the manuscript. "The problem is, it was written by Mrs. Bedford's late husband, Nick Bedford."

"Do I know him?"

I placed the picture of Nick, Bill, and the man masquerading as Jean Marcoux before him. "I believe you do, Jean Marcoux."

He glanced down at the photograph. "You must be mistaking me for someone else."

Maggie smiled. "Oh, I don't think so. You see, in the process of researching his book, Nick interviewed a Madame Marcoux. When asked if she recognized anyone in this picture other than Nick, she said she did and identified you as a person who had attended the language school they operated during the period between October 1939 and May 1940. Only she knew you as Arnholdt von Bloch. You left the language school at about the same time as the disappearance of Madame Marcoux's husband, who was later found dead at the bottom of a ravine."

"How fascinating, but pure speculation on your part. Do you have any evidence to support these facts?"

"After her husband's death, she moved to a little city called Roanne. Near the end of the war, she happened to see some German soldiers rounding up locals. The truck went to the square, where all the men were executed. Mrs. Marcoux was hiding in the church. One German soldier returned. He removed his uniform and put on civilian clothes that had been hidden behind the main altar. Mrs. Marcoux recognized the person she knew as Arnholdt von Bloch."

"Many people were caught up in the war, and I'm sure many look like me. As I told you, I was living in England during the war."

"We checked that too. There definitely was an Arnold Black who matched the age you describe as your age when you came to the US, but unfortunately, he died shortly before you arrived here."

He sat still with his hands calmly crossed on his knees.

"We are also certain you entered this country not as Arnold Black but as Arnholdt von Bloch."

He waved a hand dismissively. "And what leads you to that conclusion?"

Maggie slid a copy of the passport entry across the coffee table. "I guess you skipped the question on the immigration form that asks, 'Are you or have you ever been a member of the Nazi Party?'" Her comment seemed to amuse him a bit.

"But the bigger question is, why did a director of the CIA personally request expedited processing for you?" I said.

He brushed it all away. "This means nothing, and frankly, I don't think anyone would find what you believe to be very interesting."

I slid a copy of the photograph we'd found across the table. "Perhaps not, but the Justice Department might be interested in this." I tapped the photo.

He picked it up, glanced at it, and put it back on the table. "You have no idea how many Nazis received shelter in this country."

"Did you sleep well at night, knowing you had betrayed people like Nick and Bill and had sent innocent people to their deaths?"

His eyes were cold. "It was war."

"It was murder."

"A distinction without a difference."

"I wonder what the authorities would say if they knew about that part of your past."

He uncrossed his legs and leaned toward us, his eyes cold. When he finally spoke, his voice was hard and flat. "What makes you think they don't already know?"

The snap of his fingers echoed around the room. The door opened. In stepped Victor with a gun of some sort in his right hand, pointed directly at us.

I hated guns. I had never owned one and did not care to do so. I particularly hated having one pointed at me. I had had that experience once before, and it had not ended pleasantly.

Victor looked at Black.

Black waved his hand. "Not just yet, Werner. These people have expressed a deep curiosity about my past, so I am going to indulge them before you dispose of them."

I could not keep my eyes off the gun pointed at my midsection. Maggie, on the other hand, maintained stony eye contact with Black.

"It was indeed unfortunate that the real Jean Marcoux caught on to the fact that I was a German spy operating in the eastern part of France to assess troop movements and recruit locals to spy for us. Of course, I had to deal with him before he got a response to his inquiries. I should have stayed longer to ensure that no suspicion fell on me, but I was called back to Berlin. When the Führer called, you went, no questions asked. The spring campaign was in the planning stages, and my bosses wanted me stationed in Paris to carry on with intelligence gathering. I was fluent in German, English, and French, so it made sense. I was given a new identity as a language instructor at a small provincial school outside Paris, together with a new past, but the real objective was to get me to England to spy on the British."

He paused and shuffled his papers. "We didn't take the French seriously, but we were certain the English would be formidable. While in France, I started searching for the identity that would get me to England. It took a while to find someone who bore a resemblance to me, but I did. Ironically, it was an English headmaster by the name of Arnold Black teaching English in Northern France. He was single, slightly older than I, and from an obscure place in Northern England and had no known relatives. He was killed in a fortuitous car accident. I fortuitously found him and reported the accident. The school had no information about surviving relatives, so because I spoke English, I offered to make inquiries. The school was very appreciative and handed me all of his papers.

He was buried in France with no fanfare and was promptly forgotten by the school. The difficult part was doctoring his picture on his passport in a way that would not arouse suspicion on the part of the British, and then I bided my time.

"Fortunately for me, Dunkirk came along. I destroyed my French papers. In the chaos, no one really looked closely at my English papers or questioned why an English headmaster landed up on the beaches of Dunkirk. After arriving in England, I secured a teaching post in a small school, no questions asked. Until the US entered the war, I was able to get some information but nothing of high value, which was when I came up with my next plan. I couldn't believe I hadn't thought of it sooner. I tried to join the army, knowing that because of my supposed bad eyesight, I would be rejected, but when they found out about my fluency in three languages, they steered me to MI6, who were participating in a joint operation called Sussex."

I started to rise from my chair. Werner stepped forward. I sank back. Werner crossed his arms with gun in hand and positioned himself directly behind us. Black stood up and wandered over to the drapes, which he threw open, and for a moment, he seemingly was lost in thought. Rain pelted the windows, making rivulets out of the drops. He returned to his chair. I could see Werner's outline, his features melting, in the streams of water coursing down the window.

"They were putting together two-man teams to work with the French Resistance. I did their infantile training, and then I was dropped into France as Jean Marcoux. It didn't take much to get rid of the radio operator, and eventually, they put me in contact with Nick and Bill. All went well, from my point of view. I turned in several resistance cells, but unfortunately, I knew I was arousing suspicion on the part of Nick and Bill. I devised a plan to make my escape. It didn't take much. A fake ambush, and voilà—I was gone, presumed dead. If only I could have stayed that way.

"I made my way back to Germany and was eventually sent back to Roanne, where, as you have just pointed out, Mrs. Marcoux recognized me. I didn't know it at the time, of course. After the war, I discovered that Nick was making inquiries about me. By that time, I was living in the US, and my life had taken on some complications. I contacted him and asked him why he was making inquiries. He'd thought I was dead. I told him clearly not. He, of course, wanted to know what had happened. I suggested we meet at a restaurant near his home. Conveniently, it was located on the side of a cliff.

"We met. We had a discussion. He revealed to me what he had learned from Madame Marcoux. At that point, I realized I had no choice. I backed him toward the seating area near the battlements. I remember it was a beautiful morning—just a slight breeze, so I suggested we sit on the battlements. Below was a sheer drop. I remember looking over and thinking how lovely the trees looked all dappled in sunlight and how I hoped he would be grateful for that last sight as he fell to oblivion. I looked around. There was no one. I am a strong person. We were standing near the edge. He accused me of being a spy, among other things, which I must admit I happily acknowledged, and then, in one swift move, I lunged at him, causing him to lose his balance, and threw him over the edge."

"How did you get the manuscript?" I asked.

His cold gaze fixed on me. "I went to his home and took it. It was a terribly messy place." A look of disgust crossed his face. "But I managed to find the manuscript, or what I thought was all of the manuscript; tidied up; and left."

I could feel Maggie's body shaking. "Did it not occur to you that his wife might be at home?"

His voice was icy. "I didn't know he was married, but it

would not have made any difference. I would have disposed of her too. I had no idea he was married until a Mrs. Bedford sent me an email about some missing pages. When I took the manuscript, I did not realize that some pages were missing. I just filled in the missing portions with my own work. Her copy obviously had those pages. I was contemplating what to do about her, when you came into the picture, and once you are out of the picture, I will deal with her."

Maggie and I looked at each other. "That's hardly necessary since you already have," I said.

He looked genuinely puzzled. "What do you mean?"

It was Maggie's turn to fix him with a cold stare. "Well, you murdered her, so as you well know, there is nothing left to do."

"I have never met Mrs. Bedford, let alone murdered her," he scoffed.

"What about Lee Burnley, or, as you knew her, Leah Bernstein?" I asked

"What about her?"

"She was murdered."

"I had nothing to do with that. Unfortunately, your Ms. Whoever was a bit of a nosy parker, as the British are fond of saying. She had been doing more snooping than was healthy for her. She made the mistake of confiding to me the results of her snooping, thus putting me in something of a dilemma. I found her rather attractive for a Jew and had suggested she might like to have a bit more of a personal relationship with me. But obviously, that wasn't an option at that point, so I fired her. Apparently, someone else was not so forgiving."

"Why did you decide to publish the manuscript?" Maggie asked.

He seemed genuinely surprised by the question. "Why does anyone do anything? Surely you can't be that naive. It's called money. I have had the odd financial setback—stock market and such—and I needed cash. I read the manuscript and thought it could be a money maker. I had no idea there was a widow. So many years had gone by, and what with so many anniversaries of D-Day and such coming up, I thought, *Why not?*"

"When did you change your name from von Bloch to Black?" I asked.

"After I arrived in the States."

"Why?"

"For very practical reasons that are no concern of yours."

"Maybe the current vice president had something to do with it." Maggie interjected.

He sneered. "That man is just a pretty boy, not very smart—nothing like his father."

"I guess not since his father was the one who cleared the way for someone who obviously did not have much in the way of intelligence," I said.

He looked mildly offended. "Your feeble attempt at humor annoys me, Mr. Kramer."

I wanted to keep him talking while I tried to find a way out of our predicament. "You will never get away with this."

"Really, and what makes you think that?"

"For one thing, you and the institute are being investigated, so if we end up dead on your doorstep, it will only lead to more questions."

"Oh, if you are referring to that audit, I can assure you no auditor will find anything amiss about our books. And this will very much look like a break-in by the time Werner is through. Now I must take my leave. Werner will be taking—"

A tremendous clap of thunder interrupted him. The lamp flickered off, and the exit light dimmed, leaving the room dancing in shadows. A flash of lightning lit up the room. I saw the amorphous, featureless reflection of Werner in the window with gun lifted. His head turned toward the door, his shadow was tangled up with other shadows, and then there was darkness. For a moment, the stillness in the room was palpable, and then the lamplight flickered on again. Black was facing the window with his back to us.

"Really, Werner, we have to get them to do something about the electrical in this building." Black turned around with a smirk on his face. The smirk turned to a look of confusion. "What are you doing here?"

I heard a faint click and then a soft pop. A red blotch stained Black's forehead. He threw his head back and then toppled forward to the floor.

I whirled around. Only Maggie, a dead Black, and I remained.

Hell was there, and we were in it.

48

"Why am I not surprised to see you two here?" Without waiting for an answer to the question, which really didn't require an answer since we couldn't give him one, Mike went on. "It seems every time I turn around, you two are involved in a murder. What's the matter with you? Don't you have enough to do without getting involved in—" He tapped the table. "Let me count. Not one, not two, but three murder investigations. You are involved in more murder investigations than half the NYPD."

"Maybe four," I said.

He swore softly. "So did you get a look at who shot the man?"

We shrugged. "The room went dark for a moment, and when the lights came on, I just heard a pop, and then Black toppled over," I said. "We were the only people in the room."

The crime scene team had come and gone, and the body of Arnold Black had been removed and presumably was on its way to the medical examiner's premises. Only Mike, Maggie, and I—and the lingering smell of death—remained in the room.

"Suppose you tell me what you were doing here."

"Arnold Black is—was—doing a reading at our bookstore. He said he needed clarification on some aspects of the proposed reading and asked us to meet him here to discuss them," I said.

He waited.

Maggie waded in. "We also had concerns."

"And would those concerns be related to the manuscript you were asked to look at?"

Maggie and I glanced at each other. "Yes," I said. "Black's book bears a striking resemblance to the manuscript we have. We asked Syd to see if she could definitively determine who the author was. She couldn't affirmatively decide either way, as there was not enough physical evidence to point to one or the other. There was no doubt that at least ninety percent of the book was written by the person who wrote the manuscript and that parts of the book were written by someone else. We were asked to investigate his authorship."

"It got complicated," Maggie added.

"How so?"

"It's a long story, Mike," I said.

"My time is your time."

"Can we do it back at the shop? This place is giving me the creeps," Maggie said.

He stared at us for a moment. "You'd better have some of that nice Scotch on hand."

49

Just when I thought the evening could not possibly spring any more surprises on us, it did. We made our way through the bookstore and headed upstairs.

"Do you have something against using the elevator?" grumbled Mike.

"Not enough room for all three of us," I said.

"Besides, taking the stairs is good for your heart," Maggie said.

"My heart got a good enough workout with you two tonight to last me a lifetime."

I retrieved the key from above the door.

"That's some security system you have."

As it turned out, I didn't need it. As I went to insert the key, the door flew open.

"Bill?" I said.

"You scared the living daylights out of me!" Maggie said. "What are you doing here?"

"Goodness, child, there is no need to raise your voice. I may be of advanced age, but I can still hear. You look exhausted. What were you two up to tonight?"

"Would you mind if we exchanged pleasantries inside?" Mike said. "This landing is a little tight for all of us."

Bill peered around Maggie. "Oh, it's you, Mike." He stood to the side, and we all sidled in like three little children all in a row. The fireplace was on, and a tray of cocktail glasses sat on the counter.

Mike took a look. "At least someone has the right idea."

Bill mixed cocktails. Soon we were all settled in front of the fire.

"Why didn't you tell us you were planning to drop in?" Maggie asked.

"I hadn't intended to come by, but my meeting with the boys went longer than usual, so I thought I'd bunk in for the night."

The boys were a group of elderly baseball fanatics who get together every week during the season to discuss all things baseball. They had been doing so for, give or take, sixty years.

"You're starting a little early this year, aren't you?" I asked. "If memory serves me, the season doesn't start for a bit yet."

"Harry, Harry, you of all people should know that training season is the time to start checking everyone out so we can make appropriate predictions for the season. Besides, Opening Day is just a pitch away. But enough of baseball. What is going on here? It's not like you, Mike, to pop in for a nightcap at ye olde Used and Rare."

"It's a long story," I said.

"Not too long, I hope," he said wryly. "I'm too old for a lengthy rendition on how much trouble you two have gotten into now."

"Trouble is putting it mildly," Mike said.

I gave Bill the *Reader's Digest* version of the events of the evening. He shook his head. "I just might outlive you two yet."

"So now that we have all arrived at the same starting line, why don't you fill me in on your true involvement in this mess?" Mike said.

"As we told you before, we were approached by Mrs. Bedford to prove that the manuscript she gave us was written by her husband, Nick Bedford, who disappeared some fifty years ago. That was the fourth murder I was referring to."

Bill's lips twitched. "Fourth?"

I gave him the names of the other three. "Sally came to us after she discovered and read Black's book, which is almost an exact duplicate of the manuscript. She had been trying for years to find out what happened to her husband. When she came across Black's book, she instinctively felt that Black was connected in some way to his disappearance."

"So you were really investigating a fifty-year-old disappearance?" Mike said.

"No, not at first. Sally hoped that proving her husband wrote the manuscript might flush out more information on her husband's disappearance. That was really all she cared about."

"But everything changed with Sally's death," Maggie said. "Arthur Babcock gave us a letter she had written asking us to continue on with the manuscript attribution."

"But even if she hadn't written the letter, Babcock had every right as the executor to get to the bottom of it, since any possible copyright infringement claim became the claim of the estate," I added.

Maggie continued. "When you told us this was a murder investigation, we really didn't know what to do. I mean, we just couldn't believe that exposure for plagiarism and any associated infringement claim would be a motive for murder."

"Perhaps in the future, you might let me decide what constitutes motive. I have a specialty in the area," Mike said dryly. Bill nodded in agreement.

Maggie stood up and started pacing. "Really, Mike, think about it. It's a manuscript that is over fifty years old. We had no definitive proof it wasn't Black's manuscript, and it would have been Sally's word against his. Syd could conclude that one person wrote most of the manuscript, but who was that person? Her instincts told her that someone whose second language was English and who employed traditional English usage wrote the sections that differed and the balance of the manuscript was written by someone who employed American usage. That was about it."

"We needed something more definitive to confront him with," I said.

"And did you find it?"

Maggie said, "All we had to go on at first was a picture that had been in Sally's apartment—a picture of three men, one of whom was Dad. A picture that disappeared in between our first and second visits."

Mike's eyebrows arched, and he looked at Bill. "You?"

"As far as I know, I am her only dad," Bill said.

Mike groaned. "Don't tell me you are involved in this mess."

Bill shrugged. "Not initially."

"But Bill was away, so we couldn't talk to him immediately," I said.

"And then it got complicated again," Maggie added.

Mike said nothing.

"We checked Sally's safe-deposit box," Maggie said. "We found the same picture we had seen in the apartment, and we found a slip of paper with some numbers on it."

He tapped his fingers on his glass. "What kind of numbers?"

"They made no sense. So we decided to go to Sally's farmhouse in France to see if we could find anything there that would shed some light on the manuscript issues."

"You can imagine our surprise when the door opened, and there stood Bill," I said.

"I can't imagine why," Mike said.

"Sarcasm is not helpful, Mike," said Maggie.

"Bill gave us the history shared by the three of them, including their work with the OSS during World War II. At that stage, we were almost certain Black was the third man in the photo. He went by the name Jean Marcoux. We searched the house but found only sheets of notes and loose photos. The notes were in shorthand, and the only thing we knew for sure was that they referred to a town in France called Roanne. So we headed back to the States."

I paused to have a sip of my drink. "When we returned, we showed the bits of paper to George, who surmised they referred to editions of a French newspaper. We consulted our friend Truman, who deciphered them and found the editions."

"And?"

"One was an obituary of a Jean Marcoux."

"And the other?"

"Was a photo in the paper of a man in a German uniform standing beside Hitler. The picture is grainy, but we believe that man is Black."

"What about the sheets of paper you found?"

We were silent for a moment. "Harriet had a friend who translated the shorthand for us," I said. "It was an interview with a Madame Marcoux, who was given a picture to look at. The photo was not attached, so we could only speculate that it was the same picture of the three men we have."

Maggie continued. "Only she identified the man as Arnholdt von Bloch, who attended their language school and then disappeared not long after her husband did. She saw von Bloch only once after that, in Roanne, shedding his German uniform after rounding up and executing some locals."

"The problem was that if von Bloch and Marcoux were one and the same, von Bloch should have been dead."

Bill recounted the events of the evening when Marcoux, a.k.a. von Bloch, supposedly died.

"We were not sure if Black, Marcoux, and von Bloch were one and the same, so we had Harriet apply for a job at the institute as Black's assistant," I said.

"Bill, please tell me you didn't know about this," Mike said.

Bill shrugged.

"Oh, good grief, you three. What were you thinking?"

We stared hard at him. Maggie held up her hand. "It gets a little more complicated. We discovered that a call had been made to Sally's phone from Black's office shortly before she died. Also, Harriet retrieved some entries from his calendar."

"That's it?"

"Not exactly. When Harriet came back to the store to report on what she'd found, she was beside herself. It turns out she saw you come into the store, Mike. She wanted to know what the auditors at the institute were doing here. It turns out she recognized you as one of the auditors."

Bill looked puzzled. "Auditors?"

"We told her who you really were and cautioned her about saying anything."

Bill threw up his arms. "What are you talking about?"

"Well, Mike, what are we talking about?" I said.

His face remained impassive.

"Isn't it your turn now?"

"No, but we will talk later about why you didn't come to me then."

"We also know that Leah Bernstein is—or, rather, was— Lee Burnley and that she too was murdered. Why we don't know, but we are sure you do. We went to Lee Burnley's home because she told your friend Mila she had found something but didn't tell her what it was she'd discovered."

Bill shook his head. "That nice young woman is your friend?"

Mike ignored the question.

Maggie walked over to the desk and took an envelope from the drawer. She opened it and withdrew the three pieces of paper. "This is what we found at her place."

Mike took each piece of paper, stared at it, and then handed them all to Bill.

Bill's face clouded over. "My, my."

"So then we were certain that Black, von Bloch, and probably Jean Marcoux were the same person. I know you won't believe me, but we had decided that whatever was going on was much bigger than what we had been retained to do. Before we could phone you, he phoned us, and that's why we went to his office."

"What happened at the office? And please leave out no little detail."

"He admitted that he killed Nick Bedford and stole the manuscript."

"Why?"

"Black had heard that Nick was making inquiries about him. He wanted to find out why. After he killed Nick, he went to Nick's farmhouse. I guess he discovered the manuscript, and he packed it up and took it without realizing there was a copy. We can only surmise that he thought there was something in the manuscript that revealed something he didn't want to be revealed."

"And was there?"

"That's what we find puzzling. Three of us have read both the book and the manuscript, and even when you compare the pages that are different, there doesn't seem to be any revelations that relate to Black's background or possible activities in the war."

"Unless, after Nick had the interview with Mrs. Marcoux, he didn't have time to incorporate the new work into the manuscript," Bill said.

"I guess that is a possibility," Maggie said. "Black did intimate that he did not know of the shorthand notes."

"He insisted he had nothing to do with Lee Burnley's death," I said, "and seemed genuinely taken aback when we told him that Sally had been murdered."

"We showed him the passport documents, the letter signed by the vice president's father, and the picture, but he seemed to shrug it off," Maggie added.

Mike tapped his glass. "Did he say why the CIA expedited his entry into the country?"

We shook our heads. "Black said he changed his name after he came to the States but didn't say why. For that matter, there is very little known about his work in the US until the seventies, when he was caught doing some arms deals that involved the CIA and was ushered out the door." I said.

Bill cleared his throat. "I suspect the name change had something to do with a congressional investigation into Nazi war criminals who were living in the US and whose entry may have been facilitated by US government agencies."

It was time for another drink.

"What about this Werner or Victor character?" Mike asked.

I shrugged. "When we came to the building, he was the security officer on duty. We didn't think he was much of one, because he didn't check Maggie's bag, which, based on its size, he should have."

Mike snickered. Maggie was not amused.

"Isn't it your turn now?" she asked.

50

ike's face remained impassive. He put his glass down. I sensed he was undecided about how much he should or could tell us, so I decided to help him along.

"For instance, why are you pretending to be an auditor reviewing records at the institute?" I asked.

His poker face remained firmly in place. He took a deep intake of air. "Well, I suppose at this stage, there's no harm in telling you. Just remember, this is told to you in confidence. If you jeopardize my investigation, I can assure you the fallout will not be pleasant."

I knew he meant every word.

"My unit was tasked, along with several other law enforcement agencies, to investigate allegations that the institute was being used as a front to funnel illegal campaign contributions to various candidates—funds that would not show up anywhere."

"Let me guess. Primarily to our current VP?"

"You didn't hear that from me. The end result was that we placed two female operatives in the office as well."

"Lee Burnley and Mila Zilke."

He shrugged again. "We were and still are gathering evidence. In the course of all this, Lee Burnley disappeared and was later found dead."

"What tipped you off to Black?"

He stood up and started pacing the room. "It was a fluke, to be honest. The IRS was doing a routine audit on a restaurant services company in upstate New York. The company had become embroiled in a bunch of employment discrimination lawsuits. It attracted the feds from a payroll standpoint. In the course of that audit, they came across donations made to the institute, which raised some eyebrows."

"How so?" Maggie asked.

"For one thing, why would a restaurant services company with no foreign trade business make donations to an institute that specializes in international relations reports? For another, all the donations were made in the six months preceding an election. Curious—wouldn't you agree?"

We nodded.

"So they decided to dig a little deeper and started doing a review of the personal tax returns of the top dogs at the board and executive levels of the company. Coincidentally, several of the executives, including the chairman and CEO, had maxed out on their campaign contributions during those same election cycles. So far, nothing illegal. Then investigators got lucky. One of the executives got nervous and started talking. He alleged that the company had been approached, and it was suggested that by donating to the institute, the company could snag a further tax deduction, and the work of their favorite candidates could be furthered. So the feds smelled a rat and decided they wanted to find out if anything illegal was going on. They decided an audit of the institute was in order. They decided to add a little forensic help. That's where we came in."

"But why send Mila Zilke to us?" Maggie asked.

"That was happenstance. Mila knew Harriet through college. After Harriet phoned Mila to see if she would help decipher some shorthand notes, Mila mentioned to me that Harriet worked part-time for you, so knowing that you were working on a manuscript attribution issue that was tangentially related to the Bedford murder, I figured there was no harm in seeing what you were up to, and I told Mila to go ahead. By that time, we had removed her from the job at the institute because Lee had disappeared, and we worried that someone might catch on to what Mila was really doing there. Frankly, we saw no connection to Black at the time, other than that he had written a book on the French Resistance too. I had never met Harriet, and I must admit I wasn't at all sure it was a good idea on Mila's part to get her into the institute."

"So what does all this have to do with what Lee Burnley found?"

"Absolutely nothing. It's not connected to the audit at all. But it has definitely added a layer of complexity to this case. That is why it is so important to remember what Black said."

Maggie stood in front of the fireplace, rubbing her hands together. "The only thing that really struck us was his assertion that he had nothing to do with the murder of either Sally Bedford or Lee Burnley. He seemed genuinely surprised when we told him Sally had been murdered. In fact, he said that after getting rid of us, he would get rid of her."

"But not so surprised about Lee Burnley," I added. "He denied having anything to do with it."

Mike rubbed his jaw and looked thoughtful. "If he didn't have anything to do with their murders, who did? If he was a war criminal, why was it so important to let him into the country?"

The ticktock of the hallway clock filled the silence.

"Has the audit turned up anything?" I asked.

"Nothing."

"What?"

"Absolutely nothing. He may have implied to the upstate contributors that their contributions would be funding a campaign, but so far, we have been unable to uncover anything that looks, feels, or smells like a campaign or, for that matter, any kind of political donation."

"So if not illegal campaign contributions, what are we looking for?"

Mike loosened his tie. "And who would want Black dead, and why?"

"It doesn't make any sense. Surely if someone had wanted to kill Black, they would have wanted us dead too. After all, we are potential witnesses."

"Unless they thought Black was by himself," Maggie said. "Maybe whoever did this did not realize we were present—perhaps they were surprised and caught off guard."

Mike shrugged. "Could be, but I get the feeling they were not concerned about you two. In fact, it might have been helpful to have someone there. Black would never think someone would come after him with witnesses present."

"Something else has been bothering me all night," I said. "I couldn't put my finger on it until now. Just before Black was shot, the lights were flickering off and on, throwing shadows everywhere. When that bolt of lightning lit up the room, there was a figure behind me. I could see a blurry reflection in the window, but when I think about it now, it was more of an elongated figure. Werner was stocky. I just thought the rain streaming down the window had distorted his reflection."

"What makes you think otherwise?" Mike asked.

"Black had been facing the window with his back to us. He must have seen the reflection too. When he turned around to face us, his face changed expression. The smirk was gone. He looked confused and said, 'What are you doing here?' He already knew Werner was there, so why ask, unless someone else was present?"

"But, Harry," Maggie said, "how could anyone have entered that room without us hearing something?"

"Because whoever it was, he or she was already there when you arrived," said Mike. He looked at his watch. "Almost midnight. We should call it a night. Tomorrow I'll have one of my guys check out who had access to that particular floor."

"Should we have Harriet go to work there tomorrow?" Maggie asked tentatively.

"Absolutely. Right now, I think we have to make sure no questions are raised by the sudden absence of one worker. She should show up and act as if she knows nothing. I'll make sure I keep an eye out for her. Brief her beforehand so she knows you are okay, but she should carry on as if she is adjusting to a new set of circumstances. The place is a crime scene, so ordinarily, no one would be allowed in, but I'll handle it. Just tell her to follow whatever directions the duty cop gives her. I want her to be able to check the office out to see if she notices anything missing or different from when she left the night before. We'll all meet back here tomorrow afternoon. Until then, stay put, and for Pete's sake, try to stay out of trouble."

51

I was not really comfortable with sending Harriet into the lion's den, but she displayed more sangfroid than I would have under the circumstances.

"If you can go get yourself almost murdered, I guess I can try to help find who tried to do it," she said.

We had all been told in no uncertain terms to stay put for the day, but we weren't much help to George, who once again tut-tutted us for getting in harm's way.

"Well, George, it's not like we get advance notice from someone saying, 'Oh, I guess I'll try to shoot you tonight,'" Maggie said crossly.

I just raised my eyebrows. "I think I'll start dismantling our author table."

"No, no," George said. "This is such a good idea. Let's see if we can think of another author to take Black's place; then we'll just swap out books. Bill, I have a collector who wants to look at our first-edition set of Eloise books. Would you retrieve them for me? Harry, there are many new boxes of books to catalog. Maggie, you go get the accounts in order."

"Why me? Why do I have to do the cataloging?" I whined.

"Oh, suck it up, buttercup," said Maggie, and off she went to beaver away on the accounts.

We were just locking up, when Harriet and Mike appeared, looking like best friends of several years.

"This gal would make a great detective, Harry," Mike said. "I told her she should join us."

Harriet rolled her eyes, but I could tell she was pleased with the compliment and obviously thrilled with her new vocation as a detective.

"Well, don't just stand there. Come in and tell all," Maggie said, pointing to the conference room.

"I did as you told me," Harriet said. "I went to the institute, and sure enough, there were cops galore and yellow tape everywhere. I attempted to go in but of course was stopped by a police officer. Feigning surprise, I asked what was going on. He said it was a crime scene, like I couldn't have figured that out for myself. I explained that I was a temporary worker and had left some personal belongings in my office. 'Get in line,' he told me, and he pointed to a line snaking halfway down the block. He told me everyone who worked at the institute had to sign in there. So I did. That's when Mike—er, Detective Farmer—came up behind me and motioned for me to come with him."

We turned to Mike.

"I had already finished sealing all the audit document boxes," he said, "so I went in search of Harriet."

"Then we went to the fifth floor," Harriet said. "When I first walked in, nothing seemed to be amiss, except for the remnants of the crime scene—yellow tape marks on the floor and so on. I checked the drawers, but nothing was out of order."

"I told her to turn on her PC."

"Which I did. But when I entered my employee ID and

password, they were rejected. I tried several times but with the same result. So I asked Mike—er, Detective Farmer—if it would be all right to turn on the dragon lady's PC. I'm not sure I thought it would turn up anything, because I didn't know her password, but he thought it was worth a try. Well, I didn't have to worry, because she hadn't logged out. That was a surprise."

"When opportunity knocks, you open the door," Mike said. "I told her to check her email and document files."

"That was the next big surprise."

"Harriet, spit it out," Bill said impatiently.

"It was blank. The PC had been scrubbed clean. My guess is that is what I would have found if I had been able to access my computer."

"So we checked the filing cabinets," Mike said. "Not much in those either. We are having our forensics team go through the files we did find and work on the hard drives of both computers. And thanks to Miss Harriet, we found one more little item: a small piece of paper tucked under the executive assistant's phone, with a telephone number on it."

"Whose number?" Bill asked.

"It's a Washington area code. We are checking it out right now."

"Then we went into Black's office." Harriet was now excited.

"To me, the office looked just as it had the night before when we left," Mike said. "It was something I hadn't picked up on the night before, but Harriet saw it right away."

"I had only been in Black's office once," she said, "but I knew he had a cabinet in there with a television, because the TV was on when I was in there. The cabinet was behind the couch where Maggie and Harry were sitting. Only it seemed there wasn't a cabinet there anymore."

"Harriet mentioned that it was curious they had removed the cabinet and told me about it and where it used to be. Well, actually, it was still there. It was flush to the wall. It looked like a cabinet only when the doors were open, because they were finished on either side; when closed, the doors blended in with the wall. The cabinet had a push mechanism instead of handles, so when you pushed on the right panel, it swung open. So that got me wondering what else might be behind those panels, and sure enough, the panel next to the TV cabinet swung open too, revealing a closet big enough to conceal a person. I think when the lights went out, it was an opportunity for whoever was in that closet to come out and shoot Black."

52

"But who?" I asked no one in particular.

"That, my friends, is the sixty-four-dollar question," Mike answered.

"Black must have known something or had information about someone that was so threatening or compromising that they wanted him dead," said Maggie

"There has to be something in those records that's been missed that would give us an inkling of what is really going on," said Mike.

"By the way, that was the other interesting thing: the only person who did not show up for work today was the dragon lady," said Harriet.

Bill looked mystified. "Who is this dragon lady?"

Mike consulted his notes. "Her name is Mrs. Martha Peabody. Apparently, she had already put in for time off earlier in the week."

"Which was news to me," Harriet said.

"You'd think she would have phoned you, Harriet, once she heard the news or at least contacted the office to find out what had happened," I said.

"She couldn't have heard much," Mike said, "since we've only released the sketchiest of details, and considering her hard drive was wiped clean, she is a person of interest to us. We're trying to track her down. By the way, I'll need Harriet to report for work at the institute tomorrow. We're going to scour every sheet of paper in the place if necessary to find out what is going on there."

Harriet reported for work the next day, as instructed. Mike sat her down in the so-called audit room, where they proceeded to comb through every document that had been examined before. Her first job was to ferret out any and all information relating to the elusive Mrs. Peabody.

We should have guessed there wouldn't be much, considering the secretiveness that was all-pervasive at the institute, but even her personnel records were skimpy on detail. She was a single mother of one child, Evan, who was eighteen years old; his whereabouts were unknown. Her record showed she had joined the institute just before Evan was born and long before Black arrived there. She received regular annual increases and bonuses at Christmas, even though there were no performance reviews carried out, at least none that were in the records. The phone number on file remained unanswered. She had an address on the Upper East Side. The feds didn't have much more luck with her Social Security number.

Before becoming Mrs. Peabody, she had been one Doreen Goodman from Fishkill, New York. When she'd married Mr. Peabody and who he was remained a mystery. Her Social Security record showed she was sixty years old, which meant she'd had Evan at a later date than would have been common then.

Her résumé was sparse. She had come to the institute from
a lobbying group in Washington, DC, where she had been
employed as a research analyst, and before that, she had been
employed at a Washington law firm whose name I did not recognize. She had a liberal arts degree from a tiny state college
in Vermont. It always amazed me how little people revealed
about themselves in the course of seeking employment.

Although we had been cautioned not to indulge our
sleuthing habit, Maggie and I decided it wouldn't hurt to do
a little harmless independent investigating on our own. We
decided to try to track down the elusive Mrs. Peabody on
the pretext of needing to know what to do with the excess
quantity of Black's books now collecting dust in our store-
room. We tried the number Mike gave us but got no answer.
We trekked up to her listed address, an apartment building
at 110th and Fifth, on the border of Harlem, which was when
we found out that no one by that name lived in the building.
On a hunch, I phoned the number Harriet had found, but
the call went to voice mail immediately, with a standard
recording: "Your call has been transferred to an automatic
voice messaging service. The number you have dialed is not
available to take your call."

"You'd think she would have called in again," I said. "She
must have heard the news. Wouldn't you want to know what
was happening?"

Maggie looked up from the directory she had been perus-
ing. "She has to know something, and she can't have gone far.
The real question is, why would she fake an address?"

I stared at her for a minute. "Maybe it wasn't the address
she faked. Maybe it was the name."

"You think she used Doreen Goodman instead of her
married name?"

Back we trekked uptown. We spoke to a different doorman

and received the same skeptical look. Perhaps it was part of the training—how to look suspicious and skeptical for no good reason.

"We aren't supposed to discuss the residents," the doorman said.

"Oh, we are not asking you to gossip about the residents," Maggie said smoothly. "We just want to know if Doreen Goodman lives here."

"Nope, no one by that name lives here." Seeing our crestfallen looks, he added, "Sorry."

"Don't apologize—we were in the city and were hoping to catch up with her. We were all part of the Fishkill crowd."

"Oh, you must mean Doreen Gray. Mrs. Gray does have a home in Fishkill, but she isn't there this weekend. She said she was going to visit her kid at Brown. She's not going to be happy when she finds out they got their wires crossed. Evan thought he was supposed to meet her here."

As we walked back to the subway, I turned to Maggie and said, "Are you thinking what I'm thinking?"

"That Brown is a rather expensive proposition for someone earning an administrative assistant's salary, even if you are a senior assistant?"

"My thought exactly."

"I suppose he might be on scholarship or have received other financial aid."

We decided to pursue the thread, but it wasn't going to be easy, given all the privacy laws in place.

"Where do we start?" I asked.

"How about online directories?" Maggie answered.

We went onto the Brown website, and sure enough, they had a student and employee directory. We put in the name Evan Peabody. No results. We tried Evan Goodman. No results. Finally, we tried Evan Gray. There it was: Evan Gray was an undergraduate studying political science, and the listing included an email address.

We couldn't be sure it was *the* Evan Gray, so we turned to another source: Syd.

"What's up?" Syd asked when I called.

"We need help." I filled her in on the background.

"Hmm. Let's get a birth certificate and then go from there."

As only Syd could do, she phoned with the results a few hours later. "I did a search, and I think I've got the right Evan Gray. The timing is right. You will never guess who is registered as the father."

My ears pricked up. "Who?"

"Edmund Gray."

It took a minute for that bit of information to sink in. "Are you sure?"

"Don't jump to conclusions yet. I did an online search of Washington directories in the time period leading up to the birth of Evan Gray. Gray is a pretty common name, so I wasn't surprised by the number of Grays in the directories we searched."

I felt that familiar sinking feeling.

"But what was interesting is that we could only find one Edmund Gray with an address in Washington. And guess who else lived at that address."

"Doreen Peabody, Goodman, or Gray?"

"Right on."

"But—"

"Edmund Gray was married to someone else at the time."

I shook my head. "It doesn't make any sense. Why would a high-profile politician like that put his name on the birth certificate? And then keep an address in the same building as his mistress and newborn son?"

"Don't forget that eighteen years ago, he wasn't a player. His father was. He was a lawyer in a Washington firm. She probably worked for his father, and that's how they met. They are very similar in age," replied Syd.

"So you think he moved her out of town to cover up the fact that he fathered a child with another woman, not his wife? It's not unheard of and not illegal."

"Well, don't forget his father was contemplating a run for the presidency at that time, and maybe they didn't want to risk a family scandal."

"Were there any court proceedings for support of the child?"

"None that we could find."

"It doesn't make sense."

"It could have been a private arrangement."

"Unless we can access her bank account, we'll never know. I suppose Mike could find out for us."

That evening, Mike dropped in, and we gave him the information we'd uncovered.

"Is there something about my instructions to cease and desist amateur sleuthing that you do not understand?" he asked testily.

We shrugged.

"For your information, I have checked her financial affairs—nothing out of the ordinary. Her paycheck has been electronically deposited for years. Once a year, there's a deposit matching her bonus, and then it just as quickly goes into a savings account. She has the usual investments."

"There has to be some kind of financial connection between Gray and her. I can't believe she didn't ask for support from him for the child," I said

"You're awfully quiet, Harriet. Anything you want to add?" Maggie asked.

"You know how sometimes someone says something that triggers a memory that just sits beneath your consciousness?"

Maggie shrugged. "All the time, but I call them senior moments. You're a little young for those."

Harriet shook her head. "No, something Mike just said." She had dispensed with the Detective Farmer bit.

Mike tapped his fingers on the table. "We were just talking about her paycheck and—"

"That's it. It's the bonus. The amount of the bonus—there's a similar number somewhere in those records."

"Why is that significant?" I asked.

"Her bonus has been exactly the same amount for as long as she has been there, no matter what her salary level. It's not a percentage. It's not related to anything. I bet if we check everyone else's bonus, the amount varies from year to year, except for hers."

"Could that be the number you think keeps repeating?"

She shook her head vigorously. "No, that figure appears somewhere else. Can we get access to those files tonight?"

Mike sighed. "Just when I thought there was a drink in my future."

"Where are the files?" Syd asked.

"Locked up in the institute."

"Why don't we all go?" Maggie said.

Now it was my turn to groan, but off we went.

Two hours and much eye fatigue later, Harriet found what she was looking for. "Look at this," she said, waving a sheaf of paper in her hands. She pointed at the year-end bonus allocations. "Every year, her bonus is exactly sixty thousand dollars. Trust me. You can go back eighteen years, and there it is—the same figure."

"So?" I asked cautiously.

"Now look at the donor ledger sheets. Every year, Edmund

Gray made a donation of exactly sixty thousand dollars to the institute just before bonus season."

"He was using the institute to launder support payments so no one would know or be able to trace the paternity of the child back to him," Syd said. "That's how he successfully hid his second family."

"I think it's time to find and meet Ms. Doreen Gray," said Mike.

"I think I know how," I said.

The following morning, shortly after we opened the shop, the tinkle of the bell announced our first customer. A woman in late middle age, bundled up in a navy coat and matching gloves, strode purposefully to the front checkout counter.

"I understand you are looking for me. I am Doreen Gray."

53

"I beg your pardon?" I finally managed to blurt out.

"I am Doreen Gray," she repeated more loudly.

"Yes, we heard you," Maggie said. "We weren't expecting you."

She looked around. "So I gather."

"Perhaps we should continue this in the office," Maggie said with more aplomb than I could manage.

Mrs. Gray looked around again and waved her glove. Her eyes narrowed. A small smile formed on her lips. "This seems private enough."

So that was how it was going to be.

She turned her gaze back on us and got right to the point. "Why are you looking for me?"

"Surely you must have heard about the death of your boss," I said.

"And what has that got to do with your looking for me?"

"We were curious about why you hadn't bothered to come back to work. Surely you must be aware that as you're Arnold Black's senior administrative assistant, the police would be most interested in talking to you."

"That doesn't explain why you want to talk to me."

"As you know, Mr. Black was going to do an author's session with our bookstore. It came to our attention that the authenticity of his manuscript had been called into question. We went to the institute the night he was murdered to discuss this with him. Unfortunately, he was killed before we got any definitive information from him. We thought you might have some information about the origins of the manuscript. It is particularly pertinent because the woman who commissioned us to look into the appropriation of her husband's manuscript was herself murdered earlier, which makes hers the second, if not third, death associated with the institute."

Her eyes narrowed. "Are you suggesting I had anything to do with any of these deaths?"

"What we find interesting is that among your many last names is Gray, which is also your son's last name, and he was born just after you left Washington, where you worked for Mr. Gray, who at one time was a very senior official with the CIA and authorized the entrance of Mr. Black, a known Nazi war criminal, into the United States. We also know that his son is listed as the father on your son's birth certificate; he was married at the time; every year, he donated sixty thousand dollars to the institute; and every year at approximately the same time, you received a bonus in exactly that amount. We also believe that Lee Burnley, a.k.a. Leah Bernstein, not only discovered Black's past but also stumbled on the paternity of your son. How are we doing so far?"

She looked faintly amused and then turned on her heel and started toward the door. I thought it was game over.

She paused at the door and rummaged through her handbag. When she turned around, she held a smallish weapon in her hand and was pointing it at us. She flipped over the Closed sign on the door with one hand and walked quickly toward us.

Using her little weapon as a pointer, she said, "Perhaps it is a better idea to continue this conversation in your office."

Once we were in the office, she closed the door and motioned for us to sit down. "It really is too bad that people cannot mind their own business, but since you are so curious about the institute and me, let me satisfy your curiosity, although please remember that curiosity killed the cat, and your curiosity is most assuredly going to do you in."

I think I heard this somewhere else just recently, I thought.

She circled around the chairs we were sitting on, never taking her eyes off us. She brought her face so close to mine that I could smell the stagnant odor of cigarette smoke on her clothing.

"Let's get one thing straight. Edmund Gray is not the father of my son. The very thought that he would father my child disgusts me. Edward Gray, Edmund's father, is the father of my child. We put Edmund on the birth certificate because at the time, Edward was contemplating a run for the presidency, and the scandal of having a second family would have cratered that bid. Don't forget the Clinton scandal was barely in the history books. We agreed I would move to New York, and Edward would set me up at the institute, including, as you quite rightly surmise, ensuring I received a bonus every year that equated to what would have been awarded as maintenance for Evan. He was on the board at the time, which necessitated his coming to New York regularly, so it was easy to carry on as a family. By the time Evan was old enough to be told the truth, it didn't matter. As far as Evan is concerned, Edward is his father, and he has kept the secret. Only a few other people knew about the real paternity and what was going on money-wise at the institute. Unfortunately, Black was one of them. And then I caught

Miss Bernstein, or whatever her name is, snooping one day and insisted she be fired."

Lee Burnley certainly had known more than we thought. It was no small wonder she had become a target for some nasty business.

"I also thought your Mrs. Bedford knew. She sent a note to Black saying, 'I know who you are,' and implying that she was going to the board with relevant information. Black was such a fool. Why he decided to publish that manuscript is beyond me. It was so clearly above his intellectual level I didn't think anyone would believe he'd written it. That was when things got out of control—or, should I say, out of my control. I dealt with Ms. Bernstein first. I made the mistake of going to Edmund and insisting he send a couple of guys over there to find out what information she really had. What a fiasco."

She gave a wry laugh. "As you know, Margaret Thatcher once said, 'If you want something said, ask a man; if you want something done, ask a woman.' So I went to her house myself. She wasn't home that day, so I had a look around. I noticed she had a kayak on the side of the house, and I remembered she had mentioned she was a birder. It didn't take me long to tamper with the kayak."

"You. You killed Lee Burnley," Maggie sputtered.

"I merely facilitated her demise," she said archly. "I couldn't have her blabbing about whatever it was she'd found."

"So you didn't know what she'd found?" Maggie asked.

She snorted. "It didn't matter. I knew she knew something."

"That doesn't explain Sally," I said quietly. "She knew none of this."

"That was Black's idea."

"That's not what he said."

She ignored me. "Horrible man. He ran into financial difficulties. He was greedy and lazy. He put together a little blackmail scheme that cornered all of us. Even that wasn't enough to satiate his greed. He decided to publish that damned book. His real fear was that maybe there was something in those missing pages that would put an end to his blackmail scheme, so he threatened that if we didn't help him, he would expose us all."

"How did he find out about your money arrangements?"

"He knew about my yearly bonus—everyone in administration did. At first, he couldn't figure out how to get his hands on part of it. And he was already skimming money from the institute using those phony donations from upstate businessmen. It was only going to be a matter of time before the auditors started connecting the dots."

Really, I thought to myself.

"If only you had minded your own business and just stuck to figuring out that the man copied a whole book, you wouldn't be in the pickle you are in now."

With a calmness I certainly didn't feel, Maggie said, "You can't honestly believe that someone is not going to, as you so quaintly put it, connect the dots and figure out who is behind a string of murders."

"By the time I am done, this is just going to look like a robbery gone awry."

"Just as you hoped for with Black. Pushing your luck, aren't you?"

"I have nothing left to lose."

"What I don't get is that you covered up all manner of financial goings-on without eliminating all the people who knew. Why now?" I asked.

"I did this for my son and for Edward. I could never allow him to be disgraced by all these foolish people."

"Having children doesn't justify murdering three people."

"Do you have any children, Mr. Kramer? Because if you did, you'd be surprised what you would do for them."

"But not this, Doreen," said a voice behind us.

She whirled around to face a shadowy figure confronting her from the doorway. "Edward, is that you? What are you doing here?"

"I'm here to ask you to put down that silly gun and allow this man to take you away to somewhere safe. Someplace where you can't hurt yourself or anyone else."

Mike and Bill emerged from behind him.

She glanced wildly from one to another. "No, I cannot. I have to protect my son."

"Our son," Edward said gently. "Please give me the pistol." He extended his hand to her.

A look of panic came over her face. "Where is Evan?"

"He is with me."

"What have you told him?"

"That you are very ill and need treatment."

"I want to see him."

"He doesn't want to see you."

She let out an animallike howl and fell to her knees. Edward rushed toward her. Before he could reach her, she lifted the pistol, pointed it at Edward, and then turned the gun on herself.

54

oreen Gray survived. We were shaken.

After the ambulance departed, taking Doreen and Edward Gray to Bellevue, we gathered upstairs since our office was a crime scene temporarily. Although we had no idea what would become of either of them, we knew we could close the books on our investigation. Sally could rest peacefully in knowing we had kept our commitment to her to prove that Nick was the author of the manuscript.

If the resolution was so neat and tidy, why was I so bothered?

"For someone who managed to help solve a few murders, you're lookin' a little subdued, Counselor," Mike said. "What's buggin' you?"

"You know, Mike, I'm not sure. It just seems a little too convenient."

"Murder is never convenient," Maggie said quietly.

"Think about it for a moment," I said. "Based on a very brief voice mail from me, Doreen Gray waltzed in here, confessed to three murders, and then attempted to shoot herself."

Mike shrugged. "So?"

"She didn't have to say anything. All she had to do was come in, pick up a few books, laugh us off, and leave with a 'Good luck.' Until she confessed, the only things we knew for certain were her name, her son's name, and possibly who the father was. Even the scheme at the institute was flimsy evidence—one person gave a donation, and later, an employee received a bonus in the same amount. The only hard evidence we had was from Black, who confessed to Nick's murder but not to any others. Yet she thought Sally's murder was Black's idea."

"Which means she had no idea who killed Sally," Maggie said.

"Or maybe she did," grunted Mike.

"But who was she so desperate to protect?" I said. "I don't believe for a minute that she was concerned about Gray Senior."

We looked at each other, thinking the unthinkable.

"Evan," Maggie said softly.

"Think about it," I said. "On the day Sally died, the door-man said only one person had been to visit Sally: the delivery boy. But we found no evidence of a delivery. Peter Graber mentioned that he told the newspaper delivery boy to cut the paper off. The night we were in Black's office, the blurry vision I saw was slight. I don't think it was Doreen Gray."

"And," added Maggie, "the day we visited her building, the doorman said there must have been a miscommunication. Evan thought she was here for that weekend. He was in the city the night we went to Black's office."

Mike pulled out his phone.

55

"Hello, Evan," I said.

He did not acknowledge me. His gaze was fixed on the person opposite him.

"I'm surprised it took you so long. Please join us."

I stood in the doorway, chilled by the scene before me. Evan's father sat opposite him, his hands gripping the arms of the chair he was seated in. Perhaps the weapon confronting him was the source of his consternation.

"Why?" I asked.

Evan seemed puzzled by the question. "I had to protect my mother, of course."

It was déjà vu all over again, except for one thing: the character speaking the words was different.

"Protect her from what?" I asked.

He replied, "From all of you."

"But no one was after her."

"They were going to destroy her life."

"So you took it upon yourself to destroy them first?"

"You would be surprised what you would do for your mother."

"Mrs. Bedford did no harm to your mother."

"Oh, her," he said dismissively. "I overheard that odious man Black talking to my mother about what a nuisance she was going to be and how much unwanted attention it would focus on the institute. Then my mother said, 'Just deal with it.'" His voice hardened. "Well, I wasn't going to wait for him to deal with it."

"And Leah Bernstein?"

"Oh, that was a different story. She was too snoopy for her own good. She told my mother she had discovered something interesting."

"And that was?"

"Something about Black's past. Mother said she was really cagey about it. She started to worry about what else Leah may have discovered. So I decided to find out. Unfortunately for her, I found out who she really was and where she lived. It was nothing at all to remove the flotation cork on her kayak and disguise it. Then I waited."

"You were the paperboy."

There was silence.

"And Black?"

Evan turned his head toward me, and his eyes narrowed. "He was the most odious creep who ever walked the earth. I hated that man. Did you know he was blackmailing my mother?"

"Yes," I replied.

"But you don't know the half of it. He discovered the scheme concocted by—" He paused and then spit out, "My *father*, Edward. Every year, he forced her to hand over one half of the gross amount of the bonus and launder it, so it never showed up in his accounts. He threatened to expose both of them. Of course, Mother paid taxes on the whole amount." Bitterness saturated every word.

"My God, Evan, I had no idea," Edward said. "Your mother never said a word."

That seemed to infuriate him. He bolted out of his chair and towered over his father, wiggling the pistol in his face. "Of course you didn't. You were a god in her eyes—the father of her son, the man who would marry her as soon as you divorced the woman you called your wife. I finally realized you were never going to marry her and never going to acknowledge her or me as your true family. You betrayed us. You disgust me."

We waited.

"I decided to follow her today," Evan said. "I was afraid she was going to do something rash. I decided I had to protect her. While you were in the office, I realized that in her haste to get you into the office, she hadn't locked the door; she had just turned the sign to Closed. I was just about to intervene, when he showed up and lied to her about my not wanting to see her. It would have been kinder if you'd just taken a knife and stabbed us both in the back."

"She knew about your involvement?" Edward asked.

"I never spoke to her about any of this. Then I slipped up. She read in the paper about the discovery of a body. The woman's name was similar to that of the woman who used to work for her. I asked whether they'd found the flotation cork. There was no mention in the paper of a missing flotation cork. That was when she became suspicious."

"How did you get into Black's office without anyone knowing?"

"That was nothing," he scoffed. "I pretended to be picking up a handbag my mother had left behind. The day-shift security guard knew me and knew my mother had taken a long weekend to see me. I explained that she had forgotten it and that I'd come back to pick it up for her. He just let me in. Then it was no problem to hide until the office closed. I waited until Black left the room, and then I seized my chance. I knew about the hidden closet—my mother had shown it to me one day when Black was away. She had been working in there and let me amuse myself by watching television. I just let myself in and waited. I had no idea you and your wife were going to be there that evening or that that lout Werner would be there. At least he had the good sense to hightail it as soon as I fired my shot."

"How did you explain your absence to your mother?"

"I told her I had gone to the office to meet her, and when I got there, I realized I had the dates mixed up, so I left. I could tell she was skeptical. When she saw the news about Black, it didn't take her long to figure out the timing and put two and two together about the dead woman in the kayak. By this time, she was desperate—desperate to protect me—and that's why she went to the bookstore today to finish off what she considered to be loose ends."

I had never been reduced to a loose end before, and I didn't like the sound of it.

Evan raised the gun and moved toward his father. "But at least I can exact some measure of revenge for her." An evil smile formed on his face.

A small whoosh of air entered the room. Evan's hand went limp. His body sagged and then crumpled to the floor.

"You really have to get out of the detective business," Mike said. "I have enough to worry about with keeping myself from getting shot up. I don't have time to worry about you too."

"Now you tell me," I said.

The room was quiet now. Evan had been taken to Bellevue,

where I presumed he would see his mother sooner than he thought. His father had been taken away to give his statement about the whole sorry mess. Maggie was busy fending off reporters, all of whom she thought had something to do with the NYPD.

"I'd like to finish that drink we started a few hours ago if it's still sitting there," Mike said gruffly.

Had it really been only a few hours since we figured out Evan, not his mother, had been running around knocking off anyone he thought, mistakenly or otherwise, was out to get her? We had tried to get Edward Gray on his cell phone to help us locate Evan but had realized when no one picked up that Edward was most likely next on Evan's list. There had been only one place Evan could go, and therefore only one place Edward would have gone: the apartment where, for years, Edward had concealed his second family.

That was when we'd concocted our plan.

The rest was history.

56

I poked my head into Bill's study. A warm breeze as soft as a feather, a harbinger of the spring to come, ruffled the drapes. Bill was resting in his chair with his head slightly to one side and a book hanging limply in his hand. A mild stroke brought on by the stresses of the last few months had accentuated the frailties of old age. I tiptoed in, gathered up some papers sent askew by the breeze, and put them on his desk.

"We should talk."

The muscles in my back contracted. I had known this moment would come, and now here it was. I turned to face him. "I'm not sure we should."

He ignored me. "Sometimes events happen with no thought to unintended consequences."

"I'm not sure I like to think of someone as an unintended consequence."

His eyes fluttered open. "You're a better person than that, Harry."

I was immediately ashamed of myself but shook my head. I did not want to have this discussion.

"We can't avoid this, Harry. I need you to know." Without waiting for me to say anything, he continued. "It was a long time ago." His voice wavered. "Just before Nick disappeared, Sally was in New York on business. She sent me a note wondering if I would be in the city while she was there. I hadn't seen either of them since shortly after the war ended, when we were debriefed in Washington. By then, Nick had already proposed to Sally, and they were about to get married. They asked me to stand up for them. The picture you saw in Sally's apartment with me in the background was taken on their wedding day. I had been in love with Sally since the evening in the underground, but I was timid. I hesitated to express any interest because it was wartime, after all. Nick had no such reservations, and before I knew it, they were a couple."

He gave me a wry smile. "The old adage 'He who hesitates loses' certainly describes me. I digress, but you must allow an old man his memories."

He motioned for me to come closer. I pulled up a chair and waited.

"After the war, I met many wonderful women but could never seem to make a commitment. Law school was finally over, and I started to practice. Years went by. I only had intermittent contact with Nick and Sally, and then I received her note. I was curious to see if time had changed anything, so I agreed to meet her for a drink after work. When she walked into Peacock Alley at the Waldorf, all of my old feelings surfaced. She had barely changed. By that time, we were all in our thirties. We started talking and never quit, and without boring you with all the details, we had a one-night affair. She went home, and I went back to the business of practicing law. About three months later, she telegraphed the news that Nick had disappeared and that she needed to talk to me. I went to France. We met at the farmhouse. As soon as I walked in, I knew what she needed to talk to me about."

He closed his eyes for a minute and then, shaking his head, continued. "She was pregnant, but the child was not Nick's. She told me she had been so happy when she found out, because they had longed to have a child. What she didn't know until after Nick's disappearance was that Nick was incapable of having children. When she was going through his papers, she found a medical file. Apparently, they had been trying for some time to have a child with no success, so he'd decided to consult a doctor to determine if he was the problem, and indeed, he was. He never told Sally.

"Whatever he thought, he must have decided the child would be theirs, no questions asked. Sally told me the child could only be mine. I was stunned. She had been conflicted about whether to tell me, but after some thought, she'd decided in good conscience that she had to tell me the truth. She was very frank with me. She told me she would never be able to forgive herself or face the child, knowing what pain she must have caused Nick, and she had already made arrangements to have an abortion. I was horrified. I promised her if she had the baby, I would assume full care and responsibility for the child. Reluctantly, she agreed.

"I brought Sally back to the US with me. We couldn't marry since Nick had not been declared legally dead, and frankly, the financial consequences for Sally would have been catastrophic if she had divorced Nick. I would have married her gladly, but she was so overcome with remorse and guilt about our affair that there was no possibility of that ever happening. So we played at being married. We told everyone, including my brother, James, that we were married. James was serving overseas at the time, and as luck had it, he never met Sally. We registered the child's birth with my name listed as father and gave her my last name. Of course, as you know, that child is my Maggie."

"But who was listed as the mother?"

"Sally, of course, but we used a sleight of hand to disguise it by using Sally's middle name, Ruth, and my last name. It was difficult. Sally stayed for another three months. Once Maggie was weaned and I was set up with a housekeeper, Sally went back to France. I told everyone that Ruth was going to care for a sister in France who was very ill and would return in a few months. A few months after that, Ruth conveniently died in a car accident."

"But the portrait—"

"Just a fictionalized portrait I had made up. It actually does have some of Sally's young features. I told Maggie the same story—that her mother died shortly after her birth in a car accident in France and that she had no living relatives, to head off any curious questions."

"And the picture?"

"Sally wanted a picture for her memory, so I had a photographer come out and take one. That was the last time she saw Maggie, until she came to the bookstore to seek your help. We had made an agreement that it would be in the best interest of everyone if Sally had no further contact with Maggie. Each year, I sent pictures and updates, and I often visited Sally in France. We became the best of friends.

"When I found out from George that she had been to the bookstore, I was furious. I went to her apartment to confront her. It was purely selfish on my part; I feared if Maggie learned the truth, she would never forgive me. When I got there, she explained what she had discovered and said she was sure it was a key to Nick's disappearance. She initially sent Arthur to the bookstore, thinking that would be the way to avoid seeing Maggie directly, but when he told her you wouldn't undertake the job without meeting the actual owner of the manuscript, she tossed caution to the wind and went.

"She said if I was really dead set against her retaining the bookstore for assistance, she would withdraw her request. I calmed down. I could tell she was not well. Her pallor was off, but she attributed it to her heart problems. We spent a lovely evening together and actually talked about resuming our relationship. I told her about my upcoming wine trip, and we agreed to meet at her place later in the month. That is where you found me. I was devastated by the news of her death but even more so by the circumstances. Just when I thought Sally and I would be together for whatever time we had left, she was again snatched from me."

"Why are you telling me this now, Bill?"

"You saw the picture. But more importantly, there is a flash drive in the locked upper drawer of my desk. It has all of Sally's medical records on it, as well as mine, just in case there is a need ..." His voice trailed off.

The breeze had died. The air in the room was stifling. I looked at my watch. "It's that time. Why don't I get Maggie, and I'll make us all a drink?"

He gave me a weak smile. "I'd like that."

I rose, but he clutched my arm, so I sat down again.

"You have made my daughter very happy, Harry. I owed you this explanation. You have done so much for us."

I looked him directly in the eyes. "Thank you."

I found Maggie in the library, sitting cross-legged on the floor and sorting a pile of books for shipment to the bookstore. She looked up. "How is he?"

"Tired but ready for a cocktail. How about you?"

"I thought you'd never ask."

I helped her to the upright position. We made a tray of drinks and headed for the library. Bill was right where I'd left him.

Maggie leaned over, kissed her father on the top of his head, and gave his hair an affectionate ruffle. "Your personal bartenders are here."

He didn't stir. I put the tray down, went around to the front of his chair, and shook him gently. No response.

"Call 911."

About the Author

Born and raised on the prairies in Canada, **B. F. Monachino** fell in love with New York City some forty years ago on her first visit. Although she is a lawyer by profession, like her favorite characters, she is an avid reader and a collector of both current and rare books. This is her second novel.

Facebook.com/bfmonachinoauthor
Twitter: @bfm_author
Instagram: bfmonachino_author

CPSIA information can be obtained
at www.ICGtesting.com
Printed in the USA
LVHW092112100621
689682LV00023B/69

9 781480 897960